P9-DDG-811

FLINT MEMORIAL LIBRARY
147 Park Street
North Reading, MA 01864

THIS TOWN
IS A
NIGHTMARE

M. K. KRYS

THIS TOWN IS A NIGHTMARE

Penguin Workshop

PENGUIN WORKSHOP
An imprint of Penguin Random House LLC, New York

First published in the United States of America by Penguin Workshop,
an imprint of Penguin Random House LLC, New York, 2021

Text copyright © 2021 by M. K. Krys
Cover illustration copyright © 2021 by Shane Rebenschied

Penguin supports copyright. Copyright fuels creativity, encourages diverse voices,
promotes free speech, and creates a vibrant culture. Thank you for buying an authorized
edition of this book and for complying with copyright laws by not reproducing, scanning,
or distributing any part of it in any form without permission. You are supporting
writers and allowing Penguin to continue to publish books for every reader.

PENGUIN is a registered trademark and PENGUIN WORKSHOP is a trademark of
Penguin Books Ltd, and the W colophon is a registered trademark of Penguin Random House LLC.

Visit us online at penguinrandomhouse.com.

Library of Congress Control Number: 2021008309

Printed in the United States of America

ISBN 9780593097175   10 9 8 7 6 5 4 3 2 1

This book is a work of fiction. Any references to historical events, real people,
or real places are used fictitiously. Other names, characters, places, and events
are products of the author's imagination, and any resemblance to actual
events or places or persons, living or dead, is entirely coincidental.

The publisher does not have any control over and does not assume any
responsibility for author or third-party websites or their content.

For my mom, Phylis.

Thanks for the McDonald's dates.

1

Beacon dropped his skateboard onto the cracked New York City sidewalk and pushed off. He weaved through the crowds, past brownstones and steel skyscrapers, churches and theaters and police stations. Cars zoomed past on the street. Horns honked and people yelled out cuss words. Chilly air blew across his face, carrying the scent of hot dogs and fresh-poured concrete.

Beacon loved this board. He relished the rise and fall of the path under his wheels. He lived for the speed, came alive when he sailed past commuters and sliced across roadways. It didn't matter where he was when he was on his board. He was home.

He whizzed around a busy street corner and saw a flash of white-blond curls standing at a set of traffic lights. His heart lodged in his chest. Jane Middleton couldn't be here, in New York City . . . right?

He looked back, searching for Jane. But the girl had vanished. If she'd ever been there to begin with.

Beacon had become a paranoid mess ever since his family

had gone on the run from the Sov. Every scritch behind him was a predator; every blond-haired girl was his enemy ready to take him down. He was getting really sick of the constant fear, but unfortunately, it didn't seem to be going anywhere.

"Hey, watch it!"

Beacon turned back around just in time to avoid slamming into a construction worker. He jerked out of the way and stumbled off his board, rolling onto the concrete. The sidewalk traffic flowed around him as if he were just a lamppost and not an injured twelve-year-old boy.

"I'm okay, nobody panic," Beacon muttered. He pushed himself up and wiped off his jeans.

And found the exact place he'd been looking for.

The flashing neon sign across the street announced "Ed's Fast Cash Pawnshop." There were about eight dollar symbols on the sign, which was what propelled Beacon to pick up his board and cross the street, even though his stomach felt like it was filled with slippery eels.

As Beacon got closer to the shop, he saw a homeless man and his dog sitting in front of the building. The massive chocolate Lab leaped like a puppy when Beacon approached. It pushed its body into Beacon's legs, nearly toppling him with his eagerness to be petted. Beacon obliged, laughing as the dog's tail spun like a windmill.

"Cute dog. What's his name?" Beacon asked.

The man looked up from under the dark hood he wore low over his face. Beacon suppressed a gasp. It wasn't a man, but a kid not much older than him. His face was covered in patches of freckles, and his wild mane of blond hair hung over hard blue eyes. The maroon T-shirt he wore under his unzipped sweatshirt hung loosely on his thin frame.

The kid stared at him contemptuously.

"He's really cute," Beacon tried again. "He's a Lab, right?"

The boy said nothing.

"Good talk," Beacon muttered. He withdrew his hand and entered the pawnshop. The bell over the door jingled as he walked inside.

The place was dank and musty. Every inch of its cluttered shelves was filled with toasters and ironing boards, Xboxes and power tools and gaudy gold jewelry under smudged glass.

He approached the front counter, where a woman with a jam stain on her smock was watching a news report about unprecedented hurricanes blowing across the East Coast. Beacon pushed down the panic he always felt anytime he accidently caught one of these news reports and cleared his throat. The woman sighed heavily and looked over at him.

"Um, hi. I'm here to sell this." Beacon hefted his skateboard.

He felt his throat get tight, and he swallowed hard. He couldn't be a baby about this. His family needed money. It would be selfish and stupid to hang on to a Habitat skateboard worth hundreds of dollars when he could sell it and use the money to buy groceries for weeks.

After narrowly escaping Driftwood Harbor, Beacon, his twin sister, Everleigh, their dad, and Beacon's new friend Arthur, had driven straight to New York City, an eight-hour drive down the interstate from the fishing village. They'd planned to take out all of his dad's savings at the bank, switch out the stolen Mercury Cougar for something less likely to get them all arrested for grand theft auto, then hit the road again. But his dad's bank account had been frozen. They'd had no money for gas or food or . . . anything. So they were stuck here, what felt like a stone's throw away from the town they'd discovered was controlled by shape-shifting aliens.

"Put that here," the woman said, slapping the counter.

Beacon slid his skateboard onto the counter. He'd gotten it for his eighth birthday. He'd received a handful of newer skateboards since then, but this one was his favorite. So when they'd moved from LA to Driftwood Harbor and he could only take his most important possessions, this had been the only skateboard he'd kept.

Now he would have none.

"I'll give you twenty bucks for it," the woman said.

"What?!" Beacon cried. "This board costs over three hundred dollars brand new!"

"Twenty bucks, take it or leave it." The woman went back to

watching the news. Beacon ground his teeth.

Five minutes later, he was shuffling down the street with a twenty-dollar bill in his pocket.

Beacon walked. And walked, and walked, and walked. Soon, he was "home."

A siren wailed as he stared up at the derelict apartment building.

He couldn't believe he'd once scoffed at staying at Blackwater Lookout Bed-and-Breakfast. The inn practically looked like the Four Seasons Hotel compared to this place. Graffiti covered the crumbling brick facade. The windows that weren't broken out entirely were covered in grime and had sheets for curtains. Scary-looking men smoked on the stoop out front, and Beacon didn't think they were smoking cigarettes.

But this was the only place they could afford. The landlord hadn't cared about anything fancy like "background checks" or "identification" or . . . anything, really, as long as the rent was paid. So his dad had sold the car, and they'd used almost everything they got from it to put a roof over their heads for the next thirty days. They had about thirteen days left, and then things were going to get *really* interesting.

Beacon stepped inside. A medley of TV shows, screaming matches, and babies crying could be heard through the thin walls as he climbed up the steps to the third floor. He unlocked the door of apartment 304 and went inside.

Everleigh, Arthur, and the twins' dad were crouched over something in the cramped living room. They didn't even look up as he entered.

"Hey," Beacon said.

"Oh, hey," his dad said distractedly, running a hand over his bald patch. His tie was pulled loose and slung across his shoulder, a look Beacon was used to seeing lately as his dad and Arthur worked together on this or that.

"What are you guys doing?" Beacon asked.

"Come here. You have to see this!" Arthur said, beckoning him with a frantic sweep of his arm. He pushed up his cracked glasses and then bent over his work again.

Beacon stepped closer and peered over Arthur's shoulder. On the stained indoor/outdoor carpet was some type of thick, plastic wand with wires sticking out of the end, like an octopus on a stick.

"What is it?" Beacon asked.

"It's a PJ," Arthur said, as if that explained everything.

Arthur was Beacon's best friend and the president of YAT— Youth Searching for Alien Truth (and no, it's not YSAT, thanks for asking). Beacon had met Arthur in the woods in Driftwood Harbor after they'd moved from Los Angeles all the way to the tiny fishing village in Maine. They'd come for a "fresh start," after the unexpected death of Beacon and Everleigh's older brother, Jasper— or so Beacon had thought.

The real reason they'd come was that their dad had been recruited by the CIA to help an alien race called the Sovereign develop an antidote that would give humans the ability to breathe underwater so they'd have a chance of surviving the tsunamis and flooding soon to be caused by climate change. Only the "antidote" turned out to be an injection that turned humans into creepy, mind-controlled lemmings who worked for the Sov. They'd even gotten ahold of Beacon's own sister, who had gone from a sarcastic, moody tomboy who wore busted overalls to someone who did bake sale fundraisers with the Gold Stars and wore pink skirts.

"Ah, a PJ," Beacon said knowledgeably.

"It stands for Personal Jumpstarter," Arthur said. "I modeled it off an old TENS machine."

"Transcutaneous electrical nerve stimulation," Everleigh supplied in response to Beacon's confused look.

"My grandma bought one off an infomercial once," Arthur continued. "For her arthritis. It's a little machine that delivers small impulses through these electrodes that attach to your skin. They're supposed to be for pain relief, but I figured with a little rewiring, we could use these to Jumpstart people the Sov mind-controlled with their antidote. We can carry them as weapons. A lot more convenient than trying to get a Sov to walk into an electrically charged puddle."

During Beacon's frantic escape from the Sov's underwater UFO, Beacon had accidentally electrocuted a whole group of Gold Stars who had been chasing him. Only the electrocution hadn't killed them, like he'd thought it would, but zapped them out of their mind-controlled state.

"Isn't he a genius?" Beacon's dad clapped Arthur warmly on the shoulder. Arthur beamed.

"Wow," Beacon said. "This is really great. But are you sure we have the money for all this stuff?" He gestured at the wires and tubes all over the floor.

"There's an entire alien race coming after us," Everleigh said dismissively, pulling a strap of her overalls back over her shoulder. "I think self-protection should be a priority. Besides, we didn't spend anything on this. This is all stuff I got from the junkyard the other day. The stuff you said was useless junk, remember?"

"Oh." Beacon suddenly felt like the kid in the group project who didn't contribute anything but still got an A. Everleigh was a car mechanic prodigy, Arthur was Albert Einstein 2.0, and Beacon's dad was a freaking CIA agent. What did Beacon bring to the table?

"So where were you just now?" his dad said.

A small bit of pride shot through him as he remembered his trip to the pawnshop. He did have something to contribute.

"Getting this," Beacon said.

He produced the twenty-dollar bill from his pocket. He expected his dad to be happy, but a frown creased his forehead.

"Where did you get that?" he asked.

"It doesn't matter," Beacon said.

"Did you steal it?" Everleigh asked.

"What? No, of course not!" he said indignantly. "I just . . . sold my board." He'd muttered the last part under his breath. He blinked fast and turned away so no one would see how close he was to crying.

"You sold your skateboard?" His dad was standing now.

"We needed the money," Beacon said. "You don't have a job. Money must be running out by now. What are we going to do when the rent is due?"

"I've applied at a few places," his dad said. "I'm sure I'll hear back soon. It's all going to come together."

"Wait a minute," Arthur said, standing up. "What about my grandma?"

"What *about* your grandma?" Everleigh said, with all her usual grace and tact.

"I thought you said staying here was just temporary," Arthur went on. "You said you'd bring me back to Driftwood Harbor once everything settled down. Now you're talking about applying for jobs. That sounds pretty permanent."

"Even if we had a car to get back to Driftwood Harbor, it would be a terrible idea," Everleigh said. "What do you think is going to happen—you're just going to waltz back into town and they're going to forget about the fact that they were keeping you as a prisoner in their underwater ship, and that you broke out, and oh, that you're immune to the antidote they're giving out to try to mind-control the entire population?" Everleigh shook her head. "You wouldn't just get to go back to your normal life, Arthur. They'd find you again. They'd probably do some more freaky experiments on you, too. Or did you miss all that the last three weeks?"

"So what, then? I just never get to talk to my grandma again?" Arthur said.

"No one said anything about that," the twins' dad said.

"I haven't seen Grams in two weeks." Arthur's eyes were shiny behind his glasses. "She's probably worried sick about me."

"We'll get you back there, if that's what you really want," the twins' dad said. "But now just isn't the safest time. The Sov and the CIA are still looking for us—I saw an APB for a stolen 1968 Mercury Cougar at the precinct on the corner just last week. We need to wait until some of the heat dies down before we talk about bringing you back. Otherwise we'd just be putting everyone in danger. *Including* your grandma."

"Can't I just call her?" Arthur asked weakly.

"NO!"

Beacon, Everleigh, and their dad had all shouted it at the same time.

"Do you want to get us killed?" Everleigh said. "Because that's exactly what would happen if you did that. The Sov are *absolutely* tapping your grandma's phone. A phone call would be all it would take for them to know exactly where we are."

"I could use a pay phone," Arthur said. "At the library or something."

"They could trace that," the twins' dad said. "They'd know we're in New York. Right now the Sov probably assume we've gone to someplace like Japan, or Canada, at the very least. It would have been the smart thing to do—get as far away from Driftwood Harbor as possible. That's probably the only reason we haven't been found yet."

All of a sudden, Beacon remembered the girl he'd seen on the street corner earlier. She'd looked so much like Jane. He briefly thought about mentioning the incident to his dad, but he quickly changed his mind. If he did, his dad would probably just decide that Beacon couldn't go out without him. And there was only one thing worse than having a whole alien race and the US government after him, and that was being cooped up in this apartment that smelled like fish tacos 24-7.

Besides, he knew it wasn't really Jane. Not today, or any of the other times he could have sworn he'd seen her. He was just being paranoid. If Jane were here, she wouldn't be following him around discreetly. She'd attack him, then drag them all back to Driftwood Harbor.

"What about a burner phone?" Arthur asked. "Those are untraceable."

"Harder to trace, yes, but not impossible," the twins' dad said. "I'm sorry, Arthur, but we can't take any chances of the Sov finding us. Everleigh, would you mind getting started on dinner?"

The conversation was over.

"You mean the Mr. Noodles?" Everleigh said.

Her dad charitably ignored her barb. "Yes, thanks, sweetie. Beacon and I have somewhere to be."

"Wait, what?" Beacon said, standing up straighter.

"Grab your coat," his dad said.

2

Twenty minutes later, they were standing in front of $$$$ Ed's Fast Cash Pawnshop $$$$.

"What are we doing here?" Beacon asked.

"Getting your board back." His dad walked inside, and Beacon hurried to follow.

"But, Dad—"

"I know—you wanted to help. And that's very admirable. But you're a kid. It's not your job to worry about rent and groceries."

Beacon gave his dad a meek half smile. He wanted to argue, but truthfully, knowing his dad had a plan and he didn't have to worry about anything made a weight he didn't know he'd been carrying lift from his shoulders. Also, he was just happy he was getting his board back.

They approached the front counter.

"Excuse me?" his dad said to the woman. "My son was in here earlier today and he sold you his skateboard?"

The woman raised her eyebrows.

"It was in error," his dad continued. "We'd like it back, please."

"If it's still available," Beacon added quickly.

The woman pulled the board out from a pile of junk next to her desk and slammed it on the counter. "Forty dollars," she said.

"What?!" Beacon cried. "But you only gave me twenty for it!"

"Forty dollars, take it or leave it."

"But that's not fair! That's like, like extortion or something!" Beacon said.

Beacon's dad held out a hand to silence him.

"Listen, Karen is it?" he said, looking at her name tag. "My son is ten years old."

Beacon opened his mouth to argue that he was twelve, but his dad stepped on his foot under the counter.

"I'm sure you weren't aware of that when you accepted this skateboard, as I'm certain you know that it's illegal in the state of New York to accept an article from a person appearing to be under the age of twelve. Now, I know it's just a misdemeanor offense, and if you have a clear record, there may not even be jail time involved, but some judges like to make examples out of people, especially those seen to be taking advantage of vulnerable children, which I know wasn't your intention."

He opened his wallet and made sure Karen saw his shiny gold CIA badge while he fished around for the twenty-dollar bill.

Karen's eyes popped wide, and she sat up straight. His dad slid the money across the counter.

"So I'm sure you'd be happy to accept the twenty dollars you gave my son in exchange for the board."

The woman gulped, then fumbled for the bill.

"Thank you, Karen." His dad flashed her an insincere smile and turned around. Beacon hurriedly grabbed his board.

"That was so awesome!" Beacon whispered as they approached the front door.

He'd never seen his dad in CIA mode before. He always threw around phrases like "gross abuse of power" anytime Beacon begged him to use his badge to get what he wanted—but it was undeniably cool.

"Was it because she was abusing *her* power?" Beacon said.

"What?" His dad arched an eyebrow.

"That you used your badge," Beacon clarified.

"I don't know what you mean."

Beacon frowned at his dad. Maybe he'd misread the situation.

The bell over the door jingled as they exited the pawnshop. Beacon was about to ask his dad if he really hadn't flashed his badge on purpose, when he heard a growl. The homeless boy and his dog were back. The dog stood up alertly at the sight of them.

"Hey, little buddy," Beacon said. "Remember me?" He stretched out his hand, and the dog growled again. Beacon snapped his hand back. "What got into you?" Beacon turned to his dad. "He was friendly earlier. I don't know why he doesn't like me now."

But Beacon quickly realized that the dog wasn't growling at him. The animal slouched toward his dad like a predator stalking its prey.

"Whoa there, boy," his dad said, backing up a step.

"Let him sniff you," Beacon said. "Maybe that'll help."

"I'm not going near that thing," his dad spat.

Beacon had never heard his dad talk that way about an animal before. But he'd also never seen him cornered like this, either.

"Hey, are you going to do something about your dog?" Beacon asked the homeless kid.

The kid gave him the same hostile stare he had earlier and didn't move an inch. Unbelievable! He was just going to let his dog attack Beacon's dad.

The dog crouched low on its front paws, wiggling its butt as if preparing to leap across the sidewalk. Its jowls pulled back, revealing sharp, slobbery teeth. A low, rumbling snarl issued from its throat. The little hairs on the back of Beacon's neck prickled. His dad shrank away, bumping into a lamppost. The dog followed his movements, forcing his dad into a dingy alley. Beacon looked around for help. A few people walking by cast anxious expressions their way, but they just walked on, as if they were happy this was happening to someone else and not them.

"Tell your dog to back off!" Beacon cried frantically, turning to the homeless kid. But he was gone.

Beacon swung around and looked up and down the street. The kid was nowhere to be seen.

Another ferocious growl ripped his attention back to the alley. The dog was closing in on his dad.

Beacon didn't know what to do. Put the dog in a chokehold? But what if the dog just attacked *him* instead? That thing was huge. There was no way he would be able to fight it off.

He knew what he had to do.

He ran back to the pawnshop and crashed through the door.

"Call the police!" he screamed. "A man is being attacked!"

Karen quickly picked up a phone. Beacon turned around to run back to his dad, but paused briefly at a shelf by the door. He grabbed the first thing he laid eyes on—a weed trimmer. He yanked the pull cord on the trimmer and ran outside. The engine roared as he careened into the alley. He expected to find his dad on the ground, the dog gorging on him, a total bloodbath. But the dog was gone.

His dad calmly wiped dirt off his trousers.

"What the heck are you doing with that?" his dad called over the roar of the engine.

Beacon sheepishly lowered the weed trimmer and cut the gas. "Defending you. Where did the dog go?"

"I yelled at it and it got scared off."

"Really?" Beacon said. The dog hadn't seemed too skittish. His dad must have yelled *really* loudly for the dog to get scared. So strange that Beacon hadn't heard him. The walls of the pawnshop must have been thick. Or maybe the trimmer engine had masked the sound. "Well, that's good, I guess." Beacon shook his head. "Man, I can't *believe* that kid just took off. That dog could have killed you!"

Sirens wailed dully.

"Did you call the police?!" His dad's eyes flashed with anger.

"Well . . . yeah. I wasn't just going to let you get mauled by a dog," he said defensively.

"No, no, of course, that was the right thing to do," his dad said, softening. "But now that we're out of harm's way, we should probably get out of here. Better to stay off the police's radar. You never know who's in league with the Sov."

"I guess so," Beacon said. He still felt uneasy about his dad's sudden anger. What had he expected him to do?

Beacon started to walk, and his dad raised his eyebrows.

"Uh, Beaks?" A slight grin pulled at his lips.

Beacon looked down. That's when he realized he was still holding the weed trimmer. He felt his cheeks go red. His dad laughed, and some of the tension dissipated from Beacon's body. His dad must have just had a bad moment earlier. And wasn't he allowed? They were all feeling stressed and on edge lately.

"Oh, right. I guess I'll just put this back, then," Beacon said.

▸▸▸▸▸▸▸▸▸▸▸▸▸▸▸▸▸▸▸▸▸▸▸▸▸▸▸▸▸▸▸▸

That night, Beacon dreamed of home. In his dream, he woke up in his bed back in Los Angeles, moonlight filtering through the window onto his Tony Hawk poster. Something had woken him up, and he quickly realized what: He could hear Jasper outside his bedroom. He kicked off his sheets and crept into the darkened hall, following the sounds of Jasper's laughter floating on the air, just out of reach.

The pantry closet was open an inch. When they were younger, they would crouch inside it during games of hide-and-seek.

And he'd just seen the door move.

"Jasper?" Beacon whispered, trying to keep his voice down so he didn't wake his dad and sister.

No answer. The laughter had stopped.

Beacon crept closer to the pantry. Then he reached out and pulled on the doorknob. A massive tentacle slithered out of the door.

Beacon screamed.

"Wake up! Wake up!"

Beacon blinked open his eyes. Arthur was bent over him in the dark, his eyes huge behind his broken glasses.

"Are you okay?" Arthur asked. "You were screaming."

"I was? Did I wake you up?" Beacon mumbled.

"No, I was already awake. Couldn't sleep."

Everleigh groaned and smacked her lips together. "Everything 'right?" she said.

Beacon swallowed. "Just a bad dream. Go back to bed."

Everleigh was already snoring. His dad hadn't woken up at all. An unsettled feeling came over him. His dad was usually such a light sleeper. He famously once asked Jasper to pipe down when he made a "racket" undoing his belt when they were all sharing a tent during a family camping trip.

Beacon pushed that thought out of his head. It was good that his dad was finally getting some rest. They all needed it.

Beacon lay back down and pulled his thin comforter up to his chin.

He tried to go back to bed, but he couldn't fall asleep. The truth was, these dreams really bothered him. He used to hate the nightmares about Jasper underwater, but now he longed for any chance to see his brother's face again. In his dreams now, Jasper was always just out of reach. Just around a corner. Just out of sight. It was like the dream was designed to torture him. Punish him.

The worst part was, he knew he deserved it. He hadn't thought about his brother all day. He'd been too busy, and Jasper hadn't crossed his mind. But he knew that none of that was a good excuse. It had only been a little over a year since he died. What kind of a person didn't think about their dead brother every waking moment of the day?

Is this how it will happen? Beacon wondered. How Jasper would be forgotten? First, a day without thinking of him. Then a week, then a month, until he couldn't remember him ever being a part of their family at all? Frantically, Beacon tried to remember his brother's face. His wide brown eyes, and the dimple that popped out in his cheek when he smiled big, which he always did. Beacon tried to remember his booming and infectious laugh. And slowly, slowly, his brother came back. Beacon's breathing evened out, and he fell into a fitful sleep.

3

The junkyard was hemmed in by a chain-link fence topped with razor wire. Despite this precaution, the front gates were almost always open, revealing teetering piles of rusted-out cars as tall as two-story houses.

Dark clouds hung low over the yard, and thunder rumbled ominously. Any minute now it was going to spit.

Briefly, Beacon wondered if this was normal rain, or if it was possible the Sov were right, and there would be a collection of weather events that would devastate the planet. The reports of flash floods and other freak weather events had slowed since they'd seen the urgent news broadcast at the diner outside of Driftwood Harbor. But did that mean the floods were just a coincidence? Or was this the start of the Sov's prophecy coming true?

Beacon shook his head. He couldn't think about that right now. They were at the junkyard for a reason.

Their shady landlord was helping the twins' dad aquire fake identification so he could apply for better jobs, so Everleigh, Beacon, and Arthur had decided to spend the day gathering supplies for more PJs.

"I don't think we're going to get lucky here again," Beacon said. "This place is pretty picked over." Beacon glanced across at the others. That's when he noticed that Arthur looked pale. Well, paler than usual.

"Are you okay, man?" Beacon asked.

"Yeah, just a little lightheaded," Arthur said, touching his temple.

"I heard it helps if you eat," Everleigh said dryly.

This morning, Arthur had eaten two bites of his off-brand cereal and declared he was full.

"Loopy Fruits just aren't the same as the real thing." Arthur forced a smile. "I'm fine. Let's get this done."

Beacon was prepared to argue with him, but then Everleigh rolled up her sleeves and said, "Let's go shopping!"

The kids split up. Traversing the junkyard, Beacon couldn't help thinking about how strange it was that his dad was letting them out like this. When they'd first arrived in New York, he'd assumed that they'd be chained to the bedposts anytime their dad had to go out without them. Instead, he was letting them roam around a junkyard in an unfamiliar city by themselves. He wasn't about to lodge a complaint, but it was weird.

Beacon headed out for the far left corner. He was eager to

contribute something, especially after his failed attempt to sell his board.

Beacon ducked his head against the first few drops of rain and climbed up onto the hood of an old Ford Anglia. He peered in through the cracked windshield. Most of the cars had already been rifled through, but some of them had soda cans and filthy blankets strewn around inside. Beacon could imagine homeless people sleeping in the piled cars on cold winter nights. He left those cars alone, even if he and the others really could use extra blankets. At least they had a roof over their heads.

Beacon was fishing through the center console of a Beetle when he heard a bark.

He jerked his head up and quickly scanned the lot for a dog. But he didn't see anything. He must have imagined it, just like the Jane sightings.

Beacon shook his head and went back to digging through the console.

Then he heard it again.

He scoured the lot. Arthur was climbing a pile of scrap metal, and Everleigh was strolling out of the old security tower toward a rusted old crane. Relief trickled in, but it was short-lived. Something moved in the shadows, and Beacon realized it wasn't the crane his sister was walking toward, but a chocolate brown Lab standing next to it.

"Everleigh, stop!" Beacon yelled.

Beacon scrambled down the pile of cars, and his shoes slipped on the wet metal. He slid down, gashing his leg on a loose bolt. He hissed as he landed, limping past the pain as fast as he could over the cracked concrete.

"Everleigh, get away from that dog!"

But either she couldn't hear him over the rain or he was too far away. Everleigh bent down and stretched out a hand. All Beacon could do was watch in horror as the dog trotted up to his sister and . . . delivered slobbery kisses all over Everleigh's cheeks.

Disbelief coursed through him. Yesterday the dog had been ready to tear his dad to shreds. Now it was back to being nice again.

Beacon skidded up, gasping for breath.

"Come pet him, Beaks," Everleigh said. "He's really friendly."

Arthur had appeared sometime during Beacon's frantic screaming. He leaned over the dog.

"Careful, he's hurt," Arthur said. "Look at his nose."

Everleigh gently turned the dog's snout, revealing a wet welt across his nose.

"He doesn't seem too bothered by it," Everleigh said.

The dog's tail went round and round in response.

Beacon couldn't believe what was happening.

"That's—that's the homeless kid's dog," he said, finding his voice again. "The one that tried to attack Dad."

"This puppy?" Arthur said skeptically.

"Yes, but it was acting totally different yesterday," Beacon said. "It was snarling like it wanted to rip Dad's head off."

"You must be mistaken," Everleigh said. "He wouldn't hurt a fly." She nuzzled up to the dog, and it wagged its tail.

"I'm not wrong," Beacon said. "That thing is a vicious killer!"

The dog left Everleigh and bounded over to Beacon. It bumped into his legs, until even Beacon was forced to scratch behind its ears. The dog panted appreciatively. Beacon could practically see his argument dissolving before his own eyes.

Just then, Beacon caught sight of a maroon T-shirt. The homeless boy was watching them from behind the crane. He darted out of sight when Beacon spotted him.

"Hey! You! I see you!" Beacon ran over. "Stop!"

For a moment, it seemed like the boy might ignore him. Then he stuttered to a stop and turned around. He crossed his arms over his wet T-shirt and glared at Beacon.

"What?" the boy said defensively.

For a moment, Beacon was too shocked to speak. Mostly because he had started to assume that the kid was nonverbal.

"Thanks for helping us yesterday," Beacon said. "Your dog almost killed my dad."

"Then how come my dog's the one injured?" the boy said.

"You can't be suggesting my dad did that?" Beacon said.

"I'm not suggesting it. I'm saying it," the boy retorted.

"You've got a screw loose," Beacon said. "My dad yelled and your dog ran away. He never said anything about a fight."

But Beacon hadn't heard his dad yell, he remembered. He shoved that thought out of his head. This kid was clearly lying. He just didn't want his pet to get into trouble. They put down dogs that attacked people.

"Besides," Beacon added, "even if my dad did defend himself—which he didn't—he would have had a right. You saw the way your dog was acting. You need to control that thing."

"That *thing* is smart. It's not his fault he doesn't trust your '*dad*,'" the boy said, doing air quotes.

"What does that even mean?" Everleigh said.

"Yeah, what's up with the air quotes?" Arthur said.

The boy just glowered at them. Beacon could see they weren't going to get anywhere with him.

"Whatever," Beacon said. "Just keep your dog away from us. Come on, guys."

Beacon turned around. Everleigh gave the dog one last scratch behind the ears before she followed her brother. Arthur jogged up on the other side as they trudged toward the junkyard exit.

Everleigh looked over her shoulder, then dropped her voice to a whisper.

"Hey, are you okay?" she asked Beacon.

"What's that supposed to mean?" Beacon said.

"Did you get enough sleep last night?" Arthur asked.

Beacon snorted. "Oh, I see what's happening here. You think I'm going crazy."

"I didn't say that," Everleigh said.

"But you were thinking it. I know what I saw, Everleigh. This is the same as that time I swore I saw Jane in the water back in Driftwood Harbor. No one believed me, but I was right then, too."

"Fine, okay," Everleigh said. "I trust you."

Just then, Beacon saw white-blond curls through the wooden front gates of the junkyard. A sliver of ice went through him. He bolted for the gates, but when he got there, the girl was gone.

"What happened?" Everleigh panted, catching up to him.

"Did you see a Sov?" Arthur asked, his eyes darting around.

Beacon swallowed hard. "No. I—I thought I saw someone I knew."

"What?" Everleigh said. "Who do you know who lives in New York?"

"Someone from back home," Beacon lied. "From Los Angeles. You wouldn't know them. Come on, let's go."

They began the walk home. Beacon craned his head back, looking for Jane one last time. Everleigh might have said she trusted him, but he was starting to wonder if he even trusted himself.

Beacon used to love rainy days. Rain was a rare occurrence in LA, so it was kind of like Christmas morning when it happened. He loved watching a movie or reading a book by the fireplace, comforted by the knowledge that tomorrow would be beautiful once again.

Now, he would have killed for a nice sunny day. Not only had it been rainy more days than not the last few weeks, but this apartment was wet, cold, and downright miserable.

Beacon shivered underneath his thin blanket. He caught a whiff of something foul and realized it was his own BO. They'd escaped Driftwood Harbor with nothing but the clothes on their backs, and since they didn't have any money to buy more, they'd had to wear the same thing every day. Not only that, but they were forced to sleep fully clothed. Things were starting to get pretty funky around here.

Next to him, Everleigh and Arthur woke up, groaning. Bullet-size raindrops struck the bedroom window like they were trying to wash the apartment away. Wind whistled through a crack in the window, drowning out the sound of water dripping from the ceiling into the old saucepan they'd placed in the middle of the bedroom carpet.

Outside the room, Beacon heard the shower turn off. A minute later, his dad came in, pulling on a suit jacket over his wrinkled button-down shirt.

"You're going out?" Everleigh asked, sitting up. Her teeth chattered.

"Yep! I have an interview today. Have you seen my briefcase?"

"In the kitchen," Arthur said. His fingers trembled where they clutched his blanket.

"You have an interview?" Everleigh said. "That's great!"

"Won't pay much. It's an analyst position at a local community college, but it's something to keep the roof over our heads. See you kids later! Stay safe."

"Good luck!" Arthur called.

He was almost out the bedroom door when Everleigh said, "Wait!"

She scooped up something from the floor and ran over. She held out his tie. Her dad felt along his chest absently, then chuckled. "Oh, whoops! Thank you, Leigh."

Then he was gone.

The apartment door slammed a moment later. Beacon frowned at the spot where his dad had been standing. His dad never went anywhere without his tie. And he never called Everleigh "Leigh." That was strictly Jasper's nickname for her.

Beacon jumped up, the blanket pooling around his feet.

"Where are you going?" Arthur asked.

Beacon grabbed his sweater and shoes and ran for the door. "I forgot I have to do something. Be back soon."

He ran down the stairs two at a time and skidded out of the apartment building. He shielded his eyes and squinted through the onslaught of rain. Was he too late? Had his dad taken a cab?

Then he saw the swing of a briefcase two streetlights down. His dad was crossing the street. Beacon ran. He weaved dangerously in and out of traffic, half blinded by the glare of headlights and rain. His clothes were completely soaked through, and he was sure that once the adrenaline wore off he would be the coldest he'd ever been in his life. But right now, energy pumped through his veins. He distantly knew that he was acting strange, that he'd have a lot of explaining to do when he got back to the apartment. But none of that mattered right now. He just had to see where his dad was going.

Ever since the homeless boy had made that comment about his "dad," he hadn't been able to shake the feeling that something was off. It made him think about other strange things his dad had said and done in the last three weeks. Take schoolwork, for example. Sure, they were on the run and traditional school was out of the question. But it was unusual that his dad hadn't forced them to do schoolwork at the apartment. He hadn't asked them to do any chores, or do *anything*, really. He'd pretty much left them to their own devices.

Then there were the PB&Js. Beacon had walked into the

kitchen one night as his dad was preparing their dinner and had seen him spreading one slice of bread with jam and the other with peanut butter. Then he'd mashed the two slices together. Beacon had only ever seen his dad put the jam directly on top of the peanut butter. When Beacon asked him why he'd decided to do them that way, his dad had seemed confused for half a second before he'd made a joke about livening things up a bit, since things were so boring lately.

He'd flashed his CIA badge to get Beacon's board back, slept through Beacon screaming in his sleep, let them roam an unfamiliar city alone.

There had been countless other things, too, too insignificant to mention. But added up, those small things mattered.

He *had* to see where his dad was going.

Beacon elbowed his way through the crowd. His dad turned around suddenly, and Beacon dove behind a car parked on the street. His breaths came hard and fast. Had his dad seen him? But when he peeked over the hood, his dad was on the move again.

Beacon was more careful now, keeping close to the buildings, hiding behind lampposts and hot-dog carts and people when he could.

Finally, his dad entered a building. Beacon jogged up to the steel structure and peered in through the rain-splattered glass.

The place was full of construction workers in yellow vests and hard hats putting up framing, pouring concrete, carrying supplies. Why was his dad here? Was this the community college?

Through the glass, he saw his dad walking with a tall, brawny redheaded man in a suit toward an elevator at the back of the room. Beacon couldn't help thinking that they looked like they knew each other. His dad punched a button next to the elevator. The doors opened, and they stepped inside. When the doors closed behind them, Beacon entered the building. The buzz of drills and bang of hammers came into sharp relief.

"Excuse me." Beacon tapped one of the construction workers on the shoulder. He spun around and frowned.

"Hey, kid, you can't be in here. Skedaddle."

"Okay, sorry. Just one quick question," Beacon said. "Is this the community college?"

"Pardon me?" The construction worker was looking at Beacon as if he had three heads.

"Is this place going to end up being a community college?" Beacon clarified. "Once you're done building it?"

"None of your business, kid. Now scram."

"How about upstairs?" Beacon persisted. "Maybe there's one upstairs? Or offices, even?"

The construction worker shook his head. "Get out of here, before I call the cops."

Beacon briefly thought about charging across the room for the elevator, but he didn't even know which floor his dad was on. Besides, he'd probably just end up getting tackled.

He turned around and left. The rain fell so hard, it ricocheted off the cars and pavement. But Beacon didn't feel it.

He supposed it was possible the college was under construction, or that the interview was being held off campus. But he didn't think that was the case. His dad was lying.

There was something going on. He just had to figure out what.

4

"Wake up!" Beacon shook Everleigh's arm. She groaned and pulled a pillow over her head. Beacon yanked it off. "Ev, wake up."

She bolted up suddenly. Hair that had escaped her ponytail stuck to the drool on her cheek. "What's going on? Are the Sov here?"

"Shhh! And no. Emergency YAT meeting."

"What? How come?" she asked.

"I'll explain everything in a minute. Just meet me in the kitchen."

Beacon woke up Arthur next, and in seconds, they were all seated around the folding kitchen table, the moonlight struggling in through the grime-coated windows.

Beacon sat at the head of the table and steepled his fingers on the surface.

"Thank you all for joining me," he began.

Everleigh snorted.

"What?" Beacon said.

"Nothing. Hey, can't we turn on a light? This is weird sitting in the dark."

"No, it might wake up Dad."

"Shouldn't he be here?" Arthur said. "I thought he's part of YAT now?"

"No. This meeting is about him," Beacon said.

That got everyone's attention.

On the wet walk back to the apartment that morning, Beacon had run through every possible explanation for his dad's lie. But everything just wasn't adding up, and the more he'd thought about it, the more sure he'd been that something was going on. He'd run the last few blocks home and burst into the apartment, shouting about an emergency YAT meeting. But his words had died on his lips. His dad had been standing at the door, shaking the rain off his wet jacket. Turned out he'd taken a cab home. Beacon had had to do *a lot* of backpedaling, involving a hasty excuse about a suspicious-looking pigeon, but even then he got the distinct impression that his dad was onto him. After that, he'd stuck to him like glue, and Beacon hadn't gotten a chance to talk to Everleigh and Arthur alone for the rest of the night.

"Okay, so Dad's been acting weird lately," Beacon started. "I tried to look past it, because I can tell you guys think I'm going crazy, and honestly, I just didn't want to believe there was anything wrong. I even tried to put it out of my head when that kid at the junkyard said he didn't trust our 'dad.' Like, what kind of thing was that to say? Then yesterday Dad forgot his tie."

"He's had a lot on his mind lately," Everleigh said.

"He's *never* forgotten his tie before. And then he called you Leigh."

Everleigh shrugged. Even she couldn't deny that was weird.

"It just wasn't adding up," Beacon said. "So I followed him to his interview."

"I knew it!" Arthur said. "I knew you were lying about where you went when you ran out of here like that!"

"Shhh!" Beacon hissed. "Just listen. He said he was going to an interview for a job at a community college, right? But he went to this weird building south of here that was still under construction. He was talking to some guy, and it didn't look like the first time they'd met."

"What was the place?" Arthur asked.

"I don't know. All I know is that he lied about where he was going."

"Why would he do that?" Everleigh asked.

"This is going to sound out there, but what if"—Beacon looked over his shoulder at the dark hallway that led to the bedroom, then dropped his voice even lower—"what if Dad is still brainwashed?"

"That doesn't make any sense," Everleigh said, shaking her head. "Dad wouldn't be on the run with us if he were brainwashed.

He'd be hauling us back to Driftwood Harbor, not camping out in this apartment where dreams go to die."

"*Unless* this is what the Sov want," Beacon said.

Arthur sat up straighter. "Okay, I can kind of see what you're saying. The Sov might want to get eyes on the rebel operation."

Beacon skipped over the part where Arthur acted like the four of them could in any way constitute a "rebel operation." He was just happy Arthur was taking him seriously.

"Exactly," Beacon said. "Maybe they're trying to figure out what we know. Maybe they're trying to figure out why you're immune to the antidote. Maybe they're doing it for some other reason we can't even guess at. All I know is that Dad is acting weird. Even the dog could sense it."

"What does any of this have to do with the dog?" Everleigh said.

"You know how animals can supposedly sense the supernatural and stuff like that?" Beacon said. "I think that's why it only goes berserk around Dad. It knows something's off."

"You know what this means, right?" Arthur said.

"We need to Jumpstart him," Beacon said.

Everleigh pressed her lips together. She didn't like it, but she knew he was right. She stood up.

"So let's do this, I guess."

"Operation Silver Cougar is underway," Arthur said.

Beacon knew better than to ask Arthur what cougars had to

do with anything, never mind silver ones. As president of YAT, he insisted on giving their operations cool code names, and it was easier to just go with it.

Arthur retrieved the PJ from the living room, and the kids crept down the dark hall toward the bedroom. The apartment was so small that all four of them shared one room and rotated who got to use the bed. Tonight, the twins' dad slept on the floor. He lay flat on his back with his hands clasped serenely over his midsection. No blankets, no pillows. But it didn't seem to bother him. His chest rose and fell evenly under his pinstriped button-down shirt.

Beacon swallowed, then nodded at Arthur. Arthur clutched the wand of the PJ like a baseball bat and stepped forward hesitantly. The floorboards creaked under the carpet, and he froze. They all watched the twins' dad mutely, waiting for him to wake up and demand to know what they were doing. But he didn't stir. Beacon gave Arthur a thumbs-up. Arthur swallowed nervously before he closed the remaining distance and knelt down next to the twins' dad.

Arthur brought the trembling PJ first to the twins' dad's head, then to his chest, before he finally decided on his belly. He hovered the wand over his abdomen for a moment. Then he took a deep breath, jammed the wand into his side, and pressed the button. Arthur's body jolted as the shock traveled through the PJ.

The twins' dad's eyes popped open at the same time as his arm struck out and grabbed the wand. He yanked it out of Arthur's hand so harshly that Arthur stumbled back onto his butt. The twins' dad sat up as fast as a windup toy. Arthur screamed and scrambled back.

"What is that thing?" Everleigh said, eyes wide and horrified.

That's when Beacon saw it—it wasn't their dad's hand that had whipped out and grabbed the PJ from Arthur.

It was a tentacle.

The thick, slimy appendage stuck out from a gap in his dad's button-down shirt, the tip curling around the wand like a snake.

Beacon's brain stuttered as he took in the impossible sight.

"We have to go, NOW!" Arthur cried from the door.

The twins' dad sighed dramatically, looking down at his extra appendage.

"Well, this certainly is an unfortunate turn of events," he said. All at once, the tentacle slurped back inside his shirt. He tossed the PJ into a corner of the room and then fastened the buttons that had popped open from the tentacle's ejection. Then he calmly stood up and flattened the creases out of his slacks.

"D-Dad?" Beacon said, backing up.

"That's not Dad, you idiot." Everleigh snatched up her shoes and moved toward the door without taking her eyes off their dad. Or whoever it was.

"COME ON!" Arthur cried, jerking on his shoes.

"I had expected to hang out here a little longer," their imposter dad said. "But it looks like we'll be going back to Driftwood Harbor a bit earlier than planned."

His face twitched once before his skin went soft and wavy, like a distorted photograph. It all happened fast after that. Bones expanded, shifted, crunched into place. Muscles multiplied, ligaments stretched and reshaped. Skin darkened and smoothed, and hair sprouted across their dad's bald spot. One minute, he was their dad, and the next, he had shape-shifted into Victor, the leader of the Sovereign alien race.

Beacon had thought, worst-case scenario, that his dad had been brainwashed by the Sov. But it turned out his dad *was* a Sov.

"Run!" Everleigh screamed.

"That's what I've been saying all along!" Arthur said.

Beacon grabbed his sneakers and scrambled for the door. At the last minute, he saw the PJ in the corner. It would be a delay he might not be able to afford, but when might they get the chance to make another one? He darted left and scooped up the PJ.

"Beacon, hurry!" Everleigh screamed from the doorway. There was a clatter behind him just as cold fingers wrapped around his elbow.

"I'm running for my life here," Arthur called from the hall. "You might want to try it sometime."

Beacon yanked his arm free and tumbled through the bedroom door. Then all three of them ran through the apartment, shouting and pushing and elbowing their way into the main hall. Beacon tucked the PJ under his arm and jerked on his shoes one by one as he stumbled for the stairwell.

Beacon heard Victor behind him and panicked. He jumped the last four stairs and stumbled into a mop bucket on the landing. Stinky water sloshed everywhere. Gagging, he pushed himself up and crashed out of the doors. He looked left and right, his chest heaving.

Booming techno music blared from open windows. Men leered from covered doorways, their cigarettes glowing in the dark. A siren wailed distantly over the muted sounds of traffic.

No Everleigh. No Arthur.

"Thanks, guys!" Beacon shouted. He shoved the PJ into his back pocket and banked left, just as the apartment doors burst open behind him.

"This is only going to make things worse for you," Victor said, his calm voice carrying in the chilly autumn air.

A few people looked over at this pronouncement, but no one jumped up to help Beacon. He was pretty sure an actual squid could be chasing him through the streets and the native New Yorkers would shrug.

Beacon put his head down and kept running. The streets were a maze at night, lined with glowing signs and graffitied walls. But it didn't matter where he went. Just that he got away.

His feet slipped on wet leaves as he rounded a corner. A hot, stabbing pain shot from his ankle to his knee with each step. He pushed himself harder, past the pain, his fingers curled into sweaty fists at his sides. Sweat dripped from his matted hair.

Through a narrow alley, he spotted the familiar neon glare of Times Square. If he could get there, he would be safe. No way would Victor attack him somewhere so public. He darted into the alley, leaping over broken glass and garbage, crumpled takeout bags and cigarette butts. Something squeaked and scurried along the side of one of the buildings, and for once he was glad it was too dark to tell what it was. The end of the alley was in sight. He was almost safe.

Just then, a van with blacked-out windows pulled up, blocking the alley's exit. Beacon stuttered to a stop as the doors opened and two men in black suits stepped out.

"There!" one of the men said, pointing at Beacon. Beacon instantly recognized him as the redheaded man his dad—Victor, he reminded himself—had been visiting at the construction site. The man spoke in hurried tones into a wireless headset. The other man dashed forward with his arm raised toward Beacon, revealing the silver gleam of a device strapped to his wrist. Two narrow cylinders whizzed up and snapped into place above the device with a jarring *snap-snap* sound. Blue beams of light glowed to life inside the cylinders.

Beacon spun around and ran the other way. But Victor stepped into the alley entrance. He smiled, and his perfect white teeth gleamed.

"You've made me very angry," Victor said. "You aren't going to like me angry."

Beacon was trapped.

"You know, when the elders told me that you would be responsible for saving the planet from us, I thought you must be really extraordinary," Victor said. "Especially smart, especially talented—*anything*. But in the weeks that I've gotten to know you, I've realized you're just an average human kid."

Beacon backed up as Victor stepped closer, his shoes clicking loudly on the pavement.

"W-what are you talking about?" Beacon said.

"I would have killed you," Victor said. "But the elders said that it wouldn't work. That it would set off a chain of events far worse for our kind. So I decided to join you instead. Figure out a way to upend your plans from the inside. But you don't have any plans. I don't get it."

Beacon swallowed hard, gasping for breath. He didn't have time to try to figure out what Victor was talking about. He needed to think fast. He couldn't just let it all end like this.

That's when he saw it. A narrow metal ladder climbing the alley walls up to the roof. He had to take a chance, and he had to do it now, before those guys with their freaky weapons got much closer.

In one swift movement, Beacon launched himself at the wall. The guards were fast, but he was desperate. He climbed quickly, his sweaty fingers slipping on the cold metal.

"Don't just stand there," Victor ordered. "Stop him!"

A blue laser beam struck the brick next to Beacon's head, sending mortar crumbling below. Dust clouds rose in the air. *Bang, bang, bang.* Laser after laser. If it wasn't for all the brick dust in the alley impeding the guard's aim, he would have been dead already. As it was, the last beam had struck so close that the heat of the laser burned the side of Beacon's palm. He squinted and climbed faster.

The ladder shuddered beneath him. He glanced down through the mushroom cloud of dust. The redheaded guard was climbing after him. Beacon launched himself up the rungs faster, but a hand closed around his ankle. Without thinking, Beacon kicked hard. There was a sickening crunch as his heel connected with the guard's nose. The guard roared and fell from the ladder, disappearing through the dust. Beacon heard the thud as the guard smashed into the ground. Horror washed through him. He'd never hurt another person like that before. But then the other guard leaped onto the ladder in his place, and he forgot all about their feelings.

A deep, throaty growl filled the air. Beacon shivered. He knew that sound. He paused and squinted through the dust. The air cleared for a moment, and he saw shiny brown fur. The dog slunk toward the ladder. Its rumbling snarl sounded over the crash of Beacon's heart.

The dog launched himself at the guard. The guard yelped as he was ripped from the ladder and tossed aside like a cheap chew toy.

For a horrible second Beacon thought that he was next, but the dog spun toward Victor.

Victor took a step back, just as the dog leaped. But Victor whipped out a tentacled arm and struck the dog. It went crashing into the wall with a whimper. The dog rolled over and licked his wounded paw.

Victor stepped toward the animal.

"Hey! Stay away from my dog."

The homeless boy stood framed in the alley entrance.

5

"Ah, look who it is," Victor said, a smile curling his lips. "The prodigal son."

Shock poured through Beacon's body. Victor knew this kid?

"Didn't think you'd remember me," the boy said. "Just stay away from me and my dog," the boy said.

"And what if I don't?" Victor said. "What are you planning to do about it?"

Through the dust Beacon saw the barest glimpse of Victor's transformation. In seconds, the human was gone, and a horrible squid creature filled the alley. It stood on two powerful tentacles, towering over the boy. Its freakish limbs slithered at its sides in a ghoulish dance. The jaw on the underside of its body peeled open, and it let out a bloodcurdling scream. Beacon knew what it was: a battle cry.

Beacon expected the homeless kid to scream. To run. To faint—to do anything other than what he actually did next.

His freckled skin split like tree bark. Something heavy rolled under his skin like a snake, and a tentacle snapped out of his torso.

"Oh my God . . . ," Beacon muttered. He watched in mute horror as the boy transformed. The new creature rose, a mass of tangled limbs. It was smaller than Victor, but its constantly undulating tentacles suggested the speed it was capable of. The air crackled with tension as the two squid creatures faced off.

The smaller squid charged. Beacon was right—it *was* fast. The tentacles rippled over one another in a sickening swell of flesh. But the larger squid struck out with a powerful tentacle, and the smaller opponent went slamming into the brick with a thunderous boom. It didn't stay down long. When the larger creature approached, it struck back. Victor didn't see it coming and was catapulted across the alley. The action happened so fast, Beacon couldn't keep track. It was all hurtling tentacles and crumbling brick, sonic booms and dust.

A scream pierced the air. A woman stood frozen in the alley entrance. Beacon could suddenly see the whole thing from her point of view: Two larger-than-life squids duking it out. The woman slapped a hand over her mouth and stumbled back before she disappeared into the city street beyond. Beacon knew what would happen next. She would call the police. The media. *Everyone*. The squid creatures seemed to realize it, too. The larger one hesitated a moment before it slithered off the smaller one and retreated down the alley after the woman. Beacon saw a flash of his transformation back to human as Victor disappeared into the shadows.

The homeless kid transformed next. The process was slower than Victor's, less practiced. Beacon saw in gruesome detail the slimy tentacles withdrawing and absorbing, the skin slithering over a forming skeleton.

When it was all done, the homeless kid ran a hand through his blond mop and zipped up his hooded sweatshirt, as if he hadn't just transformed from a giant squid creature moments ago.

A siren wailed in the distance.

"Come on, let's get out of here," the boy said.

Beacon's fingers shook as he clung to the ladder. His *whole body* shook.

"I'm not going anywhere with you," he replied. "You're a Sov."

"And you're a human, but I'm not holding it against you."

Beacon swallowed hard.

"How did you know where to find me?" Beacon asked. "I saw you at that pawnshop, then the junkyard, and now here—have you been following me?"

"Yes," the boy said, without missing a beat.

"Oh." Beacon hadn't been expecting him to just admit it, and now didn't know how to reply. "Well, why?"

"Because Boots could tell your dad was Sov," he said.

So he *had* been right about the dog sensing his dad was off. He wished Everleigh and Arthur were here so he could prove to them that he wasn't crazy. But they'd ditched him.

"That's why your dog tried to attack my dad?" Beacon said.

"I trained him to alert me when a Sov is present." The boy mopped sweat from his brow. "Sometimes they blend in so well, it can be hard to tell. Since we're quizzing each other, what was Victor talking about—you saving the planet and all that?"

"I have no idea," Beacon said.

"I just saved your life," the boy reminded him darkly. "I stuck my neck out there for you. Tell me the truth."

"I'm not lying to you," Beacon said. "I don't know what he was going on about."

The boy stepped closer. He assessed Beacon for a long moment, as if he would somehow be able to tell if he was lying if he just stared at him hard enough. Then he sighed.

"So are we going to have this whole conversation with you hanging off the wall like Spider-Man, or are you coming down?" he finally said.

Beacon didn't know what to do. He didn't really trust this guy, but he *had* just saved his life. Besides, who knew how long it would be before Victor decided to come play again? And he was right—the police would be there soon, and he shouldn't be around when they arrived.

Beacon climbed down the ladder on gelatin legs. The entire alley was covered in sticky goo. The two guards lay comatose amid the mess of slime and mortar.

"What about them?" Beacon nodded toward the guards.

"What *about* them?" the boy answered.

Beacon felt kind of bad leaving them. What if they died? But he guessed that help was on the way. Besides, they *had* just tried to murder him. Didn't that make it fair? Distantly, Beacon thought back to the good old days before Jasper died and they'd moved to Driftwood Harbor, when his ethical decision-making had been limited to whether or not to tell his aunt Deb the truth that her new haircut made her look like she wanted to speak to a manager.

The boy shook his head and turned around. "Come on, Boots."

The dog stood up obediently and limped after its owner. After a few steps, it lost the limp and trotted happily behind him toward the alley exit.

Beacon raced to catch up and bumped into the boy, who had unexpectedly stopped and bent over. He braced himself on his knees as he inhaled deeply.

"You okay?" Beacon asked hesitantly.

"I'm fine," the boy said, standing up again. "Just needed a minute. Let's go."

He started walking again, and Beacon followed, picking his way through the goo. He couldn't help but notice how pale and mottled the boy looked.

"So, what's your name, anyway?" Beacon said.

"Galen."

"Well, thank you, Galen," Beacon said. "I don't know what would have happened if you hadn't come along. Probably would have been squid food. No offense," he added quickly, realizing that Galen was also a squid.

Galen shook his head. In the light of a nearby streetlamp, Beacon could see sweat trickling down his temples. Beacon was about to ask if he was sure he was okay when Galen stopped at the Sov guards' van, which was still parked at the end of the alley. Galen reached for the door handle.

"What are you doing?" Beacon asked. "Are you going to steal their car? Because I don't think that's a good idea. It probably has a GPS tracking device or something."

Galen opened the driver's-side door, and frantic moaning came into sharp focus. Beacon gasped. Galen disabled the child locks, and Beacon whipped open the rear door. Sure enough, Everleigh and Arthur were bound and gagged in the back seat.

Everleigh's face was red and sweaty from screaming so hard, and Arthur's broken glasses sat crookedly on his nose.

"Handkerchiefs," Galen muttered, peering into the back. "No chloroform, even? Must have cut the budget this year."

Beacon pulled the handkerchiefs out of Everleigh and Arthur's mouths.

"Beacon!" Arthur said. "I knew you'd save us!"

Everleigh spit hair out of her mouth.

"Took you long enough!" she said.

"Would it kill you to say thank you?" Beacon said.

"Maybe not, but why take the chance?" Everleigh said.

Galen pulled something out of his back pocket. Beacon saw a flash of metal. He registered it was a knife just as the boy advanced on Everleigh.

Everleigh gasped and pushed herself back in her seat, but Galen was too fast; he swiftly sliced the knife toward her. Everleigh looked down in shock, but no blood bloomed on her shirt. He'd just cut her bindings.

"A little warning would have been nice." She rubbed her raw wrists as Galen cut Arthur's ties next. Then he snapped the multitool closed and stowed it back in his pocket.

"We have to get out of here," Galen said. "Tweedledee and Tweedledum are waking up."

The guards in the alley were moaning and sitting up. They needed to get out of there. Victor might have been gone, but he didn't want to take any more chances with the guard's wrist lasers.

Beacon yanked Everleigh, then Arthur out of the back of the van. Then the group jogged after Galen and Boots out of the alley and onto a busy street, bustling with people and cars. It was hard to believe that life was carrying on normally for others when Battlestar Galactica had just taken place around the corner.

Everleigh appraised Galen as they walked.

"You're a Sov," she said.

"Don't deny it," Arthur added quickly. "We saw the whole thing from the back of the van."

"Then you saw that he saved me," Beacon said. "I would have been killed if it hadn't been for him."

"But why?" Everleigh said suspiciously. "If you're one of them, why save our lives?"

"I'm beginning to wonder that myself," Galen muttered.

"My sister is being rude, but she has a good point," Beacon said. "I'm grateful you did it and everything, so don't take this the wrong way, but why *did* you help me? Hey, can you slow down? Stop! Where are you going? We need answers!"

Galen sighed and turned abruptly to face them.

"Just let it go," Galen said. "You're free now. I'd recommend getting out of the city. Your cover is completely blown. It's not safe here."

"Who are you?" Everleigh said. "What do you know? And no offense, dude, but you look rough. Are you okay?"

Galen ignored her and turned around.

"You're just leaving us?" Beacon called.

"What exactly did you think, that we're going steady now or

something?" Galen said. "Yeah, I'm leaving. I have enough problems looking out for myself. I don't need a babysitting job."

"Who said anything about babysitting?" Arthur said. "We can look out for ourselves."

"Is that what you were doing in the back of that van?" Galen asked.

Arthur opened and closed his mouth.

Galen resumed walking.

Beacon saw it all happen as if in slow motion: One moment, Galen was walking down the sidewalk, and the next, he crumpled like a puppet whose strings had been released.

"Galen!" Beacon ran over and flipped the boy onto his back. Everleigh and Arthur crouched down next to him. Boots nudged past their legs and frantically licked Galen's cheeks.

"What's wrong with him?" Arthur asked.

"I don't know," Beacon said.

For a horrible second, Beacon thought the boy was dead.

"Hey, is everything all right over here?"

A man in a beanie and puffer coat walked over. Turned out New Yorkers *did* care about others.

"Do you need me to call an ambulance?" the man asked.

Galen's eyes fluttered open the tiniest bit.

He smacked his mouth, as if speaking were a monumental effort. "No," he finally said. "No ambulance."

The guy looked doubtfully at Galen sprawled on the sidewalk, then took out his phone.

"I said NO AMBULANCE!" Galen shouted.

"Jeez, fine," the man said, pocketing his phone. He grumbled about ingrates as he disappeared around the corner.

"Then what do we do?" Beacon said. "We can't just leave you here like this."

"Says who?" Everleigh muttered.

"Just drag me into a gutter and go," Galen said.

"What?" Beacon and Arthur said, at the same time as Everleigh said, "Sounds good!"

"No," Beacon said firmly. "We're not doing that. You saved our lives. We can't leave you like this."

"Back pocket," Galen said.

"What's in there?" Beacon asked.

Galen closed his eyes and swallowed hard. He was about to say something. Beacon leaned forward, his breath held so he wouldn't miss a word. But it never came.

Galen had passed out.

"Wake up!" Beacon shook his arm. "Come on, dude, we need to know where to take you!"

But the boy didn't even grimace. He was out like a light.

"Let's just get out of here." Everleigh glanced around frantically at the people walking by and casting worried looks at them. "We've spent way too long here. The cops could arrive any minute, and what if Victor or those guards find us?"

But Beacon ignored her. It was one thing to leave the guards who'd tried to kill him to die in an alley, but if he abandoned the person who'd just saved his life, he didn't know if he'd ever forgive himself.

He dug inside Galen's back pocket.

"What are you doing?" Arthur said.

"He said to go in his back pocket," Beacon said. He pulled out the knife, then a beat-up leather wallet. That had to be what he'd wanted them to find. "He probably wanted us to find his address."

"I don't think he has one," Everleigh said. "Isn't that the whole premise of being homeless?"

Beacon flipped open the wallet, and his eyes popped wide.

"Wow," Arthur said, peering over. "Is that real?"

Beacon pulled out a bill from the stack of crisp green twenties.

"Did he rob a bank?" Everleigh said. "Why does he have so much money? Never mind. We can get food now!"

She reached over and tried to snatch the bill, but Beacon held it out of reach.

"We are *not* taking his money," Beacon said. Just then his belly grumbled loudly.

"You sure about that?" Everleigh said.

Beacon stuffed the bill back inside with the others. He leafed through the wallet. He found a picture of a young brunette with a smattering of freckles on her cheeks, and a crumpled receipt for a Domino's pizza delivery, but there was no ID inside.

They'd reached a dead end.

He didn't get it. Why tell them to go in his pocket if there was nothing there to help them?

"Let's just call 911 and leave," Arthur said.

"What about his dog?" Beacon said.

"It'll go to a shelter," Everleigh said.

"Where it'll probably be killed," Beacon said.

Beacon pulled out the Domino's receipt again, thinking. And then it hit him. If he'd ordered pizza, he must have had it delivered somewhere. He inspected the receipt closer.

"243 Forest Park," he said, reading the delivery address on the receipt. He looked up. "This has to be where he lives!"

6

"For the record, I think this is a terrible idea," Everleigh said. Beacon and Arthur each had one of Galen's arms propped across their shoulders as they strained to drag his limp body down the street. Meanwhile, Boots trotted next to them, licking Galen's face and jumping in anxious circles. "We don't even know who this guy is."

"He's the person who just saved us," Beacon said, grunting with effort.

A couple rounded the corner and momentarily froze at the sight of them. Then the girl clung to her boyfriend's arm and urged him to walk faster. They both cast anxious glances over their shoulders as they passed. Beacon wanted to tell them that they weren't the ones they needed to worry about, that there were far scarier things roaming the streets tonight, but the couple disappeared around a corner.

"Arthur, hurry up!" Beacon said.

"I'm trying. He's heavy. Ow!" Arthur tripped over a crack in the sidewalk, nearly dropping Galen in the process.

"Oh, for heaven's sake." Everleigh shouldered Arthur out of the way and took his spot supporting Galen. Arthur removed his glasses with shaky fingers and swiped his forearm across his forehead.

"You okay, dude?" Beacon said.

"I just got chased by a giant squid, so I've been better." Arthur put his glasses back on. "Everleigh makes a good point. Why are we trusting a Sov?"

"Shhh!" Beacon looked around wildly, as if a Sov might be lurking in the shadows.

"Relax, we can say their name," Everleigh said. "Are we getting close yet?"

"I—I think we're here," Arthur said, looking up.

They stood in front of a huge, crumbling brick building near a subway station. All the windows were boarded up, and there was caution tape around the premises. The painted lettering on the front of the building was too sun-faded to read, but it was clear that whatever this place had once been, it had been abandoned a long time ago.

Everleigh squinted at the building. "Are you sure this is it? Maybe that lady we asked gave us the wrong directions."

Arthur shook his head. "This is it. 243 Forest Park."

"What are we supposed to do now?" Everleigh said. "We can't go in there. Who knows what's inside?"

"Well we can't just leave him out here, either. Help me set him down." Beacon and Everleigh lowered Galen to the ground. Then Beacon walked up the crumbling front steps and tested the door handle.

Locked.

He stepped back and looked up at all the boarded windows.

"Gimme a boost," he said to Arthur, running into the tall grass under one of the boarded-up windows.

Arthur cupped his fingers together, and Beacon stepped up onto his palms. He clambered onto the ledge, then pushed and pulled at the boards over the window. But none of them budged. They tried the next window, then the next, but they were all secure.

"Well, we tried," Everleigh said, a bit too enthusiastically. "I guess this is where the buck stops. See ya, Galen!"

She started to walk down the sidewalk, but sighed and spun back around when no one followed her. Beacon looked up at the building like the place was a complicated math equation. A gust of wind whistled through the old building, sending a vortex of leaves skittering into the gutters.

That's when he realized it was too quiet.

"Hey, where's the dog?" Beacon said.

He looked around, but it was nowhere in sight.

Everleigh sighed. "It went in there."

She gestured toward a narrow alley to the right of the building.

The dog was standing alertly in the shadows, next to a pile of trash.

"What's it doing in there?" Beacon said.

"Maybe it knows where the entrance is?" Arthur said. "Maybe it's waiting to go inside?"

Beacon stepped cautiously into the alley.

"Oh good, another alley," Everleigh muttered. "I'd been hoping there'd be more tonight."

But she followed her brother. This alley was even grubbier than the last. There was a yellow-stained refrigerator pushed up against the old brick, a broken shopping cart, a baby doll that was missing its eyeballs . . .

Boots yipped and spun in circles as they approached.

"This place is creepy," Everleigh said. "Let's get out of here. There's obviously no entrance."

"This has to be it," Beacon said. "The dog's going nuts."

"Well, unless there's a secret entrance or something, this is a dead end," Everleigh said.

Beacon frowned. What Everleigh had said got him thinking.

He pressed his hands along the brick.

"You've got to be kidding me," Everleigh said.

None of the bricks moved.

"Satisfied?" Everleigh said.

The dog was still going nuts. The entrance *had* to be here.

He opened the refrigerator, then gagged. A loaf of bread had turned into some kind of science experiment in the old in-unit freezer.

"That is nasty!" Arthur said.

Beacon held his breath and reached inside.

"Don't touch it!" Everleigh shrieked. "What the heck are you doing?"

Beacon was wondering the same thing when his arm grazed the mold and he felt puke rise in his throat. But then he felt it: a lever on the back wall of the refrigerator. He pulled, and the wall swung forward. Behind it was a small door in the brick wall.

He turned the handle, and the door swung open into darkness. Boots nudged his way past them and trotted off into the shadows.

"Oh my God," Everleigh said, peering over Beacon's shoulder. "There really is a secret entrance."

"What is this place?" Arthur said.

"I don't know, and I don't want to find out." Everleigh crossed her arms. "There could be Sov in there. We could be walking into a massacre."

She wasn't totally wrong.

Beacon bit the inside of his lip and stared into the shadowy passage. Bringing Galen home had seemed like the best move, but now he wasn't so sure. He wasn't sure of *anything*. What Victor had said in the alley had really struck a nerve. He didn't have a plan. He didn't know what he was doing. He was floundering from one day to the next, just trying to survive.

"Get Galen," Beacon finally said. "If there are other Sov inside, they won't hurt us if we have him."

Everleigh thought about it for a second, then uncrossed her arms.

"Cold," she said. "I love it. Come on, Arthur."

They disappeared and returned a moment later with Galen. They'd given up on carrying him upright, and dragged him across the pavement.

Beacon gingerly stepped through the door, then held it open as Everleigh and Arthur squeezed through with Galen. The passage was tight, and there was a lot of grunting and whisper-shouting as they struggled to fit Galen's dead weight through the small door. When they finally got inside, they dropped Galen onto the floor. Moonlight filtered in through the gaps in the boarded-up windows. They took in their surroundings as they caught their breath.

There was broken glass everywhere. It stuck up in jagged shards from what appeared to be tanks that once stretched around the room, all the way to the ceiling. The concrete walls were covered in vulgar graffiti and rot.

"This place is creeping me out," Everleigh said. "We got him inside. Now can we go?"

Boots appeared from the shadows, his nails clicking loudly on the concrete. He stood panting in a doorway, as if waiting for them to follow him.

"Aren't you even a little bit curious what he's hiding in here?" Beacon asked. "We've already come this far."

Everleigh sighed, but she hefted Galen up from under his shoulders.

"Well, are you going to get his feet, or do I have to do all the work?"

Beacon grabbed Galen's legs and lifted, and they trailed after Boots through a hallway littered with garbage, broken chairs, and rusted filing cabinets regurgitating soggy papers. The hall opened up into a large, empty room. Boots clicked his way around the walls, but Everleigh trudged backward through the center. She stumbled suddenly, then screamed and dropped Galen's shoulders. Her arms pinwheeled wildly. Beacon dropped Galen's legs and snagged the front of Everleigh's shirt, yanking her forward so hard, she stumbled into Beacon.

"What the heck was that?" Everleigh shouted, spinning around.

Beacon cautiously stepped forward.

Just steps ahead of them was a giant drop-off. It stretched to fill almost the entire room.

Arthur peered over the precipice.

"I think I know what this place is," he said. "An abandoned marine aquarium. That's what all those tanks were for. And this must have been a pool for the dolphins or whatever."

Beacon couldn't help thinking that if his sister hadn't almost just died falling into this thing, it would have been a neat place to skateboard.

Boots barked up ahead.

Everleigh blew out a slow breath, then dragged Galen away from the pool by his ankles. Beacon hefted Galen's shoulders this time, and they kept walking, around the pool, through a doorway, up a narrow metal stairwell, stopping to take a breath every few seconds. Finally, the dog stopped in front of a door at the top of the stairs.

"Thank God," Arthur said. "I couldn't walk a minute longer."

"*You* couldn't?" Everleigh said, dropping Galen's feet onto the stairs. "You weren't even doing any of the work."

Beacon laid Galen down as gently as he could manage on a set of stairs, then stepped forward and gripped the doorknob. He twisted, at the same time as he shoved his hip against the door. He'd expected it be jammed, and stumbled over his own feet when the door fell open easily. He sprawled onto his knees.

"I remember *my* first door," Everleigh said as she stepped around him.

Beacon's retort died on his lips as he pushed himself up and took in the room. Computers strung with twinkling Christmas lights lined the room. Unlike the rest of the building, which looked like a demilitarized zone, this place had been cleaned up. There was an old sofa with a blanket neatly folded over an arm, a mini fridge in the corner with canned goods and a few kitchen utensils stacked on top of it, and a dog bed on the floor, which Boots was already curled up on. It actually looked . . . cozy.

"So we found his lair," Everleigh said.

"Look at all this gear," Beacon said. "How's he getting power in this place?"

"He's got it rigged up to a generator," Arthur said, checking out his setup.

"Help me get him inside," Beacon said to his sister.

Everleigh hefted Galen's shoulders, and they dragged him the final stretch into the room. They dumped him onto the couch. He landed with his neck crooked at an awkward angle and his arm flopped over the side. He didn't roll over or adjust himself or . . . anything. It was creepy.

"What do you think is wrong with him?" Everleigh said.

"Maybe it was the transformation," Beacon said. "Maybe it took a lot out of him, and now his body needs to recover."

Arthur nodded thoughtfully.

"Well, at least we have somewhere to stay tonight," Beacon said.

"What?" Everleigh said. "We are *not* staying here."

"Why not?" Beacon asked.

"This isn't our place, for starters," Everleigh said.

"Technically, it's not his, either," Arthur said. "Besides, I don't think he minds." He lifted Galen's hand and dropped it; it flopped back onto the couch like it weighed about a thousand pounds.

"We don't know if this place is safe," Everleigh said. "What if this guy has roommates? What if other Sov are on their way home right now?"

"Does it look like anyone else lives here?" Beacon said. "There's just the one couch. Besides, we don't have any other options at the moment. We can't go back to that apartment—that place is Sov City. And we don't have money for a hotel. That means our only other option is a homeless shelter, and the Sov are probably watching places like that since they know we're on our own."

That was on top of the fact that shelters would make them prime targets for social workers and other Good Samaritans who might see kids on their own and decide to call the authorities.

"We'll stay here tonight," Beacon said. "Then tomorrow, we can figure out another plan."

"*Fine*," Everleigh said, as if the word had about ten syllables. "Now can we discuss the bigger issue here?"

Beacon raised his eyebrows, waiting for her to continue.

"If that wasn't really Dad," she said, "then where *is* Dad?"

Beacon's stomach went suddenly cold, as if an ice cube had melted inside him. He'd been so busy running for his life and trying to save Galen that the thought hadn't even occurred to him. Now it seemed wild, terrible, *inexcusable* that it hadn't been the first thing he thought about.

"He's still there—inside the UFO," Arthur said.

"If he's even alive," Everleigh said.

"Don't say that!" Beacon said.

"I'm just being a realist," Everleigh said. "Look at what they did to us when we were trying to escape. They clobbered our pod. They tried to kill us. Why wouldn't they do the same to Dad?"

Beacon shook his head. "No. They wouldn't do that. He's alive."

"You don't know that," Everleigh said. "Just because you want it to be true doesn't make it true."

"We have to find out," Arthur said. "We need to contact someone in Driftwood Harbor."

Beacon wanted to race to the nearest phone right now, but he forced himself to be reasonable. The streets would be teeming with the Sov and their guards right now. Besides, it was four o'clock in the morning.

"We'll go to a library first thing tomorrow," Beacon said. "Use a pay phone, like you suggested. The Sov know we're in New York now, so that shouldn't be a problem."

When no one argued, Beacon dropped onto the floor. They all settled into spots around the tiny room. It was the most uncomfortable sleeping quarters they'd had yet, but exhaustion had caught up with him, and within minutes, Beacon drifted off to a dreamless sleep.

7

Beacon woke with a start. For a minute, he didn't know where he was. Then he saw Arthur typing in front of a computer monitor strung with Christmas lights, and everything came flooding back. Jumpstarting his dad. The squid fight in the alley. The abandoned marine aquarium. He could hardly believe all of it had really happened.

"Oh good, you're up!" Arthur whispered. "Come check this out."

Beacon stretched up and joined Arthur at the keyboard.

"This guy's got, like, five firewalls on his computer," Arthur said.

"That's kind of a violation of his privacy, don't you think?" Beacon said.

"You're missing the point," Arthur said. "Why would he need such tight security?"

"Maybe he's on the run, like us?" Beacon said, remembering what Galen had said about their cover being blown.

"I think this guy is hiding something," Arthur said. "He knows a lot more than he's letting on. And check out his fridge. It's totally full. Where's he getting all this money from?"

Beacon opened the mini refrigerator. It was jam-packed with food—leftovers of the aforementioned pizza, string cheese, yogurt tubes . . . how was Galen affording this?

"Help yourself," Arthur said. "I already had some."

"Stealing from a dead man," Everleigh said. "Low."

She shoved past Beacon and grabbed a yogurt tube, then a pizza slice. It seemed like Beacon should have been happy about the unexpected meal, but all he could think about was his dad in that prison. Still, he forced himself to grab a slice of pizza. He didn't know when he'd get another meal.

Arthur typed frantically while the twins chewed their food, looking at Galen. The way he slept made a chill creep down Beacon's back. His mouth was hanging wide open like someone with one foot already in the grave.

"Should we be doing something for him?" Beacon asked around a mouthful of food.

"Like what?" Everleigh said. "Fluff his pillow?"

"I got in!" Arthur said. Beacon and Everleigh abandoned all thoughts of Galen and rushed over to Arthur.

"What is this?" Beacon said.

On the screen was an aerial view of a doorway. An armed guard stood in front of two massive wooden doors etched with an intricate design.

"Some type of security feed," Arthur said.

"Why is he watching this?" Everleigh said.

"Who's inside that room?" Beacon added.

"I don't know. Maybe we can see inside." Arthur typed some more, and the screen changed to a grid. Each of the twelve squares in the grid showed a different view.

Everleigh leaned forward.

"Oh my God. I think this is the UFO," she said.

"From Driftwood Harbor?" Beacon said, surprised.

"You know of another one?" Everleigh pointed at one of the squares on the grid, where tables stretched down the center of a large room. "That looks like the caf."

Beacon scanned the other squares and suddenly felt faint.

He pointed at a circular room lined with two-way mirrors. There was a stretcher in the middle of the room, surrounded by scary-looking medical equipment.

"That was where I woke up the night the sheriff shot me and Arthur."

"Are you sure?" Everleigh asked.

Beacon leaned forward. "Positive. That's where Dad tried to give me the vitamin injection."

A chill shuddered down his spine at the memory.

"So Galen knows about the UFO," Arthur said. "And he's spying on them."

"Not them," Beacon said. "On someone in particular."

Arthur looked over at him.

"He could watch anywhere in the ship, and he was looking at the one door. Why?"

"I don't know, but this is great," Everleigh said. "We can look for Dad."

"Can we see more rooms?" Beacon asked.

Arthur's fingers trembled in his rush to type. The grid changed again. They scoured the screen, looking for any sign of the twins' dad.

"I don't see anything. Where are the prison cells?" Everleigh said.

"They're invisible, remember?" Arthur said. "They wouldn't appear on the security feed."

That didn't stop them from trying. For the next hour, they searched the grids, until they found the hallway that led to the prison cells. But the security feed showed only an empty room.

"Maybe there's a way we can hack the system to show us the cells?" Beacon said.

"I'm a scientist, not a computer hacker," Arthur said. "I just know the basics."

"I bet *he* knows how to see the cells." Everleigh walked over to

Galen. She roughly nudged his stomach with her foot. "Hey, Alien Boy! Wake up!" she shouted.

Galen didn't budge.

"WAKE UP!" she yelled an inch from his ear, then shook his shoulders.

"Everleigh, stop," Beacon said.

Everleigh sighed. "What now, then? I'm not waiting around to find out if this guy dies or wakes up. We need to *do* something. Every minute we spend here, Dad is back there, in danger."

"We go back to Plan A," Beacon said, standing. "Let's find a library. It's time to contact Driftwood Harbor."

••••••••••••••••••••••••••••••••

The library closest to the aquarium was an ancient marble behemoth, replete with stone arches and a gargoyle, sitting awkwardly within a knot of steel skyscrapers and condos. They pushed open the heavy door and entered a large room with a polished tile floor and massive wooden bookcases fanning out from the reception area. They found a bank of pay phones in a small alcove off the main room. Six or seven people were sitting at tables, working. A man in a cable-knit sweater was reading a battered copy of the *New York Times*.

"Who should we try first?" Everleigh said.

"I still don't get why we shouldn't call my grandma," Arthur said.

"We went over this," Everleigh said. "Besides, she won't know anything about the Sov. She never leaves her house."

"We should call Donna," Beacon said.

Donna was the innkeeper at the bed-and-breakfast they'd stayed at during their brief time in Driftwood Harbor. Beacon had low-key been afraid of the surly woman before she'd revealed herself to be an ally and offered to help break Arthur out of the Sov's underwater prison. But once the twins and their dad had sneaked inside the ship, Donna hadn't come through with her end of the plan. She was supposed to create a distraction to get them out, but nothing ever happened. It was by sheer luck that Nixon had arrived and broken them out of the prison; otherwise, they'd probably still be inside those cells.

"How do we know we can trust her?" Arthur said. "She ghosted you guys."

"I don't think she ghosted us on purpose," Beacon said. "It doesn't make sense. She warned us that the sheriff was coming and made sure we were hidden in the garage until he left. Then she came up with the plan to save you. Why do all that if she was secretly working for the Sov? It would have been easier to just let us be arrested and call it a night." He shook his head. "Something happened to her."

"He's right," Everleigh said. "I think something happened. And

Donna makes the most sense to call. She knows all about the stuff going on behind the scenes, and she's on our side."

"Fine. Let's do it," Arthur said.

Everleigh found a computer that the previous patron had forgotten to log out of and googled some phone numbers. Then they huddled around one of the pay phones in the bank along the wall.

Beacon dialed the number for Blackwater Lookout Bed-and-Breakfast. His body clenched tight as the phone rang.

And rang, and rang, and rang.

Finally, it went to voice mail. He hung up quickly.

"No answer."

"What now?" Everleigh said.

"What about Nixon?" Arthur asked.

Nixon was a Gold Star, but he'd also saved them from the Sov's UFO prison, putting himself at risk in the process. Like Arthur, he was immune to the "antidote." Beacon had seen his file in the school nurse's office, which documented Nixon getting the mind-controlling injection dozens of times because he'd gone "Off-Program," a term the Sov used for when the injection went wonky. According to Nixon, he'd never been on the program to begin with. He only ever pretended to be mind-controlled so the Sov wouldn't try to hurt him. When he'd get caught acting out of line, they'd inject him again, and he'd know to be on his best behavior or risk getting exposed.

"What if they have him locked up now?" Everleigh said. "The

Sov know that he helped us. What if they also figured out the antidote doesn't work on him?"

"We have nothing to lose by trying," Beacon said.

Arthur searched for Nixon's phone number, then Beacon dialed.

They huddled around the phone again as the ringing stretched on and on and on. Beacon was just coming to terms with the fact that they'd struck out again when the ringing stopped abruptly.

"Hello?"

Beacon sagged with relief at the sound of Nixon's voice.

"Nixon? It's Beacon."

There was a silence on the other end of the phone.

"From school?" Beacon added belatedly. "I sat next to you in Mrs. Miller's class, and—"

"I know who you are," Nixon said. "I just can't believe you're calling me. Where are you?"

"In hiding," Beacon said cagily. "We need some information."

"I can't help you," Nixon said. "Do you know how much trouble I was in after that whole prison stunt? They've got me under lock and key. This conversation alone is dangerous. In fact—"

"Don't hang up!" Beacon said, then lowered his voice when the old man in the cable-knit sweater looked over. "We just want to know what happened to our dad after we left."

Nixon started to say something, but paused. Everleigh snatched the phone from Beacon.

"Nixon, tell us what you know. Where's our dad?"

"I don't know." Nixon at least had the decency to sound apologetic when he said it.

"What do you mean you don't know?" Everleigh said.

The kids gathered close to the phone to hear his answer.

"After you guys left, some guards Tasered your dad," Nixon said. "They hauled him off, and I haven't seen him since."

Beacon became uncomfortably aware of his own heartbeat. He felt so light-headed, he thought he might faint.

"You're lying," Everleigh said thinly.

"I wish I were," Nixon said. "I checked everywhere for him. The prison, the Contam rooms—I know every corner of that ship, and he's not there."

"There must be someplace you didn't think of," Arthur said. "Those prison cells were invisible. Maybe they've got him somewhere else like that? Somewhere you just can't see?"

"Maybe," Nixon said, in a tone that communicated just how unlikely he thought that was. There was a *thunk* from Nixon's end of the phone. Nixon gasped suddenly. "My mom's coming. I have to go." The call cut out.

Everleigh slammed the phone back onto the hook.

"So he's gone." She swiped her forearm angrily across her cheek.

"We don't know that for sure," Beacon said, though he didn't know who he was trying to convince, Everleigh or himself.

"We just have to face the truth," Everleigh said. "We're alone. We've *been* alone ever since Jasper died. We haven't had a dad since then, and we aren't getting one back."

The words hit Beacon like a sucker punch to the gut. He felt his future open up like a cold, dark chasm. The Sov were winning. They'd gotten their dad, and it was only a matter of time now until they got them, too.

He leaned against the wall next to the pay phone, just to give himself something to anchor him to reality. He closed his eyes and raked his fingers through his hair.

"What do we do now?" Arthur said.

"Who cares?" Everleigh said. Tears streaked down her cheeks that she wasn't bothering to conceal. That was scarier than anything he'd seen over the last month. She was giving up. On Dad. On them.

Beacon wanted to tell her not to talk like that, but the truth was, he felt the same way. They'd failed.

"This isn't over," Arthur said. "We still have options."

"Like what?" Beacon said glumly.

"Like Galen. There's something not right about that kid."

"What tipped you off?" Everleigh said. "Was it the tentacles? It was the tentacles, right?"

"He's a Sov," Arthur said, ignoring her attitude. "Yet he helped us, and he's spying on the UFO. That *has* to mean something. And I don't think it's just that he's nice guy—squid, whatever. There's something big going on here, and he knows what it is. What if something he knows can help us find your dad?"

Everleigh chewed the inside of her cheek for a moment, before she pushed off from the wall, determination returning to her eyes. "We need to get back to that aquarium and take another crack at his computer while he's still out."

•••••••••••••••••••••••••••••••••

Beacon opened the refrigerator door. Everleigh gagged and covered her mouth. The moldy bread looked a hundred times worse in the cold light of day.

"We need to get rid of that thing," Everleigh said.

"No way," Beacon said, stepping through into the secret passage. "It's a good deterrent. Someone sees moldy bread and they don't try to look further, or—"

There was a flash of steel, and before Beacon could utter another word, there was a blade at his neck.

"Move an inch and you'll regret it," Galen said behind him.

Beacon swallowed hard. He'd seen Galen's knife before. It was nothing more than a tiny blade set in a multi-tool. Something for emergencies. But it would get the job done.

He heard his sister and Arthur coming through the passage.

"Run!" Beacon screamed, making the knife nick his skin. He felt the warm drip of blood down his neck.

There was a flurry of footsteps. Everleigh burst into the room, her face contorting into a mask of rage.

"Let my brother go, and I might consider not murdering you."

"What's going on in there?" Arthur said, stepping through the door. "Who screamed? Oh . . ."

His words puttered out as he took in the scene.

"What are you doing here?" Galen demanded.

"Put the knife down." Arthur raised his trembling hands like a zookeeper trying to calm a feral animal. "We can talk about this."

"I call the shots around here," Galen said. "And I said what are you doing here?"

"Ooh, you are *so* tough," Everleigh said. "Let's see how tough you are when it's just you and me, without that knife."

Beacon wished he had half of his sister's self-confidence. She'd seen Galen transform into a giant squid, and she was *still* calling him out in a fight.

"There's no need for violence," Arthur said. "We can all talk, right?"

"I said *what are you doing here?*" Galen screamed. Spittle hit the back of Beacon's neck with the force of his words. "I want answers, *now!*"

"We brought you here," Arthur explained. "Last night, after you passed out. Some of us wanted to leave you on the street," he added, darting a look at Everleigh, "but Beacon insisted we help you, since you helped him."

"How did you find my hideout?" Galen asked.

"From the pizza receipt in your wallet," Beacon said. When Galen looked confused, he added, "I went in your back pocket, like you said."

Galen closed his eyes for a moment. Beacon could have sworn that if he wasn't holding the knife, he would have pinched the bridge of his nose. Beacon didn't get it. He'd done exactly as Galen had asked.

"How long was I out?" Galen said.

Arthur looked at his watch. "If you woke up just now? Fourteen hours, twenty-eight minutes, and thirty-seven seconds, give or take a few seconds."

"Damn," Galen said under his breath.

"Longer than usual?" Arthur asked, his voice pitching higher at the end. "That's why you passed out, right? Because of the transformation?"

"I passed out because you checked the wrong pocket."

"What?" Arthur said.

"I keep an EpiPen in my pocket for emergencies."

"You have allergies?" Arthur asked, confused.

"No," Galen said, rolling his eyes. "The epinephrine gives me enough energy to get somewhere safe before I black out. Buys me twenty minutes, half an hour if I'm lucky. If you would have checked my *other* back pocket, you would have found the syringe." He shook his head, as if angry with himself that he'd said so much. "You need to leave. NOW."

"I'm not going anywhere without my brother," Everleigh said.

In one swift movement, Galen pulled the knife away from Beacon's throat and shoved him toward his sister.

"Are you okay?" Everleigh grabbed her brother and quickly examined his neck.

"Go," Galen ordered.

Everleigh glowered at Galen.

"Come on, let's get out of here," Arthur said. Arthur pulled Beacon toward the passage, but panic flared inside Beacon's body. Galen was their last hope. Without him, they'd truly be out of options. He needed to think of a way to convince Galen to help them. If he could *just* figure out what the boy wanted . . .

It came to him in a flash. Of course—Galen's wallet. That was the key. Beacon yanked his arm free of Arthur's grip and spun around.

"We can help you find the girl."

"What girl?" Everleigh said.

"I don't know what you're talking about," Galen said, but he'd stiffened, almost imperceptibly.

"The girl in your wallet," Beacon said. "You've been keeping an eye on her. That's why you have those computers set up. You watch her."

"You were on my computers?" Galen's skin began bubbling and flowing like a current ran under it. He was a second away from transforming, but Beacon knew he was onto something. Why else would Galen be so mad?

"We just wanted to see what you were up to," Beacon said. "And now we know you were watching someone. Someone on that underwater ship. You left her behind, didn't you?"

Galen roared and advanced. Everleigh grabbed Beacon's arm, but he shook her off and stepped forward, facing off with Galen. "You ran away, but she's still there, isn't she? You watch her because you want to make sure she's okay."

Galen's eyes flashed, his fingers curling tighter around the knife "I didn't leave her behind! She didn't want to come."

A solid mass bulged underneath Galen's skin, like a baby trying to push its way out of its mother's belly. That tentacle was one wrong word away from bursting out of his skin. And if it did, Beacon didn't know if Galen would be able to stop the rest of the transformation.

"Who is she?" Beacon asked calmly. "A sister. A . . . girlfriend?"

"Just a friend," Galen said quickly.

"Has it been a while since you talked to her?" Beacon asked.

Galen looked like he might answer, but then he shook his head. "I'm not talking to you about this. I can see what you're trying to do, and it isn't going to work. Get out of here."

"She's in danger," Beacon said.

Galen tensed, and Beacon held up his hands. "Just listen to me for a second. There's something big going on in Driftwood Harbor. It isn't safe for her there. For *anyone*. If you care about this girl, you need to get her out of there."

"What are you talking about?" Galen said. "What do you know?"

"We'll tell you everything," Beacon said. "But first, you need to put that knife down."

"And stop doing that freaky thing with your skin," Everleigh added.

Galen's jaw rippled with fury. His nostrils flared and he gripped the knife tighter as he stared Beacon down. Then he sighed and threw the knife into the corner.

••••••••••••••••••••••••••••••••

A few minutes later, they were back in Galen's headquarters. They eyed each other like wary cats circling.

"Talk," Galen said.

He was still angry, but at least now he wasn't a hairsbreadth away from transforming.

"I don't even know where to start," Beacon said.

He brought Galen up to speed on everything from their move to Driftwood Harbor to stealing the car and meeting their dad in the diner the next county over, ending with the discovery that their dad wasn't really their dad, but Victor in disguise. The whole time, Galen listened, poker-faced.

"And that's pretty much it," Beacon said.

"That doesn't make any sense," Galen said. "Why would Victor pose as your dad? Why wouldn't he just kill you, or lock you up?"

Beacon remembered what Victor had said about him saving the planet.

"I don't know," he said.

Galen's eyes narrowed, and Beacon was suddenly sure that Galen knew he was lying. Maybe Galen was also thinking back to what Victor had said in the alley, and wondering what Beacon was hiding from him. Even though Beacon wasn't entirely sure what Victor had meant himself.

Galen held his stare, and Beacon struggled not to fidget.

"Okay, so now it's your turn to talk," Everleigh said, interrupting the silent standoff.

Beacon thought Galen would argue, but the boy just crossed his arms. "What do you want to know?"

"Why did you help us?" Arthur said.

Galen shrugged. "I wasn't going to just let Victor murder you. It really isn't more complicated than that."

"But you were following us for at least a week," Beacon said. "You admitted that. Why?"

"He was following us?" Everleigh said. "How come you never told us that, Beacon?"

"Because you never would have come here if I'd told you," he said.

"And that's a bad thing? He just had a knife to your throat."

"Just answer the question," Beacon said. "Why were you following us?"

Galen gritted his teeth, then sighed.

"I first saw you that day outside the pawnshop. Thought nothing of you, except that you were probably some rich kid who got his allowance cut off so he was selling his Christmas gift for spare cash. But then you came back later. I knew right away your dad was Sov. Boots can always tell."

"He trained his dog to scent Sov," Beacon explained to the others, gloating.

"Gives me a little warning," Galen said. "Buys me enough time to get away before anyone gets too close. It's how I've been able to stay out of their grasp for this long." Galen affectionately scratched Boots behind the ear.

"So Boots did his thing. He growled at your dad while I got away. But then your dad attacked Boots in the alley after you'd run for help. I whistled for Boots, he escaped, and we came back here. I got all packed up to leave town, but I couldn't stop thinking about how weird it was that a Sov was traveling with human kids who weren't on the Program. I was curious, so I went back to the pawnshop. I waited around for a bit, hoping you'd come back, but when you never did I tracked you down."

"You scented us, right?" Arthur asked excitedly.

"No," Galen said. "I got lucky and saw you when I was walking past the junkyard."

"Oh," Arthur said, visibly deflating. "So you were following us since then?"

Galen jammed his hands into his pockets. "I just wanted to see what was going on. I didn't get why this Sov was sticking around without inoculating you. And your area was crawling with Sov guards. They were posted everywhere. There were even a few on the stoop right across the street posing as homeless people."

"Oh my God, those were Sov guards?!" Everleigh said.

Galen bobbed his head.

"It was stupid of me to stick around so long. I've been on the run for twelve years, and now I was practically swimming in a sea of Sov again. I was just talking myself into leaving when you all ran out of your apartment like bats out of hell. And that's basically it," he said, shrugging. "I saw you in that alley, and I guess for whatever dumb reason I decided to help."

"Wait a minute, you said twelve years on the run—how is that possible?" Everleigh said. "You can't be much older than that."

"This body isn't his real form," Arthur said, then he leaned in close, his eyes huge behind his glasses. "Have you been on Earth since the Sov vessel crash-landed in Driftwood Harbor?"

"I'm one of the Originals," Galen confirmed with a nod.

"So you're, like, sixty years old?!" Beacon said. According to the leaked government documents, the UFO had crashed in the harbor in 1967.

"More like three hundred years old," Galen said. "If you're using the human definition of a year."

They all gaped at Galen.

"What?" he said defensively, his poker face breaking down. "I was told to make myself look approachable. Besides, three hundred years is still a baby in Sov years, so it's not like I'm being deceitful."

Beacon sensed his chance and leaped on Galen's guilt.

"I know *I* feel lied to," Beacon said. "What about you guys?"

Everleigh made a face, and Arthur said, "Huh?"

"But I know of a way you can make it up to us," Beacon went on. "A few weeks ago, the Sov knocked out our dad and took him prisoner. We checked the security feed of the ship, and we couldn't find him. Do you know how to look at the invisible cells?"

"Nice try," Galen said, the tough-guy mask slipping back on.

"Please, Galen," Everleigh said.

"No." From the steely look in his eyes, he was remembering Everleigh calling him out in a fight.

Beacon stepped forward.

"Look, I don't know what it's like for the Sov," he said. "But for us? Family is the most important thing. No matter what happens, they're the people who have your back, whom you can trust. And if you're lucky enough to have that, you hold on to it."

"We just need to know if our dad is alive," Everleigh said.

Galen shook his head, then he pushed off from the wall and fell into his seat in front of the computer.

"Thankyouthankyouthankyou!" Everleigh said.

"We owe you big-time," Beacon said.

Galen ignored them and went to work clacking away on the keyboard.

"What are you doing?" Arthur asked, looking over his shoulder.

"Breaking through a few firewalls, installing a rootkit, exploiting the vulnerabilities in their applications," Galen said distractedly.

"Is all that . . . legal?" Arthur asked.

"Do you care?" Galen responded.

Beacon darted a look at Everleigh. She shrugged.

"How do you know how to do that?" Arthur asked.

"I wasn't always on the streets."

Beacon wanted to ask him how he ended up on the streets, why he left Driftwood Harbor, and why he was on the run from the Sov like them, but he didn't think it was the right time. Not when they were so close to seeing inside the cells.

Galen pushed a few more keys, and the security feed grids appeared on the screen. Beacon instantly recognized metal bed frames and toilets hemmed in by clear, shatterproof glass.

"There it is." Galen leaned back and crossed his arms.

Beacon scoured each of the cells. Every one was empty.

"Are you sure this is it?" Beacon asked.

Galen nodded.

Beacon didn't say anything. He couldn't. This had been their last hope, and it was officially crushed. Their dad was gone.

Everleigh turned away and started pacing the room. Beacon felt a thickness in his throat that he was starting to resent. He was so tired of grief. So tired of hurting. He felt a hand land on his shoulder, but he couldn't see who it was through the blur of tears.

"There *is* one more place we can check."

Galen's voice pierced the fog.

"More prison cells?" Arthur asked.

Galen shook his head. "It's the Sov's massive on-land base."

"They have an on-land base?" Arthur said. "I thought they operated out of the UFO."

"They do. This place is more like"—Galen looked up, as if searching for the right word—"a science lab slash prison. It's where they keep their long-term prisoners."

"Is it in Driftwood Harbor, too?" Beacon asked.

"Yep. Just give me a minute."

They leaned over Galen as he typed. After a few minutes that felt like hours, a new grid appeared on the screen.

Storage rooms, filing cabinets, offices, and hallways.

They searched room after room.

No Dad.

"Let's see some other rooms," Everleigh said frantically. She tried to reach over Galen for the keyboard, but he elbowed her away. He typed something else, and the grids changed. The kids collectively gasped.

The room was a bare cube of concrete filled with so many people that they were packed together like sardines in a can. The prisoners all shared the same gaunt look and shaved heads, the same bones sticking out through threadbare, filthy clothes. Beacon could practically smell the sweat and festering sewage through the computer monitor. This place looked more like a tomb than a prison. And it would be one, soon, judging by the way some of the prisoners looked.

"Who are these people?" Everleigh asked.

"Anyone who disagrees with the Sov's policies," Galen said. "Townspeople, top military personnel, scientists, CIA agents—you name it. It seems like no one is safe anymore."

"Why are their heads shaved like that?" Beacon asked.

"Lice," Galen said, and Everleigh shivered. Arthur reflexively scratched his head.

Everleigh leaned closer, scanning the eerily still prisoners. No one fought, no one screamed or banged on the walls. It was as if they'd been drained of the will to live, of any hope of seeing daylight again.

"He's not there," Everleigh said finally. Beacon didn't know whether to feel upset or relieved. If his dad wasn't here, he was probably dead.

Then the prisoner nearest the camera turned.

"Dad!" Everleigh cried.

Every part of Beacon's body soared with happiness. But the thrill of seeing him alive was brief.

Their dad stared up at the camera. They hadn't recognized him from behind with his shaved head. He'd also lost at least twenty pounds since they'd last seen him—and he hadn't had twenty to lose. His mouth hung open, and even from this aerial view, Beacon could see how cracked and parched his lips were, how sunken and lifeless his eyes.

"What have they done to him?" Everleigh whispered.

Beacon's mouth felt suddenly dry, as if it were filled with cotton.

"What do they do with the prisoners?" Beacon demanded, speaking loudly so that his voice wouldn't crack.

"You don't want to hear that," Galen said uncomfortably.

"Yes, I do," Beacon said. "What goes on in this place?"

"Experiments," Galen said.

Bile rose in Beacon's throat, and he was suddenly close to puking. Everleigh pressed her fingers to her temples and stared at the screen while Arthur awkwardly rubbed circles into her back.

"What kind of experiments?" Beacon asked thickly.

"All kinds," Galen said. "They've had the scientists working day and night the last few weeks. There's something going on."

"We need to get him out," Everleigh said. "We have to go back."

Galen stood up. "Well, good luck with that. Can I show you to the door?"

A flood of panic washed through Beacon's body. They couldn't get tossed out now. They *needed* Galen. He knew so much more than they did, and not just about computer hacking. Having a sympathetic Sov on their side might be the advantage they needed to save their dad.

"Wait!" Beacon said. "What about that girl? You said they're turning on anyone who disagrees with the Sov's policies. What if they turn on her, too?"

"They wouldn't," Galen said.

"How do you know for sure?" Beacon countered.

"I just do." His tone left no room for argument.

Great.

Beacon floundered for another angle. "There must be other people you care about there. What about your parents?"

He'd thought this might spark a reaction from Galen, but he just sighed.

"Look, I'm sorry your dad is in there," Galen said. "It sucks, but you just have to realize there are bigger forces at work here than you can take on. You need to do what I'm doing. Just keep your head down and hope they don't find you. It's the best you can hope for."

Beacon shook his head. "Even if leaving our dad in there was an option, we can't keep doing this our whole life. Sooner or later they're going to find us. And what will the world look like then? How far will the Sov's control have reached? We have a chance now to stop things. Aren't we morally obligated to take it?"

Galen rubbed the crease on his forehead.

"I can see you're contemplating joining us," Arthur said, leaping on his moment of weakness. "This might be a good time to mention our club—Youth Searching for Alien Truth. We'd love to welcome you as a member."

"*Arthur*," Beacon said.

Arthur raised his hands in defense. "Right, sorry, bad time. We can revisit that later."

"Help us," Beacon pleaded. "Not because you care about *us*. But because you care about doing what's right."

"This is stupid," Galen said. "How are you even going to break someone out of a maximum-security prison?"

"We can iron out those details later," Beacon said. "Right now we just need to figure out how we're going to get back to Driftwood Harbor. We don't have the car anymore. Victor sold that—probably to make sure we couldn't get too far."

"Even if we did have the car, it's not like we can just drive back into town," Everleigh said. "The Sov would arrest us before we got anywhere near city limits."

"I don't know, but we have to figure something out," Beacon said. "We can't just let Dad rot in that place."

"My grandma," Arthur said suddenly. "My grandma has diabetes!"

"I'm sorry to hear that," Beacon said. "But this isn't really the time to talk about that."

"No, I mean, she has regular checkups at the hospital on the edge of city limits. If we can get there, we can sneak with her back into Driftwood Harbor!"

"Where are the three of you going to hide in her car?" Galen said.

"I don't know!" Arthur said defensively. "Do *you* have a better idea?"

"As a matter of fact, I do," Galen said.

"You do?" Beacon and Everleigh said together.

"Does this mean you're joining YAT?" Arthur asked.

Everyone looked at Galen. He pinched the bridge of his nose and closed his eyes for a brief moment. "I have a feeling I'm going to end up regretting this, but yeah, I guess I'll help you find your dad."

He didn't even finish his sentence before Beacon, Arthur, and Everleigh cheered and jumped up to hug him. Galen tolerated it for a few seconds before shoving them away.

"I'm only doing this because I think you're all going to get killed without my help," he said.

This dampened the mood a little, but Beacon still couldn't help the small smile that curled at the corner of his mouth.

"So what's your plan?" Everleigh asked.

"Do you know of another secret underground passage into town or something?" Arthur suggested. "Or maybe you have one of those pods that drive underwater? Oh! Or is it an alien trick to make us all invisible so we can just walk into town? That would be neat!"

It was Galen's turn to smile. "It's something like that."

9

"*This* is your plan?" Beacon said, plugging his nose.

The barge sat low and heavy in the water. It was about thirty feet wide, with squared off corners and a single cabin in the front. The entire deck was covered with garbage. Beacon didn't know what he'd been expecting, but it wasn't this.

Arthur gagged.

Everleigh grimaced and waved the sour smell away from her face. "Isn't there a boat that *isn't* covered in trash that we could take?"

"This is the only boat we have any chance of hiding on," Galen said. "No one's going to start digging through the trash to see if there's a stowaway on board."

"You expect us to hide *in there?*" Everleigh pointed at the heap of takeout containers and leaking garbage bags.

"Don't be such a princess," Galen said. "You're on the run. It isn't going to be all five-star accommodations." He leaped the gap from the pier to the deck.

"That's sexist, you know," Everleigh said, but she jumped after him.

"Are we sure this thing isn't going to sink?" Arthur said apprehensively. "When was the last time it was safety-checked?"

"Just get on the boat," Galen said.

Arthur grimaced, took a deep breath, and jumped.

"None of you even has anything to worry about," Beacon said. "All of you can breathe underwater. I'm the only one who's in danger here."

Still, he jumped after Arthur onto the vessel.

Galen had said the first workers usually arrived before sunrise, so they had to hide fast. They'd gotten lucky that there was a barge leaving for Driftwood Harbor so soon. If they missed this one, they'd need to wait six days for their next chance.

"All right, just . . . find a spot," Galen said. "Keep quiet, and don't come out until I say so. No matter what."

Arthur followed Everleigh to the back corner of the trash heap, while Beacon trailed after Galen. They hunkered down under the most intact garbage bags they could find.

Beacon tried to get into a comfortable position, but it turned out there wasn't one under a pile of garbage. Who knew?

"Good thing we didn't bring Boots. He would've hated this," Beacon said.

"He would have been fine," Galen snapped.

Beacon had convinced Galen that it would be better for everyone if he put Boots up in a kennel while they traveled to Driftwood Harbor. They couldn't exactly be incognito if Boots was barking at every Sov they passed. Galen had agreed, but that didn't mean he liked it.

The boat rocked on the waves. Thunder rumbled overhead. If it rained right now, Beacon was going to have to take it personally. If there was one thing worse than sitting in a pile of garbage, it was sitting in a pile of wet garbage.

The trash bags shifted, and Beacon felt something drip onto his shoulder. Garbage or a raindrop, he wasn't sure.

"I have a question," Beacon said.

Galen shot him an annoyed glance. "I said be quiet."

"The workers won't be here for a while," Beacon said.

Galen didn't argue, so Beacon went on. "Is it true about the floods?"

"Huh?" Galen said.

"The 'collection of weather events' that will devastate our planet," Beacon said, doing air quotes. He regretted it when the shift in position caused a leaky trash bag to spill mystery liquid onto his shoulder.

"My dad—my real dad," he went on. "The Sov told him that there would be a collection of weather events that would flood the earth. Storms, tsunamis, flash floods, that sort of thing. That was why they said they needed to inject us with that antidote. To help us breathe underwater until the earth could be restored."

"Oh. That," Galen said offhandedly. "Yeah, that's partially true."

"*What?*" Beacon squeaked.

"Shhh!" Galen hissed.

Beacon swallowed hard and lowered his voice. "What do you mean *partially true*?"

Galen shrugged. "Last I heard, Earth was headed for water town. Not, like, tomorrow or anything. A hundred years from now or something like that," he added, seeing Beacon's look of horror.

"Are you sure? I mean, how do the Sov even know about this?" Beacon asked.

"Some of our oldest people have developed abilities to see into the future."

"Elders," Beacon said, remembering the term Victor had used back in the alley.

Galen nodded.

"But they can be wrong sometimes, right?" Beacon said hopefully.

"They haven't been yet," Galen said.

A sinking feeling washed over him.

"But the floods aren't why the Sov were injecting people," Galen said, interrupting his internal doom spiral.

"It was to brainwash us," Beacon said, remembering his conversation with Nixon.

Galen nodded.

Beacon had so many questions, he didn't even know where to start.

"Are the Sov going to flood us?" he asked. "Can they control the elements or something?"

Galen scoffed. "No, this one's all on you." He answered the question on Beacon's face. "Climate change, man. Haven't you ever heard of it?"

"Of course I have. But it's really going to flood the earth?"

"I mean, you don't need elders to tell you that. Scientists have been warning you guys for years."

Beacon opened and closed his mouth like a fish on a hook.

"Well, this is just great!" he finally said.

They could defeat the aliens trying to take over their planet, and it might not even matter. Not because of aliens, but because of their own stupid decisions.

"It isn't set in stone," Galen said. "Destinies change all the time. There have been some positive changes. Solar power, electric cars, Greta Thunberg, all that. It could be different now. Who knows?"

Who knows.

Cool.

There was nothing much to say after that. They descended into silence again.

After a while, Galen pulled something out of his pocket. It took Beacon a moment to realize what it was: the picture of the girl he kept in his wallet. He couldn't have been able to see much, but the small amount of moonlight filtering in through the bags must have been enough.

"So, who is she, anyway?" Beacon asked.

Galen quickly turned the picture away. "Nobody."

"Oh, yeah, I keep pictures of nobody in my wallet, too," Beacon said sarcastically.

Galen narrowed his eyes at him. "It's none of your business."

"Come on," Beacon said. "You know our story. If we're going to be doing this together, isn't it fair you tell us something about you?"

Galen looked down at the picture and absently flicked the corner with his thumb. Beacon couldn't help leaning over and stealing a peek. He got a glimpse of a jeweled necklace that he hadn't noticed the first time, at odds with the girl's plain T-shirt and jeans, before Galen tilted the picture away again.

Beacon thought he'd blown it, but Galen surprised him by saying, "I met her on the ship. We weren't friends at first. I was actually kind of scared of her." He laughed a little, gazing at the picture again. "She was really serious and angry looking."

"Just to clarify, we're talking about that girl in the picture right here?" Beacon asked, pointing.

"She's scarier than she looks," Galen said. "They wanted us to choose young human forms. People are less suspicious of kids."

Beacon had so many questions about that, but Galen was finally sharing something personal, and who knew if that would ever happen again. He had to keep him talking about the girl.

"How did you meet?" Beacon asked.

"I was doing freelance work then, little hack jobs for whoever was willing to pay, when I was approached by someone asking if I would be willing to do a bigger gig. I needed the coin, so I took the meeting. Turns out they were offering a ton of money for someone to join a crew heading for Earth. They needed someone doing their IT stuff. I figured, why not, right? Easy money. So I said yes . . . not knowing that we weren't coming back."

"They didn't tell you that you weren't coming back?" Beacon said.

"They didn't tell us *anything*, really. Everyone was so secretive about the whole thing. 'IT' turned out to be hacking Earth's government files. I slowly started realizing this was a lot bigger than I'd thought. By the time I figured out what was going on, what they were planning, it was too late. We were stuck here."

"I can't believe it," Beacon said. "They basically kidnapped you."

"I guess a lot of people would have backed out if they'd known the truth." He sighed deeply. "Anyway, it didn't matter. I was stuck here, and I hated it. Underwater all day and all night. They didn't want us leaving the ship in those first years, and it was really isolating and lonely. So I started sneaking out."

Beacon sat forward. "Didn't they have security making sure you didn't get out?"

Galen grinned, his eyes twinkling mischievously. "Of course. I hacked the security system so the cams would be disabled in the pod room and took one for a little swim."

"No way!"

"It was so great being out of those walls. Like I could finally breathe again, you know? I started going out more and more, and I guess I got sloppy. I was climbing out of a pod one night and Daisy was just there."

"Daisy's the girl in your picture?" Beacon said.

He nodded. "I started rambling with all these excuses, and she told me to shut up. She said she knew that I'd been sneaking out and she wanted me to take her where I was going."

"So what did you do?"

"Daisy doesn't give people much of a choice," he said with a laugh. "I showed her all the places I'd discovered—the lighthouse, this amazing cave. It was weird at first, but soon I realized she wasn't the stuck-up snob I thought she was. She was just lonely, like me. We started going out every night, and the rest is history."

"So . . . how come she's there, and you're here?" Beacon asked.

"She couldn't leave," Galen said.

"You said before that she didn't *want* to leave. Was she a Kill Humans supporter or something?"

"Of course not," Galen spat. "She wanted to leave. She just . . . couldn't."

"Why not?"

"It's complicated."

"I have time."

Galen's jaw locked tight. The conversation was over.

Footsteps thundered on the deck, followed by voices. The workers had arrived.

The journey was cold and uncomfortable. They couldn't speak, or eat, or do anything, in case the workers heard them. So they just shivered in their trash heap and waited.

Beacon tried not to think about his dad—it only made him feel anxious and helpless. But he couldn't help it. He thought of the notes his dad left in his lunchbox each day, of the family Scrabble games everyone pretended were lighthearted fun but were actually cutthroat competitions, of his dad regaling them with the latest scientific breakthrough at work over breakfast.

If Galen noticed him crying, he didn't say.

It felt like a century later when Beacon was awoken from a fitful sleep by a hand shaking him. When he peeled open his eyes, he found Galen crouched half in half out of the trash heap.

"Come on. We don't have a lot of time," Galen said.

Beacon stood up and froze. The harbor was bustling with activity. Boats creaked on the choppy waves as fishermen called to one another in thick, guttural accents, their voices carried on the salty breeze. In the distance, residents walked up and down the cobbled streets of the main square.

Beacon ducked down.

"What are you doing?" Galen said. "I told you we don't have a lot of time."

"It's still light out," Beacon whispered harshly. "And we're right next to the town square!"

"It's the best I could do," Galen said. "This barge gets back on the water in an hour, so unless you want to go back to New York, I suggest you get off the boat."

Beacon gritted his teeth. It was too late now to start second-guessing Galen's plan. They were already here.

He pushed himself back up, plucking a banana peel from his sleeve. Everleigh and Arthur struggled out of their hiding spots. Arthur had sleep marks on his cheek, but Everleigh's eyes were red-rimmed and fiery. She obviously hadn't slept, and now wore an expression Beacon recognized instantly as her *just waiting for an excuse to snap* face.

"There are people everywhere!" Arthur whispered.

"What do we do now? We can't just walk out there," Everleigh said.

"We don't have a choice," Galen said.

"Look, I don't like it, either, but we have to do it," Beacon said. "Blackwater Lookout is a straight walk through those trees on the other side of the square. All we have to do is make it a few blocks."

"Famous last words," Everleigh muttered.

"Let's just get this over with," Beacon said. "Try to stay out of sight as much as possible, but walk slowly and casually. If we look panicked, it will call more attention to us. Everyone got it?"

"Got it," Arthur said.

The others nodded.

"All right, after these two ladies go past," Beacon whispered.

The women walked by in stony silence. Beacon shuddered. He'd forgotten how creepy the townspeople were, so devoid of emotion and life.

As soon as the women passed, Beacon climbed off of the barge. The others followed suit.

The main square consisted of a handful of buildings that branched off into four different directions. There was a bright turquoise bait shop, a long and low grocery store made of dark red brick, a clapboard-sided yellow diner with old-fashioned steel stools you could see through the big windows, and off in the distance, the towering stone church.

Beacon couldn't believe they were actually here. When they'd escaped Driftwood Harbor, he'd really been planning on never seeing this place again.

They walked down the pier, into the main square. Beacon's shoulders knotted up tight, but so far, no one was paying attention to them.

An elderly man carrying a bag of groceries walked past.

"Just out for a casual stroll!" Arthur said. The man frowned at them and shook his head, as if to say, "kids."

"Oh my God," Everleigh muttered.

Galen mashed his palm against his forehead.

"Just . . . don't talk," Beacon ground out through clenched teeth.

"What?" Arthur protested. It was hard to believe he'd once claimed to have completed hundreds of top-secret missions for YAT.

They were almost to the far side of the square when the door of Tonkin's Bait Shop and Antiques up ahead opened with a jingle. Jane and two of her Gold Star minions walked outside dressed in their characteristic blue-and-gold varsity jackets.

"Code Blue!" Beacon grabbed Arthur's arm and banked to the left.

Everleigh followed suit.

"What's going on?" Galen whispered, speed walking to catch up. "What happened to the plan?"

"Those people did." Beacon nodded toward the bait shop.

"Don't look now!" Arthur said. "They're in league with the Sov. We can't let them see us."

"Just keep walking," Beacon said. "We can cut behind the diner to get to the woods."

It took every last ounce of Beacon's self-restraint not to run toward the diner. His legs itched to get away from the Gold Stars as quickly as possible, but it would only make them look conspicuous.

Once they made it behind the building, they did run. Across a narrow dirt road, through a scrabbly patch of shrubs, and then, finally, into the forest. Twigs snapped and crunched under their boots as they pounded through the trees, ducking under branches and leaping over fallen logs. Before long, Blackwater Lookout came into view through a break in the trees.

The inn sat on a craggy cliff overlooking the ocean. Thick vines crept over nearly every inch of the yellow-stained siding and crumbling chimney. Paint-chipped black shutters snapped open and closed in the wind.

Beacon almost collapsed with relief. He couldn't believe he hadn't wanted anything to do with this place when they'd first arrived in Driftwood Harbor. Now, it felt strangely like coming home.

He pushed through the trees.

"Thank God we made it," he said, spinning around to face the others.

But something was wrong.

"Galen?" he said.

"Where did he go?" Everleigh asked.

Arthur turned in a circle, as if Galen might be right behind him. But he'd disappeared.

10

A yelp sounded from the forest, right before Galen emerged, dragging Nixon by his collar.

"This one was following us," Galen announced.

"Get your hands off of me!" Nixon shouted, trying to wrench free.

"Is anyone else with you?" Beacon asked Nixon, his eyes darting all around them.

"No. I told Jane and the others I forgot something at the bait shop. Now tell your goon to put me down." Nixon tried to elbow Galen, but the boy held him away from his body like a used tissue.

"Drop him," Beacon told Galen. "He's our friend."

"How do we know we can trust him?" Galen asked.

"He's immune to the antidote," Everleigh said.

"Immune?" Galen said.

"Yeah. I'm immune, too," Arthur piped up eagerly.

Galen frowned. "How is that possible? I've never heard of that before."

"I've been thinking about that, actually," Arthur said. "I've always assumed the antidote didn't work on me because my brain is wired differently from my epilepsy. If that's true, then there's got to be other people who are immune, too. Like maybe anyone who is neurodivergent is immune?"

"Cool theory. I'd love to discuss it not *hanging in the air!*" Nixon said.

Beacon nodded at Galen, and he released his hold on the Gold Star.

Nixon *oof*ed as he hit the ground. He pushed himself up and brushed leaves off his pants, his eyes shooting daggers at Galen.

"Are you okay?" Everleigh asked.

"I'm *fine.*"

"So are you?" Arthur asked.

"Am I what?" Nixon said.

"Neurodivergent," Arthur said, like it should have been obvious.

"I would have thought you'd know the answer to that already," Nixon said. "You know, since you *read my file.* But yeah." He shrugged. "I've apparently got ADHD." He rolled his eyes, like it was stupid, even as his cheeks turned red.

"Nothing to be embarrassed about, man," Beacon said, at the same time as Arthur said, "I knew it! About my theory, not about you having ADHD. This makes so much sense! Man, that's a big flaw in their system. There are tons of neurodivergent people. Way more than anyone realizes."

"Glad we sorted all that out," Nixon said. "Now on to the bigger issue. What the heck is wrong with all of you? What are you doing back here? I risked my butt to get you out of that ship, and now you're skulking around the middle of the town square? You were about *two seconds* away from being spotted."

"Our dad is being held prisoner," Beacon explained.

"No, he's not," Nixon said irritably. "I told you, I've searched every inch of the ship, and he isn't there."

"Not on the ship," Everleigh said. "Someplace else."

Galen made throat-cutting gestures, but Beacon said, "The Sov have an on-land base."

Nixon snorted. "No they don't. I would know about something like that."

"Maybe you'd know more if you hadn't hung up on us," Everleigh said.

"We really shouldn't be doing this out here," Beacon said, looking around warily.

"This wouldn't be a problem if we'd gone to my grams's house," Arthur said. "It's way closer."

"Your grams?" Nixon said.

Beacon didn't miss the odd note in Nixon's voice. Neither did Arthur.

"What happened to her?" Arthur said. "Is she—did she . . . ?" He couldn't even finish the sentence.

"She's alive. It's not that," Nixon said. He tugged at his shirt collar. "She's just . . . sick."

"Sick? What do you mean?" Arthur said urgently.

"I don't know," Nixon said. "They said she had a stroke, but no one's seen her in a while. Nurse Allen does everything for her. I think she lives there now. I tried to go over once with flowers, but Nurse Allen said she wasn't in a condition for visitors. I've been thinking it might be a cover. The Sov know Arthur would want to contact his grandma, so it makes sense they would keep tabs on her 24-7 to try to catch you guys."

"How do you know she isn't really sick?" Arthur said.

"I don't," Nixon said.

Arthur looked out at the forest. It was clear he was imagining running through it, straight to his grandma's house.

"It's not safe to go there right now," Beacon said. "What if Nixon is right? It could be a trap."

Nixon looked over his shoulder. "I have to get back. It's getting dark, and they're going to notice I've been gone." He shoved his hands into his pockets and disappeared into the forest.

Arthur's throat bobbed.

Beacon didn't know what to say. He wanted to offer Arthur a word of comfort, but he remembered what it was like after Jasper died, all the empty platitudes and advice he'd received, and how he hadn't wanted any of that. He just wanted someone to be there. To listen if he wanted to talk. To sit with him in his pain. So Beacon just squeezed Arthur's shoulder.

"Let's get inside," Beacon said. "It isn't safe out here."

When no one argued, he led the way to the inn, climbed the front steps, and knocked on the door. No answer.

"Try the handle," Everleigh said.

Beacon expected to meet resistance, but the door creaked open. The sound echoed through the high rafters. The kids exchanged a glance before they entered. Inside, they were met with familiar knotted wood paneling and overstuffed couches. The logs in the stone hearth were cold, and the smell of baking that usually permeated the inn was missing. It was clear no one had been here for quite some time.

"Where do you think she is?" Beacon said.

"Isn't it obvious?" Everleigh said. "She's in that prison. She must have been captured the night we tried to break Arthur out."

"We don't know that for sure," Beacon said. "We didn't see her on that surveillance footage. They could be keeping her somewhere else. Or maybe she got away."

Or maybe she's dead.

"Well, she hasn't been here recently." Everleigh ran a finger over a glass-topped table, leaving a clear streak in the dust.

Galen walked around, his boots thumping loudly on the creaking hardwood floors. He pulled back a curtain and looked outside, then turned to face the others.

"We'll stay here," he announced. "It's off the beaten track, it's big enough for all of us, and we've got a good view of the road so we can see if anyone is coming; that way we'll have a bit of a head start if we need to run."

Beacon glanced at the others. Everleigh had that familiar look on her face, like she wanted to argue but couldn't think of any good counterpoints. She shrugged haughtily, then walked into the kitchen and started digging through the fridge. Arthur just crossed his arms.

"I guess that's decided," Beacon said.

"Food is going to be a problem," Everleigh said. "Everything in the fridge is rotten."

"I can handle groceries," Galen said.

"You can?" Beacon said.

"How?" Everleigh spun around with her hand still gripping the fridge. "Oh my God. You're going to transform, aren't you? That's how you've been getting by on the streets. You transform into, like, a baker so you can walk into the bakery and take bread!"

"That's ridiculous," Galen said. "It would take way too much energy to do that every time I needed groceries."

"Then what do you do? We saw inside your wallet. We know you're loaded."

Galen shrugged. "I hack," he said defensively.

"You mean you steal?" Everleigh said.

"Only from major corporations," Galen said. "Nothing anything would ever notice."

"Well, I guess that makes it okay, then," Arthur said.

"You can starve if you'd feel better about it," Galen shot back.

"Okay, that's enough," Beacon said. "We have a bigger problem. How are we getting Dad out of that prison?"

Saying it out loud made a sinking feeling come over him. Getting to Driftwood Harbor had felt like such an emergency, but now that they were actually here, it seemed crazy that they hadn't made a plan before they came; it was as if they they'd jumped off a diving board without checking to see if there was water in the pool first.

"We need to figure out a way to get into that base," Beacon said. "Any ideas?"

No one spoke.

"This is a brainstorming session," Beacon said. "No reason to be shy. No idea is a bad idea."

"We could blow up the prison," Everleigh said.

"Except that idea," Beacon said. "*That's* a bad idea."

"I don't mean the whole place," Everleigh said. "Just, like, blow a hole in the side so people can get out."

"Any other ideas?" Beacon said. "Anything a little less likely to get everyone in the prison killed?"

He looked at Arthur, hoping he would pipe up with one of his genius ideas, but he was sullenly staring into the middle distance. Probably thinking about his grandma.

"Maybe we can we dig our way in," Everleigh said, "like that old movie where the prisoners dig a tunnel under their cell to freedom."

"I like that," Beacon said. "Would take a thousand years and probably kill our backs, but less conspicuous."

"What about the sewer system?" Galen said. "Instead of digging our way in, we could go in using the already-established drainage systems in place. I could try to find building plans online so we'd know where to locate the underground pipes."

"That's an amazing idea!" Beacon said. "What do you think, Arthur?"

He turned to his friend. Arthur swallowed, but he didn't reply.

"Arthur?" Beacon asked. "Are you okay?"

"You look all weird and pale," Everleigh said.

Arthur mopped the sweat from his forehead.

"Maybe you should sit down." Beacon pulled out a chair at the kitchen table.

Arthur took a step toward the chair. Then his eyes rolled back in his head. Beacon had just enough time to jump across the room before Arthur went down. The boy was as thin as a garden rake, but he was all dead weight as he collapsed on top of Beacon. With a great effort, Beacon wriggled out from under him and pushed himself up.

Arthur jerked and twitched on the tile, his eyes glazed and vacant.

"What's happening to him?" Everleigh said, fluttering anxiously over him. "Is this because of his grandma?"

"What would his grandma have to do with this?" Galen said.

"I don't know! Like a panic attack or something?" Everleigh said.

"His lips are blue and he's foaming at the mouth," Galen said. "I don't think it's a panic attack."

Beacon wanted to call the adult in the situation, someone who could *handle* this, but there was no one. They needed to do something. He needed to *think*.

"I think it's a seizure," Beacon said. "He has epilepsy. It's normally controlled by medication, but he wouldn't have been taking it since we left Driftwood Harbor."

He couldn't believe he hadn't realized this sooner. This must have been why Arthur hadn't been eating, why he was sweaty and shaky all the time. He was having drug withdrawal symptoms. And now his medications were fully out of his system. There was nothing to prevent him from having a seizure.

"What do we do?" Everleigh said.

"We need to turn him on his side," Beacon said. "Make sure he doesn't swallow his tongue or breathe in his own puke." That's what Arthur had said the teachers did for him when he had a seizure at school. "It's okay so long as it doesn't last over five minutes."

"How long has it been now?" Galen asked.

"I don't know," Beacon said. It felt like forever. "We need his medications."

"Awesome," Everleigh said. "I need a jet pack and a monkey butler, while we're making a wish list."

"We can get it from his grandma's house," Beacon said.

"I'll come with you," Galen announced.

Beacon nodded. "Everleigh, stay with Arthur."

"What? No! I don't know what to do. What if he stops breathing?" Everleigh sent a panicked look at Arthur.

"He won't," Beacon said. "But . . . if he does, call 911."

Their mission to save their dad would be over, but what other choice did they have?

Everleigh swallowed hard.

"Let's go," Beacon said to Galen.

They ran into the living room. Galen peeked out of the curtains. In the short time they'd been inside, the sun had sunk below the trees, casting the forest into shadow.

"Should we bring weapons?" Beacon said.

"Your weapons will be useless against the Sov and their guards. We just have to be fast. It looks clear." He turned to Beacon. "Let's do this."

They ran out of the front door, and down the long, twisting driveway of Blackwater Lookout. Through a frosty meadow and over a babbling creek. Past a run-down cemetery full of broken gravestones, and into the shadowy forest. They didn't stop until Arthur's house shone through the trees. They crouched down next to a poplar tree, gasping for breath. The house was tiny, but right now, it loomed in the dark like a giant. The front porch light flickered on and off, and shadows lurked in the windows. Arthur's grandma's car was the only vehicle in the driveway, but that didn't mean the place was safe.

"His bedroom is at the back of the house," Beacon said. "Let's try the window."

They tiptoed around to the back of the house. The grass was damp, and Beacon's shoes squelched with each step. When he got to Arthur's room, he flattened his palms on the glass and pushed up, but the window didn't budge. It was locked.

They scurried to the next window and peered inside. Arthur's grandma lay on the bed. Her puff of white hair was fanned out on the pillow, and a crocheted blanket was pulled up under her chin. A sheen of sweat glistened on her deeply wrinkled skin, and her mouth hung open just the slightest bit. It was hard to tell if she was sick, or just sleeping.

She shifted in the bed, and Beacon ducked quickly, moving to the next window. He got lucky: It was already open an inch. Beacon shoved the pane up, then pushed aside the gauzy seashell curtains. Moonlight glinted off a pink porcelain tub and matching sink.

"Give me a boost," Beacon whispered. Galen laced his fingers together and boosted him up with a little too much force. Beacon flew through the window, toppling over the ledge and onto the toilet with a clatter.

"Sorry!" Galen whispered from outside.

Beacon could barely hear over the sound of his heart pounding in his ears. He swallowed hard and cocked his ear to the doorway, waiting for any sign that someone was coming. But nothing happened.

He blew out a slow breath and pushed himself up. If he was lucky, Arthur's medications would be here.

He opened the medicine cabinet and squinted inside, but all he could find were Q-tips and Vaseline. He tried the drawers under the sink next—curlers, hairbrushes, toothpaste. No medication. He was going to have to go deeper into the house.

He peered out of the bathroom door. Beacon had been here a few times before, but the dark made everything seem sinister. The once-cheerful floral couches now looked straight out of a horror movie. Shadows lurked behind a teak cabinet full of porcelain dolls, and in the corner, a grandfather clock ticked away the seconds like a bomb about to detonate.

He wanted nothing more than to get out of this place. But then he thought of Arthur, and he steeled himself.

He tiptoed down the hall, cringing when the old floor creaked under his weight. But he made it all the way to Arthur's bedroom without incident. He quietly closed the door behind him.

If it weren't for the neatly made twin bed, Arthur's room could have been confused with a science lab. The pine desk against the wall was overflowing with beakers, test tubes, circuit boards, and even an old-school microscope like the one they used during science class. Pushed into one corner of the room was a big metal drum with a bare lightbulb sticking out of its top. The prototype for the ARD—the alien radiofrequency detector. Beacon smiled, remembering how Arthur had called this room his "headquarters."

He found the medication in the first place he checked, inside Arthur's bedside table. He silently thanked Arthur for being so organized. He squinted at the different pill bottles—Keppra, Lorazepam, and a bunch of others he couldn't even begin to pronounce. Beacon didn't know which ones were important, so he grabbed Arthur's beat-up JanSport backpack from the foot of his bed, pulled out the textbooks, and dumped all the pill bottles inside.

Now he just needed to get out of here.

A howl rang through the night. It sounded vaguely like a wolf, enough to hopefully fool anyone who heard it, but Beacon knew it was Galen. He froze. There was only one reason Galen would be so obvious—if he were trying to warn him that someone was here.

Beacon pushed up the window, just as footsteps thundered down the hall. Panic flared through him. The window was small. He would have to contort his body to squeeze out. There wouldn't be time. He made a split-second decision and dashed across the room into the closet. He pulled the door closed just as the bedroom door burst open.

He watched through the slats as Nurse Allen stepped inside.

She was a good head taller than any woman he'd ever met before. Despite her size, everything about her was sharp, from the wide-set shoulders under her scrub top to the dark hair that curled under her pointed chin. Even her expression looked as if it could cut through glass. The last time he'd seen her, her veiny hands had been clasped around the antidote syringe.

Beacon's heart raced so hard he was sure Nurse Allen and everyone else in Driftwood Harbor could hear it, but she didn't turn. She stared at the window, her eyes narrowed. He knew she was doing the mental calculations on if she'd left it open.

Beacon crossed his fingers and prayed, *Please just go to bed, please just go to bed.* But Nurse Allen spun on her heel, and her eyes zeroed in on the closet.

He was caught.

11

Nurse Allen stepped closer. She reached for the handle, and Beacon's throat knotted up tight. The closet creaked open an inch, but then a bang sounded from outside the room. Nurse Allen's head snapped up, then she scurried off.

Relief poured through him. He didn't waste any time. He rushed out of the closet. The pills rattled around with every step he took, but he didn't worry about being stealthy anymore. He tossed the backpack out of the window, then twisted and shoved himself through the small opening so fast, the wood scraped against his back. He landed with a thud, then scooped up the backpack and ran for the woods. In moments, Galen was loping along beside him.

"Thanks for that noise. Nurse Allen was about two seconds away from catching me," Beacon said between gasps for breath.

"What noise?" Galen said.

"That bang. Did you throw a rock at the window?" Beacon asked.

Galen shook his head. "I don't know what you're talking

about. I just howled so you'd know Nurse Allen had pulled into the driveway."

Beacon frowned, but he guessed it didn't matter what had caused the distraction, just that he'd gotten away.

They were leaping over a brook in the woods when Beacon first felt it: a brisk, cool breeze that made the hairs on his arms stand up underneath his sweatshirt. Before long, the wind blew in powerful gusts, tossing the trees above them from side to side until Beacon and Galen were forced to drop to the ground and cover their heads. Twigs and leaves blasted past, and Beacon knew if it weren't for the adrenaline racing through his body, he would have been freezing.

Then, just as quickly as it had started, the wind died away. Beacon coughed and staggered to his feet. Galen readjusted his sweatshirt, which had gotten twisted all around his lanky body from the wind.

"What was *that*?" Beacon asked.

"I don't know." Galen peered up at the sky. "A storm coming, I guess."

An uneasy feeling wormed through Beacon's body. That reason didn't seem to make sense. It was like the wind had just . . . disappeared. That didn't happen if a storm was on the way.

But he didn't have time to worry about it. Arthur needed him.

It seemed like they'd been gone for hours, but when they got back to the inn, only twenty minutes had passed.

Still, twenty minutes could be too long. Beacon knew better

than most people that it took only minutes without oxygen for brain cells to die. He'd found that out the hard way when Jasper had drowned.

His body tensed with dread as he walked back inside the inn. He found Everleigh in the kitchen, sitting against the wall next to Arthur, who was curled up on the floor with his eyes closed. He looked a bit paler than usual, but he didn't twitch or convulse, and his chest rose and fell evenly.

"He's asleep," Everleigh whispered.

Beacon let out a breath he hadn't realized he'd been holding.

"How long did it last?" he asked.

"About six minutes."

Too long. Would he be okay?

"Should we wake him up? Give him the pills?" Galen said.

"No, let him sleep," Everleigh said. "We can give it to him when he wakes up."

Beacon swallowed thickly, then slid down the wall next to Everleigh. Galen sat down next to him.

"You don't have to stay here," he told Galen. "There are beds upstairs."

"It's fine," he said. He curled up on the floor and made a pillow out of his sweatshirt. He was asleep and snoring in minutes.

"I wish I could be like that," Everleigh said, nodding toward Galen.

"Me too. It takes me forever to fall asleep."

"Really?" Everleigh said. "I didn't know that. Is it because of Jasper?"

"Some of it is Jasper." He closed his mouth. He was worried that what he was going to share would make him look bad, like a terrible brother, but it was eating him up inside. "Sometimes, lately, I'll forget to think about him all day. Like, we'll be so busy trying to survive that I don't remember Jasper until I'm trying to go to sleep. Then when I realize how much time has passed since I thought about him, I get all panicked. Then it's like an emergency that I need to remember everything."

Beacon felt himself go hot all over after this admission. He wished he could take it back, just stuff the words back into his mouth, but it was too late.

Everleigh turned to face him fully. "You too?"

The tension knotting up his shoulders melted away.

"It's been happening since we moved here," she said. "I feel so guilty about it. It's only been a year."

"You can't be too hard on yourself," Beacon said. "Running for your life doesn't leave a lot of room for thinking. Besides, you know Jasper wouldn't want us to spend all day feeling sad that he's gone."

Beacon was saying it to make Everleigh feel better, but it was true. He realized that he should show himself some of the same grace he'd shown his sister.

"I guess you're right," Everleigh said. "I just don't want to forget about him, you know?"

"I know . . ." Beacon crossed his legs. "I have an idea. Why don't we share memories about Jasper every once in a while? That way we make sure we never forget about him. Not that we ever would, but you know, to keep his memory fresh?"

Beacon almost suggested that they do the same thing for their dad, but he stopped himself short. That would be like admitting they were going to fail.

"I think that's a great idea," Everleigh said. She looked up for a moment, before a small smile crossed her lips. "This isn't anything big, but one of my favorite memories of Jasper was walking home after school. His friends would be there, and I felt so cool hanging out with them."

"I liked that, too," Beacon said, smiling. "He never acted like we were too young or stupid to hang out with him." Beacon thought for a minute. "I always think about our game nights with Dad."

Everleigh grinned. "Remember when we were playing Monopoly that one time?"

"And Jasper landed on Income Tax eleven times in a row?"

They laughed, then stifled the sound when Galen grunted and rolled over.

"He was furious," Everleigh whispered.

"Furious in his Jasper way," Beacon said. "He was never really that mad."

"Except about the Ian Pearson thing."

"Oh my God, I forgot about that!" Beacon said.

A few years ago, an older kid at school had decided to pick on Beacon. For months, he made Beacon's life hell. He stole his lunch, blew spitballs on him from the back of the classroom, and started up the nickname Beacon McLoser that followed him through every corridor. When Jasper found out what was happening, he walked onto their bus the next morning, even though he went to the high school, and picked Ian up by his jacket collar, so that his butt wasn't even touching the seat. He told Ian that if he ever messed with his brother again, he'd make sure it was the last thing he ever did. The police had come and given Jasper a stern talking-to that night, and he was grounded for a month, but Ian never bothered Beacon again.

They talked for hours, and eventually, Beacon drifted off to sleep.

When he woke up next, sunlight streamed through the open blinds. Beacon stretched and sat up, feeling more rested than he had in ages. Galen was nowhere to be seen. Arthur was still asleep, and Everleigh snored next to him with a puddle of drool under her face. He made a mental note to make fun of that later.

Arthur stirred on the tile.

"Is it the morning?" Arthur said, groaning as he sat up next to him. "How long was I out?"

"Like, eleven hours," Beacon said.

"Wow. Now I know how Galen feels when he sleeps for a million years."

Beacon slid the backpack on the floor over to Arthur.

"What's this?" Arthur dug inside the bag. He picked up one bottle, then another. "You got my meds?" he asked. "How?"

"Sneaked into your grandma's place last night."

"What about Nurse Allen?" he asked.

"She almost caught me. It was one of the scariest moments of my life."

"Did—did you see her?" Arthur asked. "My grams?"

"I did," Beacon said. "She was sleeping, but she looked comfortable."

Beacon could practically see the relief wash over his friend. He swallowed, his eyes shiny behind his glasses. He clutched a pill bottle. "Thank you. You didn't have to do this."

"Yes, we did," Beacon said.

"No, you didn't," Arthur said firmly. "But you did. And I appreciate it."

Beacon gave his friend a wan smile. Arthur unscrewed the lid of the bottle he was holding. He shook out two pills, then tossed them back and swallowed them dry.

"Good thing Galen wasn't down last night, too, or we would've been easy targets for the Sov," he said when the pills were finally down. He screwed the lid back onto the pill bottle.

Arthur kept talking, but his words blurred into the background. Beacon's mind had latched on to something he'd said. He stared into the middle distance, thinking. It felt as if he were on the cusp of something important, but the answers were just out of reach, as if he were a race car on a track, doing the same loop over and over.

Galen strode into the kitchen and dropped a stack of papers at their feet. Beacon startled back to reality.

"Jeez, what's wrong with 'good morning,' " Arthur said.

Everleigh groaned and rolled over. "What's going on?"

Beacon picked up the stack of papers and looked at the first page. A tingling feeling started low in his belly and spread through his chest. He flipped to the next page, then the next.

"Are these . . ."

"The plans to the on-land base?" Galen said. "Yeah."

"Oh my God!" Arthur snatched the papers from Beacon.

"Hey!" Beacon protested.

Everleigh scooted closer and peered over Arthur's shoulder, retying her ponytail as he flipped through the stack. Intricate floor plans filled every page.

"How did you get this?" she asked Galen.

"There's an old computer upstairs. I mean, *old*. Probably the first one ever made," Galen said.

"This is amazing!" Beacon said. "Now we just need to figure out the best access point."

"Page eight," Galen said, rooting through the cupboards. He opened a box of Triscuits and sniffed inside.

Beacon flipped to page eight.

"What is this?" he asked.

"It's the sewer system," Galen said.

"First a trash barge and now a sewer," Everleigh said. "You are just full of great ideas."

Galen popped a Triscuit under his shirt. There was a loud slurp sound.

"Ew," Everleigh said, but Galen ignored her.

"Their system connects with the city's system under Town Hall Road," he said. "If the plans are right, there should be a drain we can access about six feet underground. I marked the spot. Everywhere else is too close to town or too deep to dig without attracting attention."

"You did all this while we were sleeping?" Arthur said.

"Well, you slept almost as long as I do after a transformation, so it's not like it was hard," Galen said.

He had said it offhandedly, but his comment caused the race car in Beacon's head to skid off the track and burst onto the open road.

"Oh my God," Beacon said. "I just had an epiphany."

"What?" Arthur said.

"I was thinking about something earlier, and what you just said made it all click. I know how we can break into the base."

Galen stopped digging in the box of crackers and looked at him. Everleigh waved impatiently for him to continue.

Beacon swallowed and sat up straighter. He'd need to pitch this just right.

"Okay. So the Sov get wiped out after they transform, right?"

"Yeah . . . ," Galen said warily.

"So . . . ," Beacon continued. "We do the prison break after they've all transformed."

There was a beat of silence before Arthur said, "That's great, but how are we going to know when they've transformed?" There was a hint of disappointment in his voice that Beacon's plan hadn't been better.

"And they aren't going to all do it at the same time," Galen said. "The Sov here like to stay in their human form most of the time. Too much energy to flip back and forth. They're rarely in their natural form."

"We're going to lure them out," Beacon said. "Force them to transform into their squid forms—no offense, Galen. Then we'll do the prison break afterward when they're all down for the count. The whole prison will be vulnerable."

Arthur sat up alertly, like a puppy that just spotted people food. "This won't stop the guards and their guns, but if we can eliminate the threat of a squid attack, no offense, Galen, we'd greatly improve our odds of success!"

"How are we going to lure the Sov out?" Everleigh said without enthusiasm.

"We'll go out onto the water," Beacon said. "There's a boat in that tiny shed by the shore. You can take a look at it, Ev. Get it working if it's not seaworthy."

"That plan gets one Sov to come after you, maybe two," Galen said. "Not the whole crew. It isn't worth the risk for such little payoff. You'll just end up a lab rat like your dad."

"How many Sov are there?" Arthur asked.

Galen shrugged. "There were seventy-eight of us on the ship when it crashed."

"Seventy-eight?!" Beacon squeaked.

"Some might have left, like me," Galen said. "But yeah, roughly that."

Beacon didn't know why he was so surprised. It was a whole ship, and it had been on an intergalactic trip. Of course they needed a large crew to helm it. Still, knowing that there were that many giant squids in the town, and that his plan involved having them all come after them, was a bit disconcerting.

"Even if we could get all of them to come after us," Everleigh said, "how would we get away? We'd be stuck on a boat in the middle of the ocean surrounded by Sov."

"You wouldn't have to go out there at all," Galen said. "We could pretend to kidnap their queen."

"The Sov have a queen?" Everleigh said.

"That's how the Sov got their name," Beacon said, remembering what his dad had told him. "The ship that crashed here back in the sixties was a royal ship or something like that."

Galen nodded. "There's nothing more important to the Sov than protecting their queen. I could guarantee the whole crew would come out if they thought she was in danger."

"Great, except how are we going to get the queen?" Everleigh asked. "If she's so important, she's probably highly protected, right?"

"We don't actually need her," Galen said. "They just need to *think* she's in danger. So long as we make the threat convincing enough, they'll come."

"But if we don't actually have the queen, what's to stop them from just checking in her bedroom or whatever and realizing she's safe?"

"Leave that part to me," Galen said. "I can make sure she's unavailable."

"How?" Beacon said.

"Don't worry about it. I've got it covered."

Beacon frowned. But before he could ask any more questions,

Galen said, "All right, this is what we do." He pulled up a chair and leaned forward, his hands out like he was explaining a football play. "We send the Sov a message letting them know we have their queen and if they want her back they'll have to come and get her, et cetera, et cetera. We have a boat out on the water, forcing them to transform to save her. Only she won't be on the boat. They go back, scratching their heads about what happened, and that night, when they're weak, we hit the prison."

"I'm in," Beacon said instantly. He looked at Everleigh and Arthur.

Everleigh sighed. "Of course I'm in. I have to make sure my stupid little brother doesn't get killed."

"*Little* brother?" Beacon said. "You're three minutes older than me." But he was smiling.

"I'm in, too," Arthur said, sliding his glasses back on his nose.

Beacon looked at Galen.

"I mean, it was partly my idea," Galen said.

Operation Prison Break was underway.

12

Moonlight glinted off the glassy black water. For once, it wasn't windy or rainy, and the air was uncharacteristically warm. If they weren't about to embark on a mission that could very likely get them all killed, Beacon might have thought it was a beautiful night.

The plan had come together quickly after they agreed on Beacon's idea. Beacon and Galen had sneaked over to Town Hall Road and dug down to the drainage pipe. Arthur had taken on the task of making explosives to blow their way into the drainage system with a little too much enthusiasm. And Everleigh had only needed to use some sealant on the boat by the shed to get it seaworthy. Beacon had even found an inflatable raft in the garage so they wouldn't have to swim back to shore once they ditched the boat with the decoy queen inside. Then there was nothing left to do but do it. A little after 10:00 p.m. two nights later, they'd hopped into the boat.

"Okay, I think this is far enough," Beacon said. "Drop the anchor."

"Oh, thank God." Arthur clutched the ropes tied to the inflatable raft they dragged behind the boat. "My arms are getting a cramp holding on to this thing."

"We're been driving for, like, thirty-five seconds," Everleigh said. She hauled the anchor out of the bow and heaved it over the side of the boat. It splashed into the water before disappearing into its depths.

"All right, let's get out of here," Beacon said.

Arthur steadied the raft as Beacon climbed inside.

"Wait," Everleigh said. "Do you think this looks convincing enough?" She looked down at the "body" lying inside the boat.

They'd stuffed a few pillows into some of Everleigh's clothes, and then wrapped duct tape around it. Up close, it would be obvious there wasn't a real person inside.

"It doesn't have to be perfect," Beacon said. "The Sov won't know it's not their queen until it's too late. Come on."

Everleigh sighed, but she climbed into the raft after her brother. They both helped Arthur in as he struggled with his bag, then Everleigh and Beacon each grabbed a paddle and got to work, rowing fast and hard. They were on schedule so far, but they didn't want to take any chances getting caught out here when the Sov arrived.

Beacon dug a paddle into the water. They'd only been rowing for a few minutes, and his arms were already heavy and sluggish from the effort. But his sister wasn't complaining, so he just kept working. The island grew as they approached, a giant black mass that stretched for half a mile. They'd wanted to be able to watch their plan play out, and Galen had told them there was a cave on this island that had a good view of the water.

When they got so close that the paddles began digging into sand and rock, Beacon hopped out of the inflatable raft and helped his sister drag it up the rocky shore.

"Careful! We need this to get back," Galen said.

"If we ever get back," Everleigh muttered.

"We're getting back," Arthur said. "This is going to work. I have a good feeling about this."

They carried the raft over the sharp rocks.

"Let's put it over here," Everleigh said.

They dropped the raft behind an overgrown bush. Everleigh began kicking leaves and dirt on top of it.

"What are you doing?" Arthur said.

"Camouflaging the raft," Everleigh explained. "This thing can be seen from outer space."

"That'll have to be good enough," Beacon said.

Everleigh frowned. There was still orange rubber visible, but it would take ages to cover it all, and they didn't have time. She dusted off her hands, and they kept moving.

The mouth of the cave was hidden by bushes and fallen rocks. If he hadn't been looking for it, Beacon never would have known it was there.

Galen ducked inside first, and the rest of them crouched low and followed him into the impenetrable blackness. The temperature dropped as they entered the underground chamber. Beacon reached out to feel his way and could hardly see his own hand in front of his face. Ahead was the sound of water dripping into water, but it was impossible to tell how far away it was, or how deep.

"How did you know about this place?" Everleigh asked. Her voice echoed off the dense stone walls.

"I used to come here," Galen said. "To get away."

There was a sudden flurry of flapping in the darkness.

"What was that?" Everleigh shrieked.

"Probably a bat," Galen said calmly. "Get used to it. There are lots of them in here."

They hunkered down on the rocky floor and looked out at the sea through the cave entrance. Moonlight glinted off the aluminum boat swaying gently on the water. Beacon could just see the outline of the "body" lying inside the boat.

"What time is it?" Beacon whispered.

"Eleven fifty-one," Arthur said.

Six minutes since Galen's scheduled message should have gone out to the Sov.

We have your queen. Come to Deadman's Wharf, or she dies.

It was simple, but Galen had said any more details might give them away.

"And you're sure the queen won't be at the headquarters?" Beacon asked.

"Hundred percent," Galen said.

"How can you be so confident?" Beacon said. He wasn't really expecting Galen to answer—he hadn't the other million times Beacon and the others had pressed him to explain how he would be able to keep the queen away. But he needed to know. The entire plan hinged on the Sov thinking the queen really had been kidnapped. If they found her in their caf eating a burger, the whole plan would go up in flames.

"Just trust me," Galen said.

I don't even know you, Beacon wanted to say. But it was too late to argue.

A tentacle sprang up out of the water. Then dozens of squid creatures materialized, surrounding the boat. Beacon didn't breathe as he watched the aliens circle the boat, splashing and swirling, rocking the vessel violently from side to side on the choppy water. There were so many of them—and soon, they'd all be sleeping off their transformation.

It had worked!

Arthur leaned forward to get a better look. What followed happened so quickly.

Arthur slipped on the rocks. He put his hands out for balance, and Beacon and Everleigh jumped up to try to catch him, but that only resulted in him grabbing on to their arms as he fell. Then all three of them went down. Beacon hissed, Everleigh *oof*ed, and Arthur cried out as they hit the sharp rocks.

There was a stunned moment in which they all realized what had just happened. Slowly, they turned to look out of the cave. The creatures had swiveled toward the island. One of the squids opened its mouth and screamed. The sound traveled down Beacon's spine.

"Just stay still," Everleigh whispered. "Maybe they won't notice us."

Almost as if in response, the creatures dove en masse under the surface. The water rippled as they swam fast and furious for the island. For *them*.

"Get back and hide," Galen said. Then he darted out of the cave.

"Wait, where are you going?" Beacon called. But Galen had disappeared.

"He ditched us!" Everleigh said. "I knew we never should have trusted him."

There was a great splash outside the cave.

"We can point fingers later," Beacon said, grabbing his sister's arm. "Right now we just need to hide."

They picked through the sharp rocks, going deeper into the cave. Beacon wanted to run, but loose stones kept shifting underneath him, twisting his feet one way, then the other, making it impossible to go faster.

"Ahh!" Everleigh cried suddenly.

"What's wrong—" Beacon started, but then he took another step and his foot plunged into icy water.

"It's a lake or something," Arthur said.

They tried all angles, but the water stretched from rock wall to rock wall.

"There's no way around it," Everleigh said.

"Do we jump in?" Arthur asked. "Try to swim across?"

But it was too late.

Slithering, slurping sounds echoed through the cave.

Beacon spun around. He felt his sister grab his hand, her palm wet. He squeezed it. This was it. They were trapped.

"I love you," Beacon blurted out. They never talked like that to each other. But if he was going to die, he didn't want to do it without making sure his sister knew she meant the world to him.

"You're all right, too, I guess," Everleigh said.

"Have you ever thought about writing Hallmark cards?" Beacon said.

"I don't exactly love you guys," Arthur joined in. "I mean, I don't know you well enough for that. But I think highly of you, and I'm glad you're my friends."

"Same, Arth. You're a cool guy," Beacon said.

An earsplitting scream filled the tunnel. Beacon covered his ears, tears involuntarily leaking down his face at the high-pitched sound.

Through the dim light filtering in from the cave entrance, he saw a squid leap forward, then dart back from the rocks. Another squid lunged at them, but it screamed and retreated, too. One by one, the squids tried to move over the stalagmites.

"Why aren't they coming after us?" Everleigh said.

Beacon watched the squids advance and retreat again and again. "I—I think it's the rocks," he said.

"That has to be it!" Arthur said. "The stalagmites are too sharp. They'd probably puncture their skin if they tried to slide over the top of them."

"Oh, thank God," Everleigh said. "I *really* didn't want to die this way."

Beacon blew out a relieved breath. They might be trapped. But they were safe for now.

Then it happened.

It was too dark in the cave to see much of anything, but what he did see was enough: tentacles withdrawing, bones crunching, snapping, and locking into place. Blond hair sprouting like a time-lapse photo—one second, a pixie cut, the next, long tresses curling down her back.

"Well, well, well, if it isn't my old friends," Jane said, stepping forward. Then she turned to the squids. "Get in there and grab them."

A squid screamed in reply. Beacon's body tensed, waiting for the attack. But the squids just shuffled around, a strange murmur going through the group.

"What are you waiting for?" Jane barked. "I said get them!"

But the squids slithered away from the cave.

"Wait, stop! Come back here right now!" Jane called.

But they didn't listen. In seconds, she was alone. She whirled around and locked her eyes on Beacon.

"This isn't over." Then she stormed back out of the cave, her dramatic exit somewhat diminished by the fact that she slipped on the rocks several times.

Everleigh released a huge breath.

"Why did they leave?" Beacon asked.

"Maybe there was an emergency or something?" Arthur offered.

"Who cares," Everleigh replied. "Let's just get out of here."

She stepped forward, but Beacon grabbed her arm.

"Wait! What if this is a trick? What if they're just waiting out there for us to come out?"

"I don't see what choice we have," Everleigh said. "We can't stay in here forever. They could be back any minute."

His sister was right. He hated when that happened.

They cut back across the rocks, made even more treacherous now that they were covered in slimy yellow goo. The Sov were nowhere in sight. Beacon didn't know who he had to thank for this change in luck, but he ran for the raft hidden behind the bush a few feet from the cave entrance. He worried it might be gone, but then he saw the bright orange rubber peeking out from the leaves. They were going to get out of this alive after all.

"Someone help me with this." Beacon hauled on the heavy rubber. Arthur picked his way through the shrubs and grabbed the other end of the raft.

"It's stuck," Beacon said. "Put some muscle in it, Arth."

"I am!" Arthur said. "I'm a man of science, okay?"

Everleigh sighed. "Move out of the way."

A twig snapped close by, and they all froze.

Victor stepped out from behind a tree. All thoughts of the raft went out of Beacon's head. It fell from his limp fingers. He was dimly aware that he should be running, screaming, hiding—anything but standing there with his mouth gaping—but he couldn't make his body work.

A small smile played on Victor's lips as he registered Beacon's shock.

"Get back!" Everleigh cried, pushing her way in front of Beacon and Arthur. "Run, I'll stall him."

Her words shocked Beacon back to reality.

"Not a chance," he said. He hefted a large branch. Arthur looked around for a weapon and picked up a stick. It was ridiculous, but they'd go down fighting.

"It's me," Victor said. "Galen."

"Nice try," Everleigh said. "Just how stupid do you think we are?"

"Very stupid, if you can't understand what just happened. I saved you. I knew the only way the Sov would back off is if an order came from on high. So I transformed into Victor and shouted at them to forget about the kids and return to base stat. As soon as they get back they're going to figure out it wasn't really Victor who gave those orders, so unless you want to have a round two, we need to get out of here."

Beacon, Everleigh, and Arthur exchanged wary glances.

"If you're really Galen, then what did we talk about on the trash barge?" Beacon said.

"Before or after you cried silently for like an hour?" he replied.

Beacon felt his face go red before he lowered the tree branch. "Point made."

"Help me with the boat," Everleigh said, stepping forward.

"There is no boat," Galen said.

"What?!" Everleigh said.

Galen easily hefted the raft that they'd struggled to lift earlier. Sure enough, there was a giant gash down the middle.

"Jane slashed it on her way out," Galen said.

"I knew we should have hidden it better!" Everleigh cried. "How are we going to get back?" She frantically inspected the cut.

"Maybe we can swim?" Beacon looked uneasily at the black

water. It would be a really long trip. And even though the raft hadn't necessarily been a shield from the Sov, being directly in the water when the squid creatures could be lurking in its depths wasn't exactly appealing.

"There's no time for that," Galen said. "You can get on my back."

Beacon didn't have to wonder what he was talking about for long. Galen walked toward the water. As he did, a long tentacle sprouted up from his chest, its slimy skin glinting in the moonlight. He fell on all fours. His spine crunched, and he let out a howl of pain. Beacon covered his eyes. The transformation looked too agonizing to watch. That's when he knew without a shadow of a doubt that he really was Galen. Beacon had seen Victor transform, and it was seamless. This was the transformation of someone less seasoned, who still had a lot to learn.

When Beacon uncovered his eyes, a squid creature stood on the shore, half immersed in the water. Its tentacles rolled and swayed in the foamy surf.

"Oh my God, we're really doing this, aren't we?" Everleigh said.

"I mean, I'm comfortable with swimming back, personally," Arthur said. But he followed the twins as they walked toward the squid.

"Which part is his back?" Beacon made a face as he eyed the myriad slithering tentacles.

"I think just . . . choose a tentacle." Everleigh gingerly sat on a tentacle, gagging when she made contact. She grabbed hold of the writhing mass. As she did, another tentacle lifted and patted her on the head. She gasped, then closed her eyes and blew out a pressurized breath.

"I hate you," she muttered.

Beacon eyed the squid. Now he could understand why the Sov couldn't enter the cave. Its skin was so thin, it was practically translucent. Up close, he could see veins and arteries pulsing inside its body, just under the surface. He shuddered.

"When in Rome," Beacon said. He sat on the tentacle next to his sister.

"That's not the correct use of the idiom," Arthur said, but he followed his lead and sat on a tentacle.

"Did you just call me an idiot?" Beacon said.

"No, I—"

The squid jolted forward into the water. The kids screamed, scrambling to grab on to their chosen appendages. Water sluiced around them, and in moments, their lower halves were completely immersed in the frigid water.

And then they were off.

Beacon quickly forgot about how disgusting he found the squid and clung desperately to its body. He pressed his face against its gooey skin as they flew over the water, waves spraying wildly around them.

Back in LA, the twins used to go tubing on Malibou Lake with their uncle. Beacon remembered clutching the giant inner tube as their uncle drove his boat in wild circles around the lake, trying to throw them off. This felt just like that, only it wasn't fun, they didn't have life jackets, and Beacon couldn't be sure that Galen would circle back around to collect them if they fell off.

Abruptly, the water stopped spraying in Beacon's face, and his stomach finally unclenched. He pried open his eyes. Blackwater Lookout loomed above them, its roof lost in cloud cover.

The squid slid elegantly onto the shore. When his riders didn't immediately move, Galen flailed his tentacles and everyone fell off, muttering as they landed on the shore. Beacon stumbled up on stiff, shaky legs, ready to tell Galen off.

But he stopped short.

Galen didn't so much transform as wither. His squid form shriveled and shrunk, like a balloon with an air leak. Before they knew it, Galen lay on his side, water ebbing and flowing over his human body. If Beacon didn't know any better, he would have assumed he was dead.

"We need to get him inside," Beacon said.

They hauled him into the inn. Everleigh got a fire going while Beacon and Arthur stripped off Galen's wet clothes and wrapped him in warm blankets.

It was only after they'd gotten Galen comfortable and dropped heavily into armchairs around the living room that it finally occurred to Beacon what this all meant. They'd done it. If Galen was down for the count, the other Sov would be soon, too, if they weren't already. The prison's security would be weak.

Only it didn't feel like a victory. When they'd planned to break into the prison, they never thought they'd be doing it without Galen's help. Having a Sov on their side was an invaluable resource. But now they had no choice. By tomorrow, the Sov would be awake and back to their full strength. They'd probably even notice that the drainage system had been compromised. Beacon and the others would never be able to pull off a stunt like this again.

It was now or never.

13

"Should we be concerned that you know how to make a homemade bomb?" Everleigh asked, angling her flashlight at Arthur's hands.

The twins were bent over Arthur at the edge of the giant hole Beacon and Galen had dug on the side of Town Hall Road with an old shovel they had found behind the inn. According to the building plans, this was the exact spot where the underground pipes of the Sov's on-land base joined up with the city's system. So here they were. Ready to set off an explosion.

"Relax, I modeled this off an experiment I did in the fifth grade for the science fair," Arthur said. "I'm not a terrorist."

"Sounds like something a terrorist would say," Everleigh said.

Arthur just shook his head.

"Are you sure it's going to work?" Beacon asked.

"Well, to be honest, it didn't exactly work at the science fair," Arthur said. "My rocket just sort of . . . tipped over instead of launching off the table. I got a B-minus." He said this as if he were making a confession.

"So embarrassing," Everleigh said sarcastically.

"Incoming," Beacon said.

Everleigh quickly switched off the flashlight. They ducked into the grass on the side of the road as a car whizzed past. After a moment, Beacon poked his head up again.

"Coast is clear."

Arthur and Everleigh popped back up. Traffic seemed so scarce until you had to duck every time a car went past. It was starting to get annoying.

"Are you almost done?" Everleigh said, switching the flashlight back on.

"Actually, yes." Arthur pushed himself up to his knees and pulled a stub of a candle out of his pocket. "Once this is lit, we need to get way back. When the flame catches on this stuff," he said, gesturing to whatever it was he'd sprinkled over the pipe, "it's going to *blow*."

Arthur tied a rope around the candle, and then he pulled a barbecue lighter from his pocket. After three attempts, he managed to get a bright blue flame burning from the end of the long wand. He lit the wick, then gently lowered the candle into the hole. He stood up slowly, careful not to disturb the dirt. All three of them took big, cautious steps backward, then Arthur gave the rope a hard yank meant to tip over the candle, and they turned around and ran.

Beacon and Everleigh dove behind a large tree, and Arthur

tucked and rolled after them like some sort of action movie star.

They waited.

And waited.

And waited.

"Well, this is anticlimactic," Everleigh said after a few minutes had gone by.

"I don't get it. It should have worked," Arthur said.

"Maybe the candle went out?" Beacon suggested.

"That's possible," Arthur said. "It *is* a bit windy."

He stood up.

There was a blinding flash of light as the pipe exploded. Beacon saw Arthur go flying back, right before he covered his head and ducked low. Shards of dirt and metal sprayed over him, and he flattened himself farther into the cold grass. Slowly, he opened one eye. His ears rang, and a pillar of smoke and dust funneled into the air from where the bomb had gone off.

Beacon coughed, pushing himself up. He did a quick inventory to determine if he had any missing parts and was relieved to find they were all intact. Everleigh sat up warily.

"Arthur, are you okay?" Beacon asked, getting to his feet.

Arthur was lying flat on his back a few feet away, his arms and legs spread like a starfish. Soot stained his cheeks, and he stared at the sky with horror all over his face.

"I can't see anything!" he shrieked.

Beacon calmly picked up his glasses from the grass nearby and slid them onto Arthur's face.

"Oh. Awesome," Arthur said. He sat up and hoisted his bag.

"Wow, I can't believe that worked," Everleigh said. "Arthur, that was *so cool*!"

Arthur gave her a wobbly smile. If Beacon didn't know better, he would have sworn Arthur's cheeks were tinged pink. To think he'd thought Arthur was smart. No one with a brain would ever have a crush on his sister.

"Come on, let's get going." Everleigh raced over and shined her flashlight at the busted drain.

Beacon blew smoke out of his face as he peered down. Sludge shone from the bottom of a narrow pipe about eight feet below the ground. It would be a tight fit for an adult, but it was just big enough for a kid.

Without a word, Everleigh sat on the edge of the hole, then dropped down and crawled into the pipe. Arthur was next, and then it was Beacon's turn. He sat down, took a deep breath, and pushed off. It was farther down than it looked, and he landed at the bottom with a thud that rattled up his spine. Groaning, he rolled onto all fours. The pipe in front of him was narrow, dark, and coated in slime. It smelled like rusted metal and fish.

"Is everyone okay?" Beacon whispered. He couldn't see anything past Arthur's crouched body in front of him.

"We're fine," Everleigh called from up ahead, the narrow beam of her flashlight bouncing off the grimy pipes.

"All right. Then let's get moving," Beacon said.

The group inched forward.

Beacon crawled after his friends, his hands and knees instantly coated in the mystery goop. Before long, his palms stung, his knees ached, and his body was weak from the cold. He didn't know what waited for them at the end of the pipe, but if they didn't get out soon, they wouldn't be able to fight their way out of a wet paper bag. Beacon realized that was a phrase his dad would have used. He pushed the sudden image of his dad's gaunt face out of his mind and kept moving.

After what felt like an eternity, Everleigh whisper-shouted from farther up the pipe. It might have been his imagination, but he could have sworn the light seemed different ahead.

He crawled faster, and yes, it was definitely lighter. Hope bloomed in his chest, making him feel light-headed. The pipe gave way to a tall passageway. One by one, they crawled out and stood up. Pale light streamed in from an iron grille overhead. Beacon tried to peer through, but it was too high up to see much.

"Come on, Beaks." Everleigh put down her flashlight and locked her fingers together. Beacon stepped on her linked fingers. He steadied himself with Arthur's shoulder and boosted himself up, wrapping his fingers around the bars. He pushed. For a horrible moment, nothing happened, and he worried that this was all for nothing. That they would have to crawl all the way back—and *without* their dad. But when he pushed a second time, there was a popping sound, like a jar lid coming unstuck. Beacon eased the grille aside and peeked over the edge.

"What do you see?" Arthur whispered.

"It's a massive room," Beacon said. "Unfinished. Concrete floors, metal support beams all over the place. There's machinery and wires and pipes everywhere. "

"It must be the mechanical floor," Arthur said. "That's perfect."

"Is there anyone around?" Everleigh whispered.

Beacon scanned the room. It was huge—it must have taken up the entire floor of the building. But he didn't see any movement in the shadows.

"Not as far as I can tell. Push me up."

Everleigh grunted and heaved him up, and Beacon clambered through the gap. Arthur was next. Then Beacon and Arthur reached down and hoisted Everleigh through. They replaced the grille, just as Beacon heard a scrape behind them. He turned around slowly, dread prickling the hairs on the back of his neck.

A thickset woman with ruddy cheeks and Brillo Pad hair pulled into a tight bun had just emerged from a door off the main room. Beacon's fear instantly gave way to relief.

"Donna!"

Beacon had hoped they would find her, too, but he hadn't expected to do it so soon.

But Donna didn't smile or rush over to greet them, like he expected.

"What are you doing here?" She stepped forward into the small circle of light cast by a dim bulb. That's when Beacon realized what she was wearing. A freshly pressed, Sov-issue guard uniform.

"Donna, it's us," Beacon said. "We're here to get you out."

Her eyes narrowed dangerously, and she stomped toward him.

"Get away from her!" Everleigh cried. "She's had the antidote!"

But it was too late. She closed the distance between them, her fingers gripping something at her waistband: a baton.

"Beacon!" Arthur yelled. Beacon looked back, and Arthur tossed him the PJ. The wand soared through the air, end over end. Beacon caught it, just as Donna pulled out her own weapon. Blue electric light flared from the end of the long steel baton.

She thrust her weapon toward Beacon. Beacon panicked and raised the PJ up like a sword, blocking her. Their wands met in the air with a resounding clang. Donna smiled then: cold, dark, cruel. Fear shot through him, but before Beacon could react, she depressed the trigger.

A sudden, intense jolt of pain went through his body. His stomach clenched and his arm lost feeling, his legs turning to gelatin beneath him. If that was the effect of the baton when it hadn't even touched his skin, he didn't want to think about what a direct hit would feel like.

The PJ fell from his fingers with a clatter, and Beacon dropped to his knees.

"Beacon!" Everleigh cried, running over.

"Run," he grunted.

But even as he said it, Beacon knew his sister would never listen. Everleigh was as loyal as she was stubborn.

"You'll pay for that," Everleigh told Donna, her hands curling into fists.

In one swift movement, Everleigh rolled across the floor, picked up Beacon's PJ, and landed on her feet again. But Donna was deceptively fast. She slammed into Everleigh, knocking her to the ground. The PJ went clattering across the floor. Donna bent down and pressed her knee into Everleigh's chest, the baton gripped tightly in her hand.

"Please, Donna, we don't want to hurt you," Everleigh gasped out.

"I think you're a little confused about who's getting hurt here," Donna said.

Just then, a shadow fell over Donna. She started to turn, but it was too late. Arthur jammed the PJ into her side and depressed the trigger. Donna's body went rigid as the jolt traveled through her. Her eyes rolled back in her head, and she went as limp as a rag doll, collapsing on top of Everleigh. Everleigh cried out as Donna's full weight landed on her, knocking the wind out of her. Beacon struggled to his feet and staggered over, and then he and Arthur shoved Donna off his sister. Everleigh rolled to her feet.

"Are you okay?" Beacon asked.

"Just crushed a few ribs, but who needs those, right?"

Everleigh sat up and dusted herself off. Then they all looked down at the innkeeper. She lay completely still, facedown on the concrete floor. Then Donna's arm twitched. They gave her a wide berth as she rolled over onto her butt. She blinked up at the kids, a stunned looked on her face.

Beacon stepped forward hesitantly. "Donna? How are you feeling?"

She smacked her lips together, then swallowed heavily.

"Do you need water?" Arthur said. "I was really thirsty after I was jolted."

He reached into his bag and pulled out a water bottle, bringing it to her lips.

Lightning fast, she snapped out her arm and grabbed Arthur's wrist.

"It's me, Arthur," Arthur yelped. "We're here to help you. You're not under the Sov's control anymore!"

But Donna didn't listen. She grabbed Arthur's throat with her other hand. Her face was chillingly wooden as she squeezed his neck. Arthur sputtered and choked, grabbing uselessly at her hands. His lips turned a sickening shade of blue.

"Let him go!" Beacon screamed. He pulled at Donna's arms, trying to loosen her grip on Arthur. "Donna, it's us! Stop!"

But if anything, her fingers only dug more deeply into Arthur's neck. His eyes fluttered closed. She was going to kill him.

14

There was a flash of movement in Beacon's peripheral vision, right before Everleigh cracked Donna's baton into the side of her head. Donna went down. A pool of blood seeped from her temple onto the tile. Arthur dropped to his knees and sucked in deep, wheezing breaths.

"Are you okay?" Everleigh asked.

"W-why didn't it work?" Arthur gasped.

Beacon's mind went into a tailspin. Arthur hadn't had a chance to test his invention on anyone, so it was possible it was defective. But the kid was a genius.

"Victor," Beacon said suddenly, the puzzle pieces clicking together.

Of course. He didn't know why he hadn't thought of it sooner. "Victor developed the PJ with us. He knows everything about it. He must have told the other Sov about the electrocution glitch, and they updated the antidote."

"So the PJ wasn't defective," Arthur said.

"More importantly," Everleigh said, "PJs aren't going to work anymore—electrocution won't jolt the lemmings out of being mind-controlled. We're totally screwed! How are we supposed to get hundreds of people out of here if they don't want to go with us?"

"I don't know," Beacon said. "But this is our only chance to get Dad out."

Arthur stood up. He shoved the water bottle and PJ back into his bag, then threw the bag over his shoulder.

Everleigh looked down at Donna's still body. She hesitated for a moment before she bent down and laid a palm over the innkeeper's chest.

"Is she . . . ?" Arthur said.

"She's alive," Everleigh said. "Barely."

"You had to do it," Beacon said. "She was going to kill him. You saved Arthur's life."

Everleigh swallowed roughly and stood up. She cleared her throat.

"Which way?" she asked Arthur, suddenly all business.

He consulted the map from his pocket. "I think we're on the first mechanical floor," he said. "If this is east, which I'm pretty sure it is, then that must mean the prison is . . ." He spun around and faced the opposite direction. "That way."

They set off, sneaking down hallways and up narrow stairwells. The place was quiet and still, like a graveyard at night. Darkness hung over the building, save for the neon emergency lighting throwing green beams across the tiled floors.

Beacon kept expecting to run into people, but there wasn't even a sleeping guard at the security desk they slid past. But the place couldn't really be empty. The thought that the Sov were here, somewhere, was somehow creepier than if the place had been packed with squids. Beacon couldn't help thinking about the monsters lurking in the dark, about a tentacle whipping out to drag him into the shadows.

He focused on the fact that his dad was here, somewhere, and kept moving.

They were just passing through a darkened rotunda when he heard a noise. Beacon froze.

"Shhh!" he said, gesturing for the others to stand still. Everleigh and Arthur stuttered to a stop, their backs turned to each other, their ears cocked to the hallways branching out all around them.

They stood there. One moment. Two. No sound but the crashing of Beacon's heart.

Just then, clacking boots echoed from down one of the corridors, and a voice said, "Hurry up, we don't have all day."

He recognized that voice.

"Quick, hide!" Beacon grabbed Everleigh's and Arthur's arms, and they ducked into an alcove. They flattened themselves against the wall. After a moment, Beacon peeked out and saw Nixon's wiry black curls come into view. He wasn't alone. Perry walked behind him. His biceps bulged under his Gold Stars letterman jacket as he roughly dragged a prisoner forward. The girl stumbled, blinking against the neon lights. Nixon knocked on a door farther down the hall. The door whooshed open, and Perry shoved the girl inside before the door closed again.

Perry turned, and Beacon ducked back into the alcove.

"I think I saw someone over there," Perry said.

The spark of fear inside Beacon's belly ignited like it had been doused in gasoline.

"There's no one covering this floor but us," Nixon said. "You know that."

"No, man, I swear I just saw something by that alcove," Perry said.

There was a heavy sigh. Boots squeaked on the tile. Beacon's whole body tensed as Nixon rounded the corner. His eyes went wide at the sight of the three of them. His jaw flexed before he called, "Just like I said, there's no one here." He stared daggers at Beacon before he turned around and joined Perry again.

"They won't need any more participants for a while," Nixon said. "Get down to the queen's rooms in the west wing and help Sumiko guard the doors. And don't screw up," he added. "Victor won't trust us to be Junior Guards if you let anyone get in or out."

A moment later, Nixon reappeared.

"What are you doing here?" he snapped.

"Oh, you know, we were just in the neighborhood," Everleigh said sarcastically. "What do you *think* we're doing here? We're trying to get our dad out. The real question is, what are *you* doing here?"

"Trying to free prisoners," Nixon said.

"Oh really? Because from here it looks a little different," Everleigh said.

"I was going to get them out once I got rid of Perry," Nixon shot back.

Everleigh snorted.

"Look, if I went around acting like the Terminator trying to free all the prisoners, I'd just end up one of them," Nixon said. "I have to be smart about this. Do you know how tough it was to get the Gold Stars assigned here? We weren't even supposed to know about this place. I've been working hard to find out as much as I can. I've been doing my patrols by Sov meeting rooms to try to get inside info and . . . it's bigger than we ever thought."

"What do you know?" Beacon said eagerly.

"Things are bad." Nixon looked around before lowering his voice even further. "The Sov are planning a blitzkrieg attack on the planet. They're going to douse everyone in toxic rain. That's what they're testing in there." He jerked his head at the door. "I think they're close, too. I overheard the scientists talking about it. We need to stop them before it's too late. We have to find the

Rainmaker. I've scoured the whole place, but it must be hidden or something."

"Wait, slow down," Everleigh said. "What are you talking about?"

"*Blitzkrieg,*" Arthur said. "It's a method of offensive warfare designed to strike a swift, focused blow at an enemy, using the elements of speed and surprise, often with the help of air superiority."

"In English," Everleigh said.

"Surprise attack," Arthur said. "Happens so fast and from so many fronts that the enemy doesn't have a chance to respond."

A shiver traveled down Beacon's spine.

Everleigh shook her head. "I don't get it. I thought the Sov wanted to keep us 'docile and complacent,'" she said, doing air quotes.

It was a good point. Nixon had told them that the Sov's elders had predicted that, far into the future, humans would attack the Sov and take over their planet. So instead of waiting around for that to happen, the Sov had decided to deal with the problem now. Only they couldn't just kill all the humans, because that would start up a war with another alien race that didn't take too kindly to genocide. That's why the Sov began inoculating humans with the antidote—so they could make sure humans never got smart enough to figure out space travel, while keeping the other aliens off their back.

So why this sudden change of plans? Why kill humans?

"The elders had a new vision," Nixon said. "Something about someone saving the planet. I guess they decided to head us off at the pass after all."

Beacon suddenly felt like he could puke. Victor's words that night in the alley came roaring back.

"You know, when the elders told me that you would be responsible for saving the planet from us, I thought you must be really extraordinary. Especially smart, especially talented—anything. *But in the weeks that I've gotten to know you, I've realized you're just an average human kid."*

Could the Sov have been talking about him? Was he really going to save the world? Scarier yet, was he responsible for the Sov's decision to forget about Plan A and drop acid rain on the Earth instead?

Beacon tried to keep the anxiety out of his voice when he asked, "What else did you hear? Did they say who would save the world?"

"That's all I know," Nixon said. "There's only so many times I can patrol past the same meeting before people start getting suspicious."

"Sims?"

Nixon straightened at the sound of a guard's voice down the hall.

"Coming, sir!" Nixon called. Then he lowered his voice again. "There's a supply room down that hall." He nodded toward one of the corridors branching off the rotunda. "There should be hazmat suits inside."

Then he turned around and hurried away.

"Wait!" Arthur whispered. "What do we need hazmat suits for?"

But Nixon disappeared.

"What do hazmat suits have to do with anything?" Arthur repeated.

"I don't know," Everleigh said. "But we've *got* to see what's inside that room."

Beacon pushed down the overwhelming urge to just sit down on the floor and rock himself until all of his problems went away and crept across the rotunda with the others.

There was a small window in the top of the door. Beacon stood on his toes and peered through the glass.

The room was bathed in blue and red neon lights. There were vials of brightly colored liquid in metal trays on every surface, and along the back of the room were three huge glass cylinders, each containing a prisoner. They looked out at the scientists moving around the room in orange full-body hazmat suits, gas masks on their faces and giant oxygen tanks strapped to their backs. Beacon had thought that all the life had been drained out of the prisoners, but now he knew it wasn't true: There was a flash of fear visible in their otherwise lifeless eyes. Whatever they'd been brought here for, it wasn't good, and they knew it somewhere deep down.

"What do you see?" Arthur asked.

"It's some kind of lab," Beacon whispered.

A woman in a hazmat suit walked carefully with a vial of blue liquid held away from her body with a set of tongs. As Beacon watched, she placed the vial in a little machine on the side of a giant cylinder with a girl inside. The machine closed around the vial, then slid slowly up the side of the cylinder, like an elevator crawling to the top floor of a skyscraper. The girl backed away from the vial, but there was nowhere to go. Blue liquid began spraying through the top of the cylinder. The girl screamed and shielded her face, frantically trying to wipe away the liquid. She fell to her knees, coughing and sputtering. Then she collapsed against the glass. Her body was motionless.

The scientists nodded happily. The door to her cylinder was opened and one of them scooped her up and carried her through a door at the back of the room.

Beacon ducked down, swallowing past the bile in his throat.

She couldn't be dead. The Sov wouldn't do that.

Except he knew that they would.

"What's going on?" Everleigh asked.

"They're—they're testing something on the prisoners," he muttered. "I think one of them was just killed."

"Let me see." Arthur edged up on his toes and peered through the window.

Everleigh took a peek, then steeled her jaw. "We have to do something."

She was right. Beacon just wanted to find his dad and get as far away from this town as possible. But he couldn't let these people die.

Beacon looked through the glass again. There were two prisoners remaining, each in a cylinder. They needed to figure out a way to release them. Beacon bit his lip, thinking.

Just then, a scientist walked to the shadowy back corner of the room, where black metal bars took shape. Beacon couldn't believe he hadn't noticed it before. Dog cages. They were the same as the ones his aunt Deb used for her mastiffs when she was kennel training them. Except it wasn't dogs inside these cages. Dirty fingers clutched the black bars. As he watched, the scientist opened one of the cages and roughly yanked a prisoner out.

Beacon felt the blood drain from his head.

"Dad!"

"What?!" Everleigh shoved Beacon aside and looked through the window, just as the scientist dragged their dad into the empty cylinder.

"Oh my God! We need to get in there." Everleigh reached for the keypad next to the door, but Beacon grabbed her hand.

"We don't know the code to open that door, and we don't have any weapons. All you're going to do is get those scientists to call the guards, and then we'll all be in one of those things."

"So, what, we just let them kill our dad?"

"Of course not," Beacon said. "We just have to be smart about this."

"The supply room," Arthur said. "Nixon said there were hazmat suits in there."

He really was a genius.

They found it quickly. The supply room was a small, sterile room filled with clothing racks. They each grabbed an orange hazmat suit and shoved their arms and legs inside, then pulled on the hood and zipped one another up.

"Let's go!" Everleigh said.

"Wait, they were wearing these." Beacon tossed Everleigh an oxygen tank backpack. She caught it against her chest, making an *oof* sound at the unexpected weight.

"Don't throw that! Do you want to set this place on fire?" Arthur shrugged out of his regular backpack and into the oxygen one. He tried to shove the PJ into his pocket, but it was too big.

"Just ditch it," Beacon said. "It's useless, anyway."

With a pained sigh, Arthur stuffed the PJ and his bag into an empty shoe cubby. Everleigh strapped the respirator over her nose and mouth.

"I think they wore the masks *under* their hoods," Arthur said.

"Who cares?" Everleigh said. "It doesn't have to be perfect, just passable. Let's go."

They ran out into the hall. Beacon knew they should walk, that running looked suspicious, but they didn't have time to waste.

They reached the lab. Beacon took a deep breath, then knocked on the door.

After a moment, the door slid open. A scientist squinted at the three of them in their inexpertly applied gear.

"Change of shift," Beacon said, deepening his voice.

"We don't change shift for another three hours." The scientist looked at his watch.

"Change of plans." Beacon shouldered past the scientist. Everleigh and Arthur pushed in after him.

Beacon risked a glance at the cylinder his dad was now inside. Seeing him there steeled his nerves. He held himself up straighter and turned to the nearest scientist.

"I need this one released," he said. "On Victor's orders."

"What for? We were about to test the latest batch," the woman said.

"I didn't ask," Beacon said. "You got a problem with it, you can take it up with Victor. Open the hatch."

"The hatch? You mean the access panel?"

"Exactly," Beacon said. "No time to waste."

The scientist nearest him stepped closer, squinting into Beacon's hazmat suit. "Who are you? I don't recognize you."

"You wouldn't. I'm new," Beacon said, turning away. The scientist grabbed his shoulder and spun him around.

"Can I see your identification?"

Beacon felt around his hazmat suit, even though it had no pockets, and he *definitely* had no identification. "I must have forgotten it."

Another scientist standing near a bank of computers picked up a phone and began speaking in fast, low tones. Beacon needed to get his dad out *now*. He frantically looked around for something to smash the glass.

But it was too late.

The doors slid open, and someone stepped into the lab.

Victor.

15

For a moment, Beacon thought he must be imagining things. How could Victor be here? They had assumed he would return to Driftwood Harbor to attend to his world domination plans after his cover had been blown impersonating their dad. But shouldn't he be sleeping like the rest of the Sov?

Then he wondered if this was just Galen impersonating Victor again, like back at the cave. But that wasn't possible. Galen was sleeping off his transformation.

Then it hit him.

Of course Victor wouldn't be asleep. He was the leader of the Sov. He wouldn't have gone after the queen on the lake along with everyone else. That would be like the president personally defusing a bomb instead of sending out a bomb squad.

"You're really becoming thorns in my side." Victor stepped forward. His tone was casual, but his shoulders pushed back and his eyes were glaring black pools that pinned Beacon to the spot. "I'm beginning to think I should have just killed you and dealt with the consequences. And let me tell you, there were many, *many* times I was tempted those few weeks we lived together."

"Yeah, well, you weren't such a great roommate, either," Beacon shot back.

"And your peanut butter and jelly sandwiches suck!" Arthur added.

Victor ignored them and took another step into the room. It was the middle of the night, but his hair was slicked back and there wasn't a single wrinkle in his crisp, pressed suit. "You know, I should really be thanking you right now."

Beacon knew it was a trap, but he still couldn't help asking, "For what?"

"We needed new test subjects." Victor smiled coldly. "Nancy, kindly put the intruders in the cages."

The woman took a step toward Beacon.

"Don't even think about it!" Everleigh yelled from somewhere behind Beacon.

Beacon looked over his shoulder. Everleigh had yanked the respirator off one of the scientists. The man was white as chalk. He sent a panicked look to Victor, his mouth frozen in a perfect O of surprise. Everleigh held up a vial of the mysterious blue liquid.

"Back away from my brother, or I'll smash this thing,"

Everleigh said. "And your colleague here dies."

Everleigh could die, too, Beacon thought—she hadn't exactly taken care putting on her respirator. But he couldn't say anything, or he'd risk ruining whatever plan Everleigh had up her sleeve right now.

The scientist hesitated, looking between Everleigh and Victor.

"You don't follow orders from human children, Nancy," Victor said calmly. "Now do as I say."

Nancy took another step toward Beacon.

"Fine by me," Everleigh said, raising her hand.

"Stop!" Nancy froze and raised her hands in defense. "Just, please. Put that down."

"I won't ask you again, Nancy," Victor said through clenched teeth. Beacon had thought Victor's calm composure was chilling, but his rage was absolutely *terrifying.* "I said put. The children. In the cage. Or you'll regret it."

His face rippled, but he didn't transform. Beacon didn't get it. Victor could end this whole conversation by changing into his squid form. That's when it occurred to Beacon that he *couldn't* transform— not when the rest of the Sov were down for the count. Then he'd be leaving the whole base vulnerable while he slept. The realization galvanized him.

"He won't hurt you," Beacon told the woman. "It's too late to get new scientists." He had no idea if any of this was true, but from the way Victor's jaw clenched, he must be onto something.

"But my sister?" Beacon forged on. "She will *definitely* hurt you. Trust me. Just let my dad out of that thing, and we'll be on our way. No one has to get hurt."

"You don't know what you're talking about," Victor said.

Nancy looked from Victor to Everleigh. Everleigh smiled darkly, a warning all over her face. *Go ahead,* she said. *Test me.*

The scientist closed her eyes for a brief moment, then she raced over to the cylinder.

"STOP! WHAT ARE YOU DOING?" A tentacle burst out of Victor's shirt like a rocket, spraying buttons all over the room.

"I wouldn't do that if I were you!" Everleigh warned, shaking the blue vial. "Not unless you're really, *really* sure this stuff won't kill you, too. How much do you trust your scientists?"

Victor stole a glance at the nearest scientist, then let out a roar of rage as his tentacle slurped back under his shirt.

Nancy punched buttons on the side of the cylinder.

"Don't even think about calling your guards right now, or I promise I will smash this thing," Everleigh threatened.

Victor practically vibrated. If they ever crossed his path after they left this place, they were totally dead meat.

The door slid open, but their dad didn't move.

"Dad, come on," Everleigh said, waving frantically.

But he still didn't budge.

"He's had the antidote," Beacon said.

And they couldn't use the PJ on him.

"What now, geniuses?" Victor sneered.

Beacon swallowed his rising panic. He told himself to stay calm. That they would find another way to jolt him out of his mind-controlled state once they escaped this place. But he could see from the look on Everleigh's face that she was worried, too.

"Tell him he has to come with us. And obey our commands," Arthur said.

"Well, go on." Everleigh shook the vial.

"You have to go with them," Nancy said grudgingly. "Obey their commands."

At her order, their dad stepped out of the cylinder. Beacon couldn't help it. He rushed forward and embraced his dad, not caring about Victor or the fact that his dad was brainwashed or that they might never get out of this building. They'd found him.

"The other two as well," Everleigh said. "And the people in the cages."

"No," Victor said.

"Do it now!" Everleigh commanded.

"You will *not* take anyone else." Victor stepped forward, the front of his suit billowing like there were a pair of raccoons fighting underneath it. He seemed to be seconds away from transforming.

Beacon cut Everleigh a look that said everything he was thinking. *Don't push it.* This had always been about rescuing their dad. If they blew it and Victor transformed, none of them would get out of here.

Everleigh clenched her jaw.

"Fine. Come with us," she told her dad.

The twins' dad slogged toward her like an overworked circus animal.

They backed toward the exit.

"Open the door," Everleigh ordered.

One of the scientists punched a code into the panel, and the door whizzed open behind them.

"Let's go," Everleigh commanded. She waved Beacon, Arthur, and her dad out of the lab, still firmly gripping the vial of blue liquid. Her eyes settled on her dad for a moment longer than the others before she ripped them away. After the last of them had exited, Everleigh looked at Victor.

"You're evil, and I hope karma comes for you," she said.

The door closed.

Awesome. They definitely wouldn't be the target of a revenge killing now.

"Let's get out of here," Arthur said. "He's probably already calling for backup."

"What about the Rainmaker?" Everleigh said.

"Are you kidding me?" Beacon said. "You just royally ticked off the leader of the Sov. We don't have time for that."

"If Nixon is right, none of this will matter if we don't find that thing," Everleigh said. "We'll all be dead."

She was right. It was starting to become a habit.

"Hold on," Arthur said, pulling out the building plans. "It's got to be a huge machine if it's going to eradicate everyone on the planet, right? So we'll find a large room." He scanned the plans, then pointed. "There. It's the largest room in the building, and it's nearby. Just down the west wing."

"Then let's go." Everleigh turned to her dad. "Follow us. As quickly and as quietly as you can."

They set off. The twins' dad hobbled along after them, his bare feet slapping the tile. Beacon tried not to look at him. Tried not to think about the disturbingly blank stare on his face as he followed Everleigh's commands like a puppy. That was a problem for after they saved the planet.

A crackle came over the PA system. Victor's voice echoed through the halls. "Initiate the sequence."

An alarm began blaring. Overhead, a red light flashed across the white walls.

"Um, what's 'the sequence'?" Beacon said.

"I don't think we want to know," Everleigh said. "Where is that room?"

"Left here," Arthur said.

They started to bank left, but Everleigh skidded back, holding out her arm to stop the group from advancing.

Beacon peeked around the corner.

Perry and Sumiko stood importantly in front of a set of large wooden double doors at the end of the hall. Their gold and blue varsity jackets shone under the harsh fluorescent lights.

"Gold Stars," Beacon whispered. "I can see a baton on Perry's belt. Sumiko probably has one, too. What's the plan?"

"Blitzkrieg." Everleigh pushed away from the wall.

"Wait!" Beacon said, but she strolled out around the corner, her hazmat suit crunching as she walked. Beacon ground his teeth and followed his sister.

Perry stood up straight as Everleigh approached.

"Where have you been?" Everleigh demanded. "Victor's been trying to reach you for the last twenty minutes. Haven't you heard the announcement?"

"What?" Sumiko said. "Of course I heard, but—wait, what's that in your hand?"

Everleigh paused for a moment. She'd clearly forgotten she was still holding the vial of blue liquid.

"One of the samples, of course," she said, recovering.

"Why is it out of the lab?" Sumiko said. "Is that why the alarms are going off?"

"You would know the answers to all of this if you had just answered Victor's calls," Beacon said.

"Did he radio? I didn't hear anything." Perry reached for his radio, just as Everleigh grabbed the baton from his belt. Before he could react, she jammed the baton into his abdomen and depressed the trigger. Perry's mouth opened, as if to say something, before he dropped like a sack of potatoes. Sumiko had her baton out, but she wasn't fast enough. Everleigh jabbed her in the shoulder before she could even raise the weapon. Sumiko joined Perry on the ground.

Everleigh stepped over her body and turned the door handle. But it was locked.

"Maybe one of them has keys?" Arthur said.

Everleigh handed the vial to Arthur.

"What? I don't want this!" he shrieked.

"Relax, it's just deadly acid rain." Everleigh patted down Sumiko's pockets and pulled out a key ring. "Bingo!"

"Hurry!" Arthur held the vial as if it might leap out of his hands if he didn't grip it tightly enough.

Everleigh tried three keys before the lock snicked.

She scooped up Sumiko's baton and tossed it to Beacon. He couldn't help looking at his dad then, waiting for him to tell him that he was too young to be handling a weapon and that he would only end up hurting himself. But of course, his dad didn't say any of those things.

Everleigh gripped her own baton as she cracked the door open and peered inside. Beacon looked over her shoulder. There was a huge four-poster bed in the middle of the room, covered in silky sheets and too many pillows to count. Elegant furniture that looked like it might break if you actually used it was dotted around the room, and the floor was covered with a thick, intricately woven rug. Candles flickered in sconces on the damask-covered walls.

"What is this place?" Everleigh said.

Beacon looked around, and the realization dawned on him. "It's the queen's bedroom."

"Wow, so embarrassing to only have one crystal chandelier in your bedroom," Everleigh said sarcastically.

Thundering footsteps suddenly echoed down the corridor behind them.

"Someone's coming!" Arthur said.

"Help me get them in here or they'll know something's up." Everleigh grabbed Perry under his armpits, as Beacon grabbed his feet. They hauled him through the doors, then went back for Sumiko. Meanwhile, their dad just stood there waiting for orders.

"Get in," Everleigh commanded her dad. He shuffled inside, then they closed the door behind him and locked it.

Beacon pressed a finger to his lips. They went still, listening as the footsteps on the other side of the door grew louder, then retreated. When a minute passed and no other sounds could be heard, Arthur blew out a huge breath.

"That was close. Who do you think that was out there? Do you think the Sov are awake yet?"

Beacon shuddered. "I hope not."

"Ditch your suits," Everleigh said, tossing her respirator onto a divan. "They'll be looking for people dressed as scientists."

Arthur carefully laid down the vial on a nearby desk. Beacon ditched his baton. Then he and Arthur threw off their backpacks and respirators and unzipped their hazmat suits.

"What are you doing here?"

Beacon froze, the nuclear suit pooled around his ankles.

A girl stepped out of a bathroom and into the room.

She was paler than in the picture, sickly looking, as if she belonged in a prison and not in this lush room. But Beacon instantly recognized the girl from Galen's wallet. Daisy.

"I said what are you doing here?" Daisy said, casting a suspicious gaze at the twins' motionless dad. "And what have you done to my guards?"

Her guards.

Beacon's eyes landed on the necklace at the girl's throat. The oval emerald was big enough to break a window, and it didn't look fake.

The truth slammed into Beacon like a freight train.

This was why Galen had been afraid of Daisy before they became friends.

Why she couldn't leave the ship when he'd run away.

Why Galen could make sure the queen was off the ship during Operation Moonlight Serenade.

Daisy was the Sovereign queen.

16

"I said *what* have you done with my guards?"

Even though she was as thin as a fence post, the girl had an imperial tone to her voice that made Beacon's back go ramrod straight. She had the air of a person who was used to giving commands and having them obeyed without question.

Everleigh kicked her suit off her leg and gripped her weapon.

"We're the people with the batons," she said. "And we're looking for the Rainmaker. Where is it?"

"I don't know what you're talking about," Daisy said.

"Don't play stupid with us. It's obvious you're the Sov queen. Why else would they put you up in a room like this? We need to know where the Rainmaker is."

Daisy lifted her chin. "I don't know."

Everleigh switched on the baton. The wand glowed blue, and electricity popped and fizzed from its tip.

Daisy stepped back, fear widening her eyes.

"I don't know anything about their plans. No one tells me

anything, I swear! I was only brought here a few days ago. I don't even know what this place is."

Beacon remembered the security feed Galen had been watching from the aquarium. It'd been inside the underwater ship. She wasn't lying—at least not about just coming to this base. Was it possible she hadn't known the real reason they came to Earth, either, like Galen?

Beacon grabbed Everleigh's arm and lowered his voice. "This is Daisy. Galen's friend—the girl from his wallet."

Everleigh gave the girl a suspicious look.

"Galen?" Daisy said, perking up. "Is—is he here? Or is this just another trick?" Her eyes went almost as dark as her tone.

"Trick?" Beacon said.

"Like that message I got to go meet him at our spot in the forest, only no one was there. I got in so much trouble for that when Victor couldn't find me anywhere."

"What are you talking about?" Everleigh said, but the pieces clicked together in Beacon's head.

"The boat. That's how Galen made sure the queen was MIA when we lured the Sov out onto the water."

"Galen really is here, then?" Daisy said.

Arthur opened his mouth to speak, but Everleigh elbowed him in the stomach.

"Don't tell her anything. She's our enemy," Everleigh said.

"Galen said we can trust her," Beacon said. "He's sacrificed a lot to help us."

"Well, Galen left out a bit of key information," Everleigh shot back. "Like the fact that his best friend is the queen of his entire alien race."

"She's telling the truth," Beacon said.

"How do we know?" Everleigh retorted. "Of course she'd lie. She doesn't want us to ruin her precious world genocide plans."

"I have nothing to do with their plans," Daisy said.

"I guess we'll find out about that." Everleigh glared at her.

"*Everleigh*," Beacon chastised.

Everleigh glowered at her brother. Then she blew out an annoyed breath, switched off the baton, and turned haughtily to the queen.

"How do we get out of here? Arthur, give her the map."

Arthur started to dig in his pocket, but Daisy help up a hand.

She closed her eyes and pinched the bridge of her nose for the briefest moment before she said, "Behind the wall hanging." She gestured to a large tapestry on a far wall.

"Arthur?" Everleigh said.

Arthur walked over and pulled back the tapestry, revealing a door.

"What is it?" Everleigh said.

"A door," Daisy replied. "I'm sorry, I thought you were familiar with them."

"You know what I mean," Everleigh spat.

Daisy crossed her arms. "It's an escape tunnel. They must have put it in for my safety in case of emergency. They tried to hide it from me with that tapestry, but I found it when I was putting my things away."

"Great. Get your coat," Everleigh said. "You're coming with us."

"What?!" Daisy cried, her arms falling to her sides again.

"You didn't really think we'd let you go, did you?" Everleigh said. "We have miles to cover if we're going to get out of here without getting caught. If we have the queen, no one can hurt us."

Daisy's eyes narrowed dangerously at Everleigh.

"You have no idea who you're dealing with," she said darkly. "No idea what I'm capable of."

"Yes, yes, you can turn into a squid, we're all very impressed," Everleigh deadpanned, rolling her eyes. "Now get your coat, or you're going to get *very* cold." She pointed the baton at her.

Daisy stomped over to a wardrobe and grabbed a jacket. It was several sizes too big, and Beacon immediately thought of the photo of her Galen carried in his wallet. She'd been healthy in the picture, happy. What had happened to her since then?

"And take that thing off." Everleigh nodded at her necklace.

Daisy's hand went up to her throat, fingering the emerald hanging on the delicate gold chain.

"No," she said defiantly.

"Just let her keep the necklace," Beacon said.

"It could have a tracking device or something," Arthur said. "I agree, she should take it off."

"I *can't* take it off," Daisy said.

"We'll see about that." Before Daisy could react, Everleigh reached out and yanked on the chain. The necklace should have snapped, but Daisy jerked forward.

Everleigh tried again. She wrenched on the chain as hard as she could.

"Ow!" Daisy cried, grabbing her neck. "Stop that!"

"Why didn't it break?" Everleigh demanded.

"I told you, I can't take it off! It's a part of me."

"Arthur, do you have any tools on you? Pliers, or something like that?" Everleigh said.

"That isn't going to work," Daisy said. "The necklace is a part of me."

"What is that supposed to mean?" Everleigh said.

There was a knock on the door.

Beacon's eyes widened with alarm.

"Daisy, are you okay?" Victor said.

Everleigh held the baton held up to Daisy's neck.

"Tell him you're fine," she ordered.

Daisy lifted her chin, her eyes flashing with challenge as she watched the door.

"Daisy? It's Victor," the man said. "Your guards aren't here. I wanted to check that you're okay."

"*Tell him you're fine*," Everleigh said.

Daisy ground her jaw, her nostrils flaring as she looked at Everleigh's weapon.

"Daisy, if you don't answer, I'm coming in!" Victor called.

Daisy cleared her throat. "It's fine," she said weakly. "I'm fine. I was just . . . resting."

"Are you sure?" Victor said. "There's been a containment breach. Nothing for you to worry about, of course, and we're getting it all under control. But we wanted to make sure you're okay."

"I'm perfectly fine," Daisy replied.

"Okay, great. I'll have extra security posted at your door. Just stay put."

"Thank you," Daisy said.

"Good," Everleigh whispered. "Now let's go." She pushed the baton into Daisy's back. "Lead the way, *your highness*."

Daisy stalked over to the far wall. She flung aside the tapestry and opened the door to the secret passage. Beacon saw a dirt floor and naked rock walls before the narrow tunnel fell away into shadow. She hesitated.

"Go!" Everleigh demanded.

The girl took one step through the doorway.

"Help me!" she screamed at the top of her lungs.

Victor banged on the door. Through the thick wood, they could hear shouts about master keys.

Beacon closed his eyes for one brief, frustrated second.

"You idiot," Everleigh cried. "Come on, let's go! Everyone move it!"

Beacon grabbed his dad's arm and pulled him through the doorway into the passage. He realized he'd left Sumiko's baton on the floor, but it was too late to go back for it. Arthur ducked in after them. Then Everleigh shoved Daisy through and slid inside, pulling the tapestry back down as she did. The door to the secret entrance had just clicked shut when the doors to Daisy's room burst open.

Everleigh clamped a hand over Daisy's mouth, then jammed the baton into her side.

"Scream like that again, and I'll drop you with this," Everleigh whispered.

Daisy cut her a vicious look, but she did as she was told.

They ran, their boots pounding on the dirt. But it didn't seem to matter how urgently Everleigh commanded their dad. He was weak and tired, and he lagged behind.

"Hurry!" Beacon whispered urgently.

They needed to be faster. It would only be a matter of time before Victor figured out that they'd used the emergency escape.

They pushed forward through the cold, dark passage. Despite the chilling temperature, sweat rolled down Beacon's skin in thick, salty beads. His throat was raw, and he'd kill for a moment to lean up against the wall and catch his breath. But distance was all that mattered right now.

He heard a gasp behind him and turned to see Daisy on the ground and Everleigh shoving her with the baton.

"What's going on?" Beacon asked, falling back.

"She's playing possum," Everleigh said.

"No I'm not," Daisy spat. "I'm *tired*."

"Are you okay?" he asked, bending to help her up. Beacon had been so worried that his dad wouldn't be able to handle the run, but he hadn't even thought about the girl. She might have been the queen, but she was as frail as some of the prisoners he'd seen back in the lab. "Here, take my arm."

But she elbowed his hand away and pushed herself up, wiping dirt indignantly from her nightgown.

Daisy settled to hobbling along beside them. It was obvious she was in pain, but she followed their grueling pace without complaint.

Soon, they'd reached the end of the tunnel. A narrow ladder on the wall fed up to a large hatch in the ceiling.

Everleigh took in a sudden sharp breath. "What was that?" she said.

"What was what?" Beacon asked.

"Shhh!" Everleigh held up a finger to her lips.

They listened. Faint footsteps could be heard in the tunnel behind them.

"They're coming," Everleigh said. "Hurry, Beaks! I'll cover you." She pointed the baton at Daisy.

Daisy sighed and crossed her arms.

Beacon climbed up the ladder and grabbed the rusted metal lever. Dirt rained down from the ceiling as he pushed up on the door. It groaned open, and cool air filtered in through the small gap. Beacon pushed the door a few inches wider and peered outside.

They were in the woods. Thick, old trees were packed so tightly together that the moonlight barely penetrated through to the forest floor.

No guards. No Sov.

"The coast is clear." Beacon shoved open the hatch all the way.

He climbed out and turned to the side, dusting off his hands.

And stared straight down the barrel of a gun.

17

Beacon stumbled back, his hands up.

"Don't shoot!" he cried.

"Beacon?" a familiar voice said.

The gun moved an inch to the side. Beacon's vision focused, and he saw a puff of white hair, a deeply lined face, and pale blue eyes—only now, they weren't glassy or unfocused. They were alert, clear, and calculating.

"Grandma?" Arthur said from behind him. He stumbled out of the hatch and stepped forward slowly, his mouth slack. Everleigh, their dad, and Daisy pushed out after him.

"Arthur!" His grandma lowered her weapon. "I had a feeling you were back when Beacon broke into the house the other night and stole your medications." She pulled Arthur into a tight hug, pressing her cheek into the top of his head. Meanwhile, Arthur just stood there, his arms flat against his sides, too stunned to react.

"You knew about that?" Beacon said.

"The whole of Driftwood Harbor knew about that. You came

in like a bull in a china shop. You would have been caught if I hadn't distracted Nurse Allen."

"That was *you* who made that noise?" Beacon said.

"Okay, *what* is going on?" Arthur said. "Grams, what are you doing here?" He took in his grandma's dark green fatigues, her shiny black boots, and the black paint smeared under her eyes. "Why do you have a gun? How come you're out of bed?"

"We have a lot to talk about," his grandma said. "But right now, we need to get out of here, if those footsteps are what I think they are." She shucked her backpack, then began digging through its contents, urgently taking out items.

Everleigh raised her baton.

"Oh, for heaven's sake, put that down before you hurt yourself," Arthur's grandma said. "And you might want to back away from that hatch if you value your eyebrows." She jumped up suddenly and shouted, "Fire in the hole!" She threw something at the hatch.

There was a mad scramble, right before an explosion sounded. The hatch ignited in a fiery ball. The noise reverberated through the woods like a thunderclap. Beacon coughed, backing away from the billowing flames.

"Everyone okay?" Arthur's grandma asked.

Beacon searched through the smoke. Arthur was still staring at his grandma like she'd sprouted a beak and feathers. Everleigh fanned smoke out of her face, and Daisy stared at the dwindling fire with her mouth twisted in a horrified expression. Meanwhile, his dad just stood there like a mindless lemming. It was hard to be relieved that he was safe when he was barely a shell of a human.

"What did you do that for?" Everleigh cried.

But the answer to that soon became clear.

The hatch was destroyed. What was once a metal door was now a pile of rubble. Victor and the guards would need to dig their way out to get to them, or else circle back through the queen's room.

"That'll hold them off for a while, but we better get out of here." Arthur's grandma hitched her backpack onto her shoulders. She stopped suddenly, spotting Daisy.

"Oh, this is Daisy," Arthur said.

"She's . . . a friend of a friend," Beacon added lamely.

But Arthur's grandma ignored them.

"I recognize that necklace," she said, stepping toward Daisy.

Daisy clasped the jewel at her throat protectively and backed up.

"What do you know about the necklace?" Everleigh asked.

"It's the source of power for all of the Sovereign, of course," Arthur's grandma said easily, as if it were obvious.

"What?!" Beacon, Everleigh, and Arthur shrieked together.

"A little louder," Daisy whispered sarcastically. "I don't think the people at the back heard you."

"What does that even mean?" Beacon said.

"Why didn't Galen tell us about this?" Everleigh said.

"Yeah, that's a pretty big thing to leave out," Arthur said.

"We can talk about everything later," Arthur's grandma said. "All that matters right now is that we get out of here before Driftwood Harbor's finest show up. Now kindly give me some space so I can hog-tie the queen."

"What?" Daisy cried.

But the old lady was fast. Before they knew it, Daisy was bound and gagged.

"Can't have you running away on us, now can we?" Arthur's grandma said with a cheery smile. "All right, let's go. Up and at 'em!"

She motioned with her hand, and the group stumbled into action.

Beacon had no idea what was going on. He half wondered if he was asleep, and this was all a fever dream.

Arthur's grandma moved silently through the forest. Barely a twig snapped as she frog-marched the queen between the trees. Meanwhile, the kids tripped and blundered through the pines.

"Where are we going?" Beacon asked. But Arthur's grandma only pressed her finger to her lips and picked up her pace. An uncomfortable feeling wormed through Beacon's body. She was Arthur's grandma. She'd saved them from Victor and the Sov guards just now. But why had she been in the woods in the first place?

Why did she have weapons and bomb supplies?

Everleigh must have been thinking the same thing, because she grabbed Beacon's arm and fell back from the group.

"I don't like this," she whispered.

"Me neither," Beacon replied.

"I say we bail," she said. "Get back to Galen."

"What about Arthur? No way he's going to leave his grandma."

Arthur loped alongside his grandma as she led the charge through the woods, nary a limp in her step. Beacon shivered. Either she'd been miraculously cured of all of her health issues overnight, or she'd been lying to everyone. Either way, he wasn't sure he could trust her.

"We can't leave Arthur," Beacon said. "And what about Daisy? Arthur's grandma's not just going to let us take the Sov queen with us. You saw how she reacted when she saw her necklace."

"There's something really weird about that thing," Everleigh said, looking ahead at Daisy tripping and stumbling through the woods. "The necklace legit *wouldn't* come off, and you saw how thin the chain was. It should have snapped easily."

"We have to find out what she knows," Beacon said. "Besides, this is Galen's friend. We can't ditch her with Arthur's grandma after everything he's done to help us. We don't know if we can trust her."

"We don't even know if we can trust *Galen* right now," Everleigh shot back. "Why didn't he tell us Daisy was the queen? Or that she had some freak necklace that powers his whole species?"

"Would *you* advertise that?" Beacon said. "I mean, come on. It's like painting a target on their back. If what Arthur's grandma said is true and it's the source of all their power, it would be the easy way to wipe them all out. Just destroy the necklace and BAM."

Beacon mimed an explosion with his hands.

Everleigh's eyes widened. "Actually, that's a really great idea . . ."

"No, it's not," Beacon said. "Remember what happened when you tried to take it off her? She said it's a *part* of her. You'd have to kill her."

Everleigh shrugged.

"You don't mean that," Beacon said. "We're not like them. We don't just go around killing innocent people."

"Who said she's innocent?" Everleigh countered.

"She's Galen's friend," Beacon reminded her.

Arthur's grandma turned around then, squinting at them in the dark. Everleigh huffed and trudged forward.

They walked in silence. After a while, Beacon realized it had started to snow. It began with a few wet snowflakes gently dancing in the breeze, melting as soon as they touched Beacon's skin. Then the air turned crisper, the wind picked up, and snow blew in icy gusts, coating everything in white. Beacon's body locked up tight, making his skin shrivel under his jacket. He'd never felt so helpless. He was freezing and he was wearing a jacket. He couldn't imagine how cold his dad must be in his tattered clothes and bare feet.

"Are we almost there?" Beacon asked Arthur's grandma. "He can't go much farther like this."

"We're close," she said.

Beacon didn't see an end in sight.

Just when he thought the weather couldn't get worse, a gust of cold air swept through the forest. In moments, a gale-force wind roared through the trees. Beacon ducked, right before a branch flew through the place his head had just been.

"Get low!" Arthur's grandma called.

They crouched down on the snow-coated forest floor. Beacon gulped for air, but the wind blew into his face so viciously, it knocked his breath out of rhythm, like when you put your head outside the window of a fast-moving car. What was going on?

Through a gap in the trees, Beacon saw the glint of metal against the charcoal sky above a large clearing up ahead. At first, he thought he was seeing things. Or maybe that the wind had picked something up. Then more and more metal came into view, and a ship materialized. Not just one ship, he realized. A whole fleet. They hovered in the air over the clearing, blotting out the light of the moon.

"Is it the military?" Beacon asked, even though he didn't think that was quite right. The ships were a little too angular, a little too sleek, like what a fighter jet might look like a hundred years from now.

Arthur's grandma shook her head, erasing any doubts about what these were. Alien ships.

That's what had been causing the wind.

Beacon felt the blood drain from his head. Hundreds of UFOs. This was worse than he'd imagined. Way worse.

One by one, the ships began lowering to the ground in the clearing.

Arthur's grandma pressed a finger to her lips, then motioned with her head to keep moving. She hoisted Daisy to her feet with shocking agility and pushed through the forest.

The group forged ahead through the raging wind. Beacon could hardly see, let alone see where they were going. Before he knew it, a barn took shape. Beacon almost let out a cry of relief.

"Help me with this," Arthur's grandma said, slinging her gun across her back. Arthur ran up to help his grandma slide back the giant iron bolt on the barn doors, then they all filed inside. The wind stopped abruptly as the doors were pulled closed behind them. The barn was dark, save for the pale moonlight that struggled through the cracks in the wood. Beacon could just make out a ladder rising to a loft filled with hay. The smell of musty fur and animal droppings clung in the air.

Someone turned on a light, and Beacon shielded his eyes from the sudden brightness. He turned around to check out the place and yelped when he was met with a pair of huge black eyes. A giant gelding hung its head over the side of a wooden pen. It pawed the door impatiently, then whinnied, ears pricked and tail swishing. Beacon backed away from the pen, bumping into his dad, who just stood there, shivering, not even bothering to rub warmth into his arms. Whatever they'd done to the prisoners went deeper this time. It was as if they'd been sapped of life. Beacon fought down the dread that rose in his body.

"What was *that*?" Everleigh said.

"Did you see all those ships?" Arthur said.

"Of course I did—I've got eyes," Everleigh shot back. "Daisy, what are all those ships doing here?"

"I thought the underwater UFO was the only ship in town and your people had no way back," Arthur said.

"And what about the necklace?" Everleigh said. "Is it really true it powers all of the Sov?"

"Quiet down, everybody!" Arthur's grandma's voice was low, but it cut through the din like a knife through warmed butter.

She stepped toward Daisy. Daisy raised her chin defiantly, and Arthur's grandma's lips turned up a bit at the corners, as if she liked the spunk she saw inside the young queen.

"Please, tell me," Arthur's grandma said, pacing in front of the queen, "how it can be possible that I've been working behind the scenes for years, carefully planning my next move, and you three almost ruined everything in a single night?"

She turned abruptly, facing Beacon, Arthur, and Everleigh. Beacon stood up straight. The way she looked at him, it was hard to believe she was the same lady who'd croakily offered to make Arthur and him sandwiches when he'd come over to visit.

"I don't get it," Arthur said. "What's all this about?" He gestured at his grandma's clothes and gun. "Are you, like, some type of rebel operation?"

"Something like that," she replied. "I've been watching the changes happening in our town for over sixty years. I wanted to do something, but anyone who spoke up ended up disappearing or becoming one of their robots. I quickly learned that I would need to take another approach if I was going to reclaim Driftwood Harbor. I've been working undercover since then, slowly finding out more, doing what I can to fight back. You'd be surprised how loose-lipped people can be around an infirm old lady." She winked. "Nurse Allen was a thorn in my side when the Sov first sent her to spy on me, but I've learned a lot from just listening in on her phone calls when she thinks I'm asleep. Easiest spying I've ever done."

Arthur gaped at his grandma, but Everleigh refused to back down.

"Look, I'm sorry we ruined your plans," she said, "but I'm not sorry we freed our dad. He would have been killed."

"What about the rest of the prisoners in the base?" Arthur's grandma asked. "They'll be under tighter lock and key than ever before."

"We tried to get them out, but Victor refused," Everleigh said. "He's the leader of the Sov, and he's really scary."

"You think I've lived in Driftwood Harbor for over sixty years and I don't know who Victor is?" Arthur's grandma cocked an eyebrow.

"Then you know how scary he is," Everleigh said. "We had to leave the other prisoners behind, or we wouldn't have been able to get our dad out, either."

"And we couldn't let them kill our dad," Beacon added.

"Every one of those people is important to someone else," Arthur's grandma said. "Those other prisoners are someone's brother, sister, mother, father, husband, wife. And now they don't have a hope of escape. I'd been planning a rescue operation for a year, but they'd see me coming from a mile away now. There's no way I'd get close to them."

Beacon's chest filled with something so big, there was no room for his lungs to expand. Victor was obviously wrong about him. He wasn't destined to save the planet. He wasn't destined to save *anyone*. Even his dad hadn't been rescued, not really. He was still a robot.

"We're sorry," Everleigh said. "But I'm not sure what you think we should have done. Ask around if anyone had already started a secret rebel organization before we stepped on any toes?"

Arthur's grandma frowned, but didn't argue.

"Besides, our mission wasn't a total failure," Beacon said. "We wouldn't have found out about the Rainmaker if it wasn't for breaking in."

"The what?" Arthur's grandma said.

A small bit of pride trickled in from knowing something she didn't. Beacon filled her in on the Rainmaker. As he spoke, a worried crease grew between her eyebrows.

"We wanted to destroy it," Beacon finished, "but we couldn't find anything like that on the base, and then we ran out of time."

"The Sov's army," Arthur's grandma murmured. "Of course."

"What do you mean?" Beacon asked.

She blew out a frustrated breath.

"You didn't find that Rainmaker on the base because it isn't *on* the base," she said.

Beacon almost nodded in understanding, just because he felt stupid admitting he still didn't get it. She must have noticed, because she clarified.

"Their ships have been coming and going for the last few weeks. I knew they were planning something big. Now I know it's *the ships*."

"The Rainmaker," Arthur said. "It isn't a single large machine, like we thought. It's hundreds of smaller ones."

"You mean those UFOs?" Everleigh said, catching on. "That

makes sense. They're going to douse the cities all at once, so no one has a chance to escape or fight back. That's the blitzkrieg Nixon was talking about."

"That explains why they're using human prisoners, too," Beacon said. At Arthur's grandma's confused expression, he added, "The Sov can see the future, right? Not every little thing, but certain calamitous events. If the Sov kill all the humans, other aliens in the galaxy would be angry. They must be planning on using humans to man their ships so no one else can accuse them of committing genocide. That way they can wipe us out and avoid taking the blame."

"But wouldn't the other aliens realize they're using Sov UFOs?" Arthur asked.

"Haven't you noticed these ships look different from the underwater one? They look like military fighter jets. That *can't* be a coincidence. They probably built these ships to mimic ours so it would all check out if the other aliens found out what happened here."

A heavy silence fell over the barn, the only sound that of the horse stamping in the cold.

"What are we going to do?" Everleigh finally said.

"We have to find out when they're going to strike," Arthur's grandma said. She spun on the queen once again. "Tell us what you know."

Daisy moaned into the gag. Arthur's grandma pulled out the handkerchief. Daisy spat and huffed indignantly.

"I told you, I don't know anything," she said.

"We can *help* you remember," Everleigh threatened.

"Everleigh!" Beacon said. "She doesn't mean that," he added to Daisy.

"I'm not lying!" Daisy cried. "I don't know what my people have planned. I'm just a figurehead for them. I don't have any actual real decision-making power. If Victor could remove my necklace and wear it himself, trust me, I would have been dead a long time ago."

Despite her ferocious tone, there was an air of sadness in her voice that cut straight through Beacon. It must have cut through Everleigh, too, because her shoulders relaxed.

"You really can't take it off?" Arthur asked.

Daisy shot Everleigh a dark look. "No. I really can't."

"So what happens if you die?" Everleigh asked. "What? I'm just asking the obvious question," she added in reply to their horrified expressions.

"If I die, then my people are in a load of trouble," Daisy answered darkly. "This jewel is the linchpin for our kind. Everything we do is powered by it—our ability to transform, to see into the future, even our ability to breathe," she said, clutching the jewel tightly.

"So the Sov—you're like regular humans without that jewel?" Arthur asked.

Daisy shook her head. "Our kind has always had access to our abilities, but everything changed when our ancestors found these jewels beneath the earth on our home planet. They quickly learned that wearing one of these greatly enhanced our powers. It didn't take long before everyone had a jewel of their own. We began to rely too heavily on them, and soon the jewel stores had been depleted. But due to our quick evolution abilities, we had evolved to become entirely dependent on the jewels. That's how the queen came to be. Our ancestors discovered that by connecting the power of all the jewels to one person, we could get away with using just one to enhance the abilities of the entire population. Using this method, we were able to preserve the dwindling supply for many more years, but . . . now this is the only one left." She let the emerald go. It thumped heavily against her chest. "I think Victor hoped we might find more here, but . . ." She shook her head.

Beacon frowned. He couldn't imagine having that much power and responsibility *literally* resting on your shoulders.

"Why you?" Arthur asked after a moment. "No offense," he added quickly. "I'm just wondering why you're the queen."

"I don't know," Daisy said, shrugging a shoulder. "All I know is that the previous queen's jewel began losing its power, as they all do eventually. A queen's life fades away as the jewel loses its power, and even a new jewel can't revive her. So the elders proclaimed that they needed to raise up a successor. The moment I was born, they slapped this thing on me. It isn't like I wanted to be trapped in a jail my whole life."

"Jail?" Everleigh said. "Your room looked pretty cozy if you ask me."

"Oh sure, I've always had chandeliers and fancy clothes and all the food I could ever want, but if I tried to leave?" Daisy raised an eyebrow. "See how fast they'd chain me up. This is the longest I've been away from my guards in years."

If someone had told Beacon he'd feel sorry for the Sov queen, he would have told them to stop sniffing glue. But he really did feel for Daisy. What she described wasn't a life. It was a gilded cage.

"We're not going to hurt you," Beacon said.

"Oh yeah? That why you hog-tied me?" Daisy shot back, but there wasn't any heat in her words.

"Grams?" Arthur said.

Arthur's grandma pulled a multi-tool out of her pocket and whipped open a knife.

But before she could cut Daisy free, something thumped on the roof.

18

The barn went deadly quiet, save for the sound of the gun being cocked. Beacon squinted into the rafters, his heart racing.

A shadow passed over a hole in the roof. There and gone so quickly, he thought he might have imagined it.

"What was that?" Arthur said. His grandma shushed him.

So Beacon hadn't imagined it.

The Sov were here.

Arthur's grandma trained her gun at the ceiling. Everleigh powered up her baton and walked in a circle around them as she leveled the wand at the rafters.

Their ragged breathing filled the barn as they listened for any sign of where the attack would come from. But there was nothing but the sound of the wind howling through the trees.

Thump, thump, thump.

A gunshot split the air, and a jumble of screams and yelps filled the barn. Smoke poured out of the barrel of Arthur's grandma's gun.

"Did you get it?" Arthur whispered.

"I don't know," she replied.

A moment later they got their answer.

A rafter was punched out of the ceiling. The loose board tumbled end over end into the barn. A tentacle whipped inside. Before Beacon knew what had happened, the lightbulb shattered, and they were plunged into darkness. Moonlight slanted in where the board had been, and when Beacon's eyes adjusted to the dark, he saw a Sov clinging wetly to the inside wall of the barn.

"Shoot!" Everleigh yelled.

The squid retreated. Gunshots fired, and Beacon shielded his face as the booming sounds went on and on. Finally, the gunshots stopped. He opened his eyes. For a moment, he thought they'd gotten it. Then a tentacle slithered over the gap in the roof. The squid moved down the wall so quickly that Arthur screamed and leaped out of its way as more gunshots followed its path. The creature vaulted around the room so fast, they could hardly track its movements. It leaped from rafter to rafter, dripping slime over everyone. A tentacle reached out, trying to capture the queen. Everleigh grabbed on to Daisy and pointed her baton at the squid.

Beacon looked up at the roof. Any moment now, the rest of the squids were going to show up, and then they were totally *screwed*.

But as the chaos continued inside the barn and backup never arrived, a slow realization came over him. Backup wasn't coming. Which didn't make sense. Why would a Sov be acting alone to save the queen?

Then it hit him.

This wasn't just any Sov trying to save Daisy.

"Galen," he whispered, before he shouted, "Hold your fire!"

Beacon tried to leap in front of the squid, but Everleigh yanked him back by the hood of his jacket.

"Are you nuts?" Everleigh screamed at him.

Taking advantage of Everleigh's distraction, the Sov whipped out a tentacle. Its slimy appendage coiled around the queen's waist and pulled her to its body like they were doing some kind of freak salsa dance.

And then the creature was gone, disappearing back through the gap in the roof.

Beacon ran to the door.

"Beacon, come back!" Everleigh shouted. But he didn't stop.

The forest was covered in a blanket of white. It was easy to see which direction Galen had gone. There was a long, thick squid-print in the fresh snow, leading into the woods.

Beacon put his head down and ran. Snow filled his shoes, but he didn't care, couldn't care until he caught up to his friend. Until he explained.

Trees flashed past in a blur of white and brown.

"Galen, come back!" he shouted.

He banked left, running hard. He jumped over fallen branches, slid over patches of fresh ice. He thought he'd slipped again when he felt his feet go out from under him. But then a tentacle wrapped around his chest, and he was pinned against the rough bark of a tree, dangling several feet in the air.

The squid—Galen—drew up on its hind tentacles, towering over him. Its mouth opened, and Beacon saw the row of grotesque yellow fangs dripping with slime. He had no trouble imagining what they would feel like slicing through his skin.

"It isn't what it looks like," Beacon said. "We weren't going to hurt her! Arthur's grandma is on our side!"

He was just about to say, "She didn't know you were with us," when another tentacle wrapped around his neck, cutting his words short. It squeezed, and Beacon coughed, then . . . nothing. He couldn't make sounds come out, couldn't breathe, couldn't get air.

A beady black eye stared unblinkingly into Beacon's. Beacon clawed desperately at the tentacle, but it was no use. Black spots danced in his eyes, his vision going blurry at the edges.

The mouth opened wider, and the squid let out a powerful roar that blew the hair back from Beacon's face. He closed his eyes against the force, waiting for those razor teeth to pierce him.

"Beacon, where are you?" Everleigh shouted nearby. The squid startled.

Just as quickly as it had grabbed him, the tentacle let go. Beacon thumped to the ground with a bone-jarring thud. He felt along his neck, his throat raw and burning. Galen was gone.

"Beacon! Are you okay?" Everleigh ran up, sliding to her knees in the snow in front of him. Arthur and his grandma were there suddenly, shouting questions, while his dad walked calmly behind them.

"Oh my God, what happened?" Everleigh said.

"Why did you go after it?" Arthur said.

"It was . . . ," Beacon started, then erupted into a coughing fit. He swallowed past the burning in his throat and tried again. "It was Galen."

"What?" Everleigh said.

"It can't have been him," Arthur said. "He's sleeping."

"Well, he woke up," Beacon said grimly.

"Who's Galen?" Arthur's grandma said. "Will someone please tell me what's going on?"

"That squid that kidnapped the queen?" Beacon said. "That was our friend."

"Your friend?" she said, eyebrows lost in her hairline.

"I know it seems hard to believe," Beacon said, "but he rescued us from more than one Sov attack, and he helped us find our dad. Except now he thinks we betrayed him."

"Oh God." Everleigh shoved her hands into her hair. "Daisy was tied up! We shot at him!"

"But we weren't going to hurt Daisy," Arthur said anxiously. "He must know that."

"He definitely doesn't know that," Beacon said. "He made that clear when he almost strangled me. And now we have a *big* problem."

"Our most powerful ally hates us now?" Everleigh said. "Yeah, we got that."

"Worse," Beacon said. "I think Galen might switch back to the Sov's side now."

"What?" Arthur and Everleigh shrieked together.

"Think about it," Beacon continued. "The only humans he's probably *ever* connected with kidnapped his best friend, hog-tied her, and threatened to kill her. He's probably out for revenge now. I wouldn't be surprised if he helped the Sov attack us."

"He wouldn't do that," Arthur said. "Would he?" He looked uncertainly at Beacon's throat, still purple with ligature marks.

"I didn't think so before, but after he almost killed me just now? Yeah. Definitely possible," Beacon said.

Everleigh stood up. "We have to find him. Once we explain everything, he'll understand."

"I don't know how we're going to do that now," Beacon said. "He can change into any form he wants to evade us. We're like sitting ducks."

"But he transformed," Everleigh said. "He has to sleep now. That gives us time."

"Unless he uses his EpiPen," Beacon said, recalling what Galen had said about the shot giving him extra time before he passed out. "Each shot gives him almost half an hour, and I know he brought a load with him from New York for just in case."

Everleigh muttered under her breath and paced in the snow. "Okay, we just need to think like Galen would. He wants to attack us, but he left the barn. Why leave?"

"Well, it was one of him against a whole bunch of us," Arthur said. "And we had weapons. Maybe he went for backup?"

"He doesn't need backup. He's a squid!" Everleigh said.

"My grandma got a few good shots off at him. She could have easily taken him down," Arthur said.

Arthur and Everleigh argued with each other, but their words faded away as Beacon thought. The answer came to him suddenly.

"The ships," he muttered. "There's a whole fleet of them just sitting right there for the taking." Beacon pushed himself up. "We need to get to that clearing."

"If Galen is awake, then that means the rest of the Sov are probably awake, too," Everleigh said. "It's too dangerous."

"It's a risk we have to take," Beacon said.

"But what about Dad?" Everleigh said.

"Grams can watch him," Arthur offered.

"Oh, you don't think you're going anywhere without me, do you?" Arthur's grandma said. "You kids would be Sov soup if it wasn't for me."

"Then who's going to look after him?" Everleigh asked.

They all looked at the twins' dad then. He stared blankly ahead, as if he were a robot waiting for his next command. Which was kind of exactly what he was at the moment, Beacon realized darkly.

"He'll come with us," Beacon said. "After everything we went through to save him, we shouldn't be splitting up, anyway. We stick together from here on out."

Everleigh couldn't argue with that, so she just sighed.

And that's how, ten minutes later, they found themselves hunkered down at the edge of the forest, looking out into the clearing filled with a whole fleet of alien UFOs.

"Traditionally I think you're supposed to run *away* from the people trying to kill you," Everleigh said. "But I could be wrong."

"Shhh!" Beacon hissed.

"Any sign of them?" Arthur whispered.

Beacon scanned the fleet. He would have thought the place would be packed with the Sov and their guards, but there wasn't anyone in sight. The ships hovered over the frosty grass. The clearing hummed with electric energy, like the calm before a storm.

That's when he saw it: a ship at the back of the clearing. While all of the other ships' windows were dark, there was one with pale orange light glowing from inside the cabin's windows. The neon lights of a control panel flickered on, illuminating the lion's mane of hair bent over it.

"Over there!" Beacon whispered. "Galen's in that one."

He started to get up, but Everleigh grabbed his arm.

"Look." She nodded toward the far right edge of the forest. He didn't see it at first. Then there was movement in the trees. Beacon ducked, watching as people emerged from the forest's edge.

Two, four—dozens, no, hundreds of people, and they were all walking toward the ships.

"What in tarnation . . . ," Arthur's grandma muttered under her breath, squinting into the dark.

"Are those Sov guards?" Arthur whispered.

But that didn't seem right. There was something off about the way they were walking, too upright, too stiff, too . . . controlled. Beacon's chest tightened. He knew that walk, those mannerisms.

Just then, the moonlight in the clearing shifted, and he got a better view of the person closest to him. It took Beacon a moment to recognize him without a cigarette dangling from his lips, but he remembered those ruddy, wrinkled cheeks inside a tow truck the day their car had broken down on their way into Driftwood Harbor.

Mr. Murray.

"It isn't guards," Beacon whispered. "It's the prisoners. The townspeople. Everyone who's had the shot."

As he watched, Mr. Murray tripped over a tree root and fell to the ground. It had to have hurt, but he popped back up as if propelled by some otherworldly force. Blood seeped down his chin, but he didn't even try to wipe it away.

Beacon looked over at his dad, lying down in the snow because he'd been told to do it. He hadn't sat up to peer over the snowdrifts like the others had when the townspeople arrived. It was as if he were incapable of making decisions now unless someone told him exactly what to do.

"Look, there's Mrs. Miller!" Everleigh whispered, pointing at a dark-haired woman with a hooked nose and a black skirt suit.

"And there's Sheriff Nugent," Arthur said.

"What are those ones doing?" Arthur's grandma said, pointing. "Looks like they're carrying something."

Beacon squinted at two townspeople carrying either end of a long, clear tube. When they got closer, Beacon saw bright blue liquid sloshing around inside the tube.

"It's the acid rain," Beacon said.

"But they were still testing it!" Everleigh said.

"Initiate the sequence," Arthur muttered, repeating Victor's words. "Victor must have accelerated the plans because of our attack."

The twins and Arthur exchanged a sober look.

"I just don't get it," Arthur's grandma said. "Why would the townspeople be doing this? Don't they realize what's happening?"

"They don't," Beacon said. "The Sov did something to them. Something worse than before. It's like they're drones now—they just do what they've been told. And I think they've been told to kill everyone."

"It's starting," Arthur whispered.

Beacon gulped hard, pushing down the panic.

"We need to get to Galen," Beacon said. "We don't have a hope against the Sov without him and Daisy."

He stood up.

"What are you doing?" Everleigh tried to grab her brother.

Beacon shook her off and stepped forward, his shoulders pushed back, his pace slow and robotic.

"Are you crazy?" Arthur hissed. "Get down!"

"Young man, get back here this instant!" Arthur's grandma whisper-shouted.

Beacon ignored them all and walked.

There was a scuffle behind him, and a moment later, Everleigh, Arthur, Arthur's grandma, and his dad were all walking next to him, copying his mechanical body movements. Arthur's grandma had ditched her gun, and Beacon couldn't see Everleigh's baton anywhere. He *really* hoped that his plan hadn't gotten them all in a whole lot more trouble.

"Stop looking around," Beacon warned Arthur out of the side of his mouth. "Just stare ahead."

"I'm sorry, but it's hard not to look," Arthur whispered back. "My alien subreddit would *lose their minds* at all this. I mean, look at those *ships*!"

"Please stop looking at those ships," Beacon said. "You don't see anyone else gawking at them, do you?"

At least his dad didn't need lessons on how to walk like a robot.

Soon, they were surrounded by townspeople. Beacon felt as if the walls were closing in, even though he was in a big, open clearing. There were so many townspeople, and so few of them. If the townspeople were ordered to attack . . .

He pushed the thoughts out of his head and forced himself to walk the same speed as everyone else, even though all he wanted to do was run.

They were almost to Galen's ship.

"Hey, you!" a voice said.

Beacon's heart skipped. From the commanding tone in the man's voice, he knew there were now guards scattered among the townspeople. He didn't dare risk a glance at the others for fear it would tip off the guards that they weren't under their control. He kept walking, hoping that the guard was speaking to someone else, or at the very least, that he would lose interest in them. But the guard stomped over, his boots crunching in the snow.

"Stop right there!"

19

Beacon glanced around the clearing. They would have to run. But where? The place was swarming with Sov and townspeople under their control. They'd never get away.

"We are in deep trouble," Arthur whispered. He was trying not to move his lips as he talked, like a bad ventriloquist.

"I knew I shouldn't have left the gun behind," Arthur's grandma muttered under her breath.

The guard stomped up Everleigh eyed the baton at his waist, her fingers twitching—

"I need you lot in the G75 Halo," the guard said.

It took Beacon a minute to register what the guard was saying. He hadn't discovered their ruse. Every part of him tingled with relief.

"Are you stupid or what?" the guard said. "The G75 Halo. NOW!"

Beacon slipped his eyes to the left. Everleigh and Arthur were frozen next to him, apparently as unsure of what to do as he was. Arthur's grandma's eyes darted around the clearing, trying to spot the G75 Halo. Even the twins' dad didn't move. He apparently hadn't gotten the memo on ship subtypes, either, having been a lab rat—the Sov probably didn't plan for him to survive the experiments they performed on him.

"Oh my God—the G75!" The guard spun Beacon around and shoved him toward a ship. "Go, all of you."

The others stumbled along next to him while the guard muttered under his breath about how he'd told everyone humans were too stupid for this, but no one ever listened to him.

"I knew we shouldn't have rushed into this," Arthur's grandma said. "Slow and steady wins the race."

"Slow and steady gets doused with acid rain," Everleigh said.

"Just keep walking," Beacon said.

They reached the ship—presumably the G75 Halo, since the guard wasn't racing over to ask what was wrong with them. Beacon eyed the ship. From the edge of the forest, they'd looked tiny. But standing right in front of one, the gleaming silver body stretched high over his head, the size of a poor man's yacht.

"What now?" Arthur said.

"Is G.I. Joe still watching us?" Everleigh asked.

Arthur's grandma glanced over and quickly snapped her attention back to the ship. "Very much so."

"He's not going to leave until we get inside," Everleigh said.

"How? I can't find the door," Beacon said.

He inspected the body for a handle, but he couldn't see one anywhere.

"Is there a button somewhere?" Arthur's grandma felt along the body of the ship.

Beacon sneaked a glance over his shoulder. The guard was stalking toward them.

"He's coming!" Beacon said.

All around them, townspeople were boarding their ships without incident. How were they getting on?

"Open up!" He kicked the side of the ship.

There was a slick beep noise, just before the body of the ship cracked open. A set of stairs glided down, green light glowing on the snow.

Voice command! Why hadn't he thought of that?

"Go, go, go!" Beacon whispered under his breath. Everleigh jumped up the steps, followed by Arthur and his grandma.

"Get in, Dad," Everleigh ordered. The twins' dad climbed up, too. Beacon forced himself to walk on slowly after them, even though all he wanted to do was run.

"Close the doors," Beacon said when he was halfway up the steps. The stairs began moving up. He jumped into the cabin and had just enough time to see the guard's suspicious gaze before the door closed.

The interior of the ship was small and dark. A leather bench seat curved around a complicated-looking panel of dials and switches that glowed with neon lights. Through the foggy front windshield, he could see the other ships powering up.

Now that they'd found temporary protection, they had a bigger problem to face.

How were they going to get to Galen with that guard outside?

Arthur peered out a small porthole in the ship with his hands cupped around his face. "His ship is taking off!"

Beacon shouldered him out of the way and looked outside. Sure enough, Galen's ship had risen into the sky. It hovered above the tree line before shooting out of sight. Everything in him deflated. After all they had done, it was going to end like this. Trapped in a ship they couldn't fly, completely helpless while their planet was attacked.

"This isn't over," Everleigh said.

Beacon spun around. Everleigh sat on the leather bench seat, buckling a five-point harness around her shoulders.

"What on earth do you all think you're doing?" Arthur's grandma said.

The harsh tone of her voice would have had Beacon flying out of the seat, but Everleigh was practically Olympic caliber at flouting authority, and she just carried on.

"You can't be serious," Beacon said. "This is a little more complex than a pod, Ev."

"And more dangerous, too," Arthur added. "If you screw up,

we're crashing. Like, an airplane crash. You've heard about those, right?"

"Then you better buckle up," Everleigh said. "Power up computers."

Nothing happened.

"Power up the engine," she tried again. A hum went through the cabin as the computers booted up instantly and the screen flared to life. A cluster of little green dots appeared on the otherwise black monitor, with one outlier set apart from the rest.

"These are the ships," Beacon said. "That's got to be Galen, there!" He pointed at the sole green dot moving away from them.

"This is a very bad idea," Arthur's grandma said. "Young lady, I suggest you stop what you're doing and—"

"Take off!" Everleigh said.

The ship rose seamlessly into the air. Arthur's grandma let out a yelp. Beacon's stomach dropped as the trees beneath them grew steadily smaller. It wasn't anything like riding in an airplane. The engine didn't rumble, and there was no turbulence. The ship just . . . sat in the sky. Somehow, that was more disconcerting than if they had been rocking all over the place. He kept having to check out the window to make sure they really were still in the air and the engine hadn't given out.

He just hoped this ship was as easy to navigate as it seemed. Or else they were in big trouble.

"Put us back on the ground this instant, young lady," Arthur's grandma shouted.

"Sorry, I only take orders from my dad. Dad, do you have a problem with me hijacking this ship?" Everleigh asked, turning to him.

The twins' dad stared straight ahead.

"He doesn't have a problem with it." Everleigh swung back to Arthur's grandma and gave her a faux-innocent smile.

"Sit down and put on a harness," Beacon ordered his dad as he and Arthur fell onto the bench seat and buckled their own harnesses. Arthur's grandma grumbled and sat down, too.

Around them, more and more ships were taking to the sky. Soon, it would be impossible to tell which one was Galen's among all the others.

"Follow that ship!" Everleigh pointed at the outlier ship.

The ship didn't move.

"It can't see what you're pointing at," Arthur said. "Go . . . northeast!" he commanded. The ship didn't budge.

"You're not inspiring a lot of confidence in your abilities," Arthur's grandma said.

"There must be a way to do this manually," Everleigh said, considering the control panel.

She pressed a button.

Beacon expected the windshield wipers to come on, or music to blare, like what had happened the day Everleigh decided to try to drive the pod. But as far as Beacon could tell, the button was useless.

"Huh, weird. Nothing happened," Everleigh said.

"That we *know of*!" Arthur said. "That could be the button to release the toxic rain!"

That didn't deter Everleigh from pressing more buttons. Now the wipers *did* turn on. The bench seat slid forward, and hot air blasted out of overhead vents.

"Oh, for heaven's sake!" Arthur's grandma said.

Finally, the ship shot ahead so fast, they slammed back against their seats.

"Sweet!" Everleigh said. "Turbo-boosters."

"Galen's this dot here." Arthur pointed at the screen. "Hurry, he's getting away!"

"Ten-four," Everleigh said.

This time, Beacon was ready when the vessel shot across the sky. It didn't take long for them to leave the clearing behind. They sailed over a sea of pines, and soon, they were gaining on the ship. Galen must have realized it, too, because his ship darted forward suddenly.

"Where did he go?" Beacon squinted through the dash.

"He's over there," Arthur said, pointing. "By those mountains!"

"I don't see anything," Arthur's grandma said. "One moment." She pulled a pair of glasses out of her pocket and slid them on her nose. "Where?"

"So you really wear glasses?" Arthur said. "That wasn't an act?"

"Don't be silly, why would that have been an act?" she said. "Where's his ship?"

Arthur shook his head exasperatedly and pointed again. Beacon leaned in close. He could have used a pair of those glasses himself. Galen's ship was barely a speck in the sky. He never would have seen it if they hadn't had the radar.

"On it," Everleigh said.

Their ship rocketed forward. They glided over snowy orchards and wheat fields, highways and rivers, closing the distance between them so fast, it was as if they were inside a video game.

"This is actually kind of fun," Arthur's grandma admitted.

"See?" Everleigh said. "You just need to trust me." She smiled smugly and leaned back in her seat.

Just then, Galen's ship spun impressively toward the ground, then shot between two mountain peaks.

"What the heck!" Everleigh sat up straight again.

"Well, what are you waiting for?" Arthur's grandma said. "Go after him."

"A minute ago, you didn't want me flying this thing, and now you want me to go *through there?*" Everleigh said.

"Can you do it?" Arthur asked hopefully.

Everleigh looked at the spindly gap between the mountains, then shook her head.

"It's too narrow. I wouldn't trust myself in there."

Beacon slammed his palms on the dash.

He'd gotten away.

Everleigh cruised up and over the mountains. "It's okay," she said unconvincingly. "We'll just fly over him. He's got to come out the other side sometime, right?"

She was about to punch a button on the dash when Arthur's grandma said, "Now wait just a minute." She leaned forward and pointed at a ship on the radar, growing closer by the second. "We might not have lost Galen after all."

Beacon whipped around and looked through a rear window. A ship was cutting a path straight toward them.

"How could Galen be behind us?" Everleigh said. "Did he loop around or something?"

"Why would he come back after he was trying to get away?" Arthur said.

The ship grew closer and closer. Beacon squinted at the other ship's windshield. At first, he thought he was seeing things again. That his paranoia had gotten the better of him. He squeezed his eyes shut for a second, but when he opened them, Victor was still there, dark hair slicked back from his face and eyes locked on their ship with a steely determination.

"That's not Galen," Beacon said. "It's Victor."

Panels at the center of the propellers on either side of Victor's ship grinded and rotated open, and two long silver barrels pushed out from inside. Beacon realized that they were missiles, just as the twin rockets shot toward them.

"Everleigh, watch out!" Beacon screamed. Everleigh took one glance out the window before she sent the ship into a dive.

The ship plummeted toward the earth. Instinctively, Beacon shot out a hand across his dad's chest, like *he* was the parent. He was going to need a lot of therapy when this was over.

The harness dug sharply into Beacon's chest. He was starting to wonder if a seat belt had ever burst open from pressure, when Everleigh finally leveled the ship out.

"What the heck was that?" Arthur shouted between gulps of air.

His grandma was frantically rooting around for her glasses, which had fallen off in the drop.

"It's Victor," Beacon said, swallowing the bile in his throat.

"What is he doing?" Arthur said.

"Trying to kill us is my best guess," Everleigh said.

Just then, another missile came rocketing toward them. Everleigh tried to twist the ship out of the way, but not in time. The rocket struck them in the tail. The ship jolted hard before listing violently to the left.

"Well, he's succeeding," Beacon said. He clung to his armrest as another rocket blazed past them, narrowly missing.

"We must have that button, too," Arthur's grandma said. "Hit 'em, E!"

"Hold on," Everleigh said, pressing a few buttons. She grinned, the moment before two rockets blasted out of their own ship. Victor hadn't been expecting it. He barely had time to slide out of the way as the missiles soared past his craft.

"Yes!" Arthur cheered.

"Now we're back in business!" Arthur's grandma pumped her fists in the air.

But it was too late.

Their ship jolted. Beacon slammed forward so hard, he felt his brain slide around in his head. The vessel spun like an amusement park ride. Cloud, tree, sky, mountain—images blurred past so fast, Beacon couldn't make sense of what was happening.

"Do something!" Beacon screamed.

"I'm trying!" Everleigh shouted back.

The ship righted, but it rocked from side to side, and they bumped up and down so hard that Beacon's teeth chattered. Smoke poured out of the engines. The snow-dusted ground veered up at them.

"Hang on tight!" Everleigh said. "We're going down!"

Beacon dug his fingers into the armrests and hooked his feet around the bench seat legs, as if that would somehow help him.

The ship skidded against the frosty grass once, before they were airborne again. Then it crashed for real. Beacon felt the impact all the way through his body. Ice shards and dirt sprayed up all around them, pieces of the ship flying off. And then everything stopped.

Coppery blood pooled in his mouth. Lights flashed, and he was sure that alarms were going off, too, though he couldn't hear them over the ringing in his ears.

Everleigh appeared in front of him. Her lips were moving for a good minute before her voice pierced the fog.

"Are you okay?" she shouted.

Beacon took in a cramped breath, then nodded. "Dad . . ."

He groaned and peered over at the bench seat next to him, but his dad wasn't there. Beacon searched the ship and saw him waiting mutely by the door.

"He's fine," Everleigh said. "I already looked him over. Come on, get up." She unclipped his belt as Arthur released the buckle on his own harness next to him, shouting for his grandma.

"I'm fine, quit your hollering," his grandma said, fumbling with her harness. "You don't get to be my age by being fragile."

"Okay, so, that could have been worse," Everleigh said. "No one's too badly hurt, right?"

"I wouldn't speak too soon." Arthur pointed into the sky.

Victor's ship was coming right for them.

20

There was no time to run. No time to leap out of the way. No time to do anything but watch in horror as Victor's ship sliced through the air, its missiles pointed right at them.

Beacon was waiting for his imminent death, when he saw a flash of movement to his left. A moment later, something whizzed just over the top of their ship, inches from their front windshield. Silver glinted all around them. Another ship.

"What the . . . who's that?" Arthur said.

Victor's ship flew in angry zigzags, trying to take aim at them. But wherever he went, the newcomer did, too, blocking him. Even from a distance, when the ship zagged just enough to the side, Beacon could see the angry red splotches spreading up Victor's neck, and cold fear bloomed in his belly. He'd once had a teacher get rashes like that when she was angry, and it was always a bad sign. Whoever was flying that ship obviously didn't know who they were messing with.

Beacon tried to get a look at the new ship's driver, but he could only see the back of the ship.

"Why doesn't Victor just end this and shoot them!" Everleigh said.

"Maybe he doesn't want to damage another ship?" Arthur said.

"I can't see why he would care about a single ship when he's got hundreds of them," Arthur's grandma said.

The new ship turned then, and Beacon saw the mop of blond hair and freckles occupying the driver's seat. Galen.

He'd come back to save them.

"Victor *can't* shoot," Beacon said. "The queen's on that ship."

This was the third time Galen had saved his life. If they somehow got out of this alive, Beacon would owe him several fruit baskets.

Beacon's relief quickly gave way to panic. Galen couldn't block them from Victor forever. Sooner or later Victor would figure out a way to get past him.

Just as Beacon had this thought, twin hatches opened up on either side of Galen's ship. Massive metal cylinders whizzed out of the openings. Victor couldn't shoot Galen's ship, but there was no reason Galen couldn't shoot his.

Victor realized this and quickly retreated, narrowly avoiding one of the rockets that Galen had sent his way. The missile blasted through the sky, exploding against a mountain. An avalanche of rocks and snow went tumbling down the rock face. Victor's ship hovered in the sky a moment, before it zipped up and away, speeding out of sight.

Beacon raked a shaking hand through his hair.

"Is everyone okay?" Everleigh asked.

"I can't tell if I have asthma," Arthur said between gasps for air.

"Deep breaths, honey, you'll be okay." Arthur's grandma rubbed circles into his back.

"Beaks, you good?" Everleigh asked.

Beacon gave a weak thumbs-up.

Their dad just stood by the door, completely unfazed. Beacon guessed that in this instance having no feelings wasn't the worst thing in the world.

Outside, Galen's ship touched down. The hatch peeled open, and Galen stepped out. Daisy walked down the stairs behind him, wrapping a blanket around her shoulders. Even dressed in a nightgown and covered in grime from the secret passage, she managed to look regal as she surveyed the landscape.

"Open the doors!" Beacon shouted, slamming his palm against the metal interior of the ship.

The door opened and stairs whizzed out. Beacon didn't even wait for them to extend all the way before he jumped down.

"You came back!" Beacon slammed into Galen in the biggest bro-hug ever.

"I can't leave you guys alone for five minutes without you almost getting killed," Galen said.

Everleigh rolled her eyes. "I was *just* about to lay the smack down on Victor before you swooped in."

"*Riiiight.*" Galen squinted suddenly, looking behind Beacon. "Hey, is that . . . ?"

Beacon turned, too, then grinned a bit. "Yeah, that's my dad."

"You got him out? Way to go!" Galen stepped forward and extended a hand. "I've heard a lot about you. I'm Galen."

The twins' dad just stood there.

"Shake his hand, Dad," Everleigh said.

He did as commanded. A confused look washed over Galen's face as they shook, and Beacon could feel his cheeks going red. He fiddled with the zipper of his jacket.

"Yeah, he isn't himself. Arthur's PJ doesn't work anymore."

Whatever Galen was going to say next died on his lips when he spotted Arthur's grandma. His eyes darkened about three shades.

"What's *she* doing here?" he said.

"That's my grandma," Arthur said defensively.

"Yeah, well, your grandma tried to shoot me," Galen said. Which, fair enough.

"I am sorry about that," Arthur's grandma said. "I didn't realize you were on our side. All I saw was a Sov attacking, and I shot."

"You ran off before I got a chance to explain everything," Beacon said. "We didn't betray you and we didn't plan to hurt Daisy—"

Galen held up his hand to stop him, then took a deep breath. "I know."

"You . . . do?" Beacon said.

"Daisy explained. But I already knew, even before that. I read your mind," Galen added, seeing Beacon's confused look. "Back in the forest when I was, uh, choking you. Sorry about that, by the way."

"You can read minds?!"

"All the Sov can. Not every thought, and you need to concentrate pretty hard and be close to the target, but I could tell you were being truthful when you said you weren't going to hurt Daisy. Even if I didn't really want to believe it at the time. I was pretty mad."

It all made sense now. Why Galen had believed him that night in the alley when he'd told him he didn't know what Victor meant about him saving the planet. Why Galen had suddenly decided to trust them at the aquarium, when he'd initially greeted him with a knife. Why he'd let Beacon go in the forest.

A new thought occurred to him: This must be how the Sov guard had been able to take Jasper's form that night back in the underwater tunnel. He'd read his mind.

Shock and indignation warred inside him.

"Then I talked to Daisy in the ship, and she told me everything," Galen went on. "She said you were kind to her. Most of you, anyway," he added, shooting a look at Everleigh. "And that you have only the best interest of your people at heart."

Even though Beacon was disturbed at this new mind-reading revelation, he couldn't help the small smile that formed.

"Also that you smell," Galen said, smirking.

"Not just you," Daisy said. "All of you. Seriously, do humans not bathe?"

Arthur sniffed under his shirt then gagged. "I can't argue with that."

"Hey! It was your idea to get on that trash barge, Alien Boy," Everleigh said, but she smiled, too.

"As much as I'd love to continue this," Arthur's grandma said, "by now those ships have probably doused half of the Eastern seaboard with toxic rain."

Her statement cut like a knife through the lighthearted moment. Even Everleigh had the decency to look ashamed.

"She's right," Galen said. "We'd better get out of here. Victor's probably getting reinforcements as we speak. Come on, Everleigh. I'll teach you how to drive one of these things properly."

"Hey, I was managing just fine on my own," Everleigh said.

"That's what you call that?" Galen teased. They all boarded his ship.

Well, almost everyone.

"Board the ship," Beacon told his dad. It was starting to feel like he had a dog.

All that was missing was a wagging tail as his dad obeyed the command and walked up the steps onto Galen's ship. Galen watched the whole thing with a deepening frown.

"No offense or anything," Galen said, not taking his eyes off the twins' dad. "But this is weird."

Beacon knew his dad was acting odder than usual for humans the Sov brainwashed, but having it pointed out by someone else made him feel sick.

"It was the same with the townspeople back in the clearing," Arthur's grandma said. "Those people were more than the usual docile and compliant we see after someone's been given the antidote."

"It's like they're totally droned out," Arthur agreed. "Like they're computers instead of people."

Beacon wanted to tell everyone that his dad was *right there* and they could stop insulting him anytime now. But who was he kidding? His dad wasn't there. Not really.

Was it permanent? Would they ever figure out a way to get him back? Or was that night in the Sov's underwater tunnel all those weeks ago the last time he'd really had a dad?

One look at Everleigh told him she was thinking the same thing.

"We know the Sov updated the antidote because the electrocution glitch no longer works," Arthur said. "But it seems like they changed more than that. You saw Donna—she wasn't as bad as your dad. We didn't even realize she was a lemming until she attacked."

"And what about the scientists?" Everleigh said. "They weren't like Dad, either. They actually cared about each other. Even the Gold Stars have more going on up here." She tapped her temple.

"I have an answer for that," Daisy said sheepishly. "The antidote has different levels of strength. For the different things the Sov need you for."

Everyone turned to her. "They can't brain zap scientists, or they wouldn't be able to do the kind of critical thinking needed for science," she explained. "But if you're a lab rat and they plan to do painful procedures on you, it would be helpful if you didn't fight back or complain. Each human they inject has had their antidote adjusted to a level that suits their 'use.' Now that Victor's enacting his plan for domination and doesn't need the brainwashed humans to blend in anymore, it seems he's turned most of the antidotes up to full throttle."

A sick feeling coiled inside Beacon's stomach. He couldn't help imagining all the things his dad had been through. All that he might have been through if they hadn't saved him.

"I'm sorry," Daisy said. "I've never agreed with what they're doing. I want to do right by my people, but they aren't upholding the values the Sovereign used to stand for. No one deserves to be exterminated."

Beacon was surprised by the anger in her voice.

"It isn't your fault," Beacon said. "There was nothing you could do."

"I tried. I really did," Daisy said. "But when I spoke up, they just locked me in my room."

Daisy fingered her necklace.

Beacon didn't know what to say. But then Galen powered up the ship, cutting off his thoughts.

"Buckle up," he said, breaking the tension.

There wasn't enough space on the bench seat for all of them, so Daisy folded down extra seats along the sidewalls. Everyone snapped into their harnesses as Galen got the ship airborne again.

Beacon tried to put what Arthur had said about his dad being like a computer out of his mind, but every time he tried to think of something else, his mind veered back to it, like a bowling ball bouncing off the bumpers. For some reason, it got him thinking about what he'd seen in Nixon's file the day he and Arthur had broken into Nurse Allen's office. All the dozens of injections Nixon had received because he'd gone "Off-Program."

"Hey," Beacon said, thinking out loud. "So you know how kids are called 'Off-Program' when the antidote goes wonky and they can't control us anymore?"

Everyone but his dad swung around to look at him. He instantly felt stupid and was sure they would laugh at his theory. But they were all waiting for him to talk, so he took a deep breath and went on. "Well . . . what if that injection *is* a program?"

"What do you mean?" Arthur asked.

"What if the Sov install a mind-control program in humans via the injections, instead of using a disc or whatever?"

For a solid ten seconds that felt like a century, no one said anything. Beacon just sat there, feeling stupid and hot. Then Daisy said, "Well, I *have* overheard my guards talking about participant software."

"Really?" Arthur said.

"Yeah, I'm sure I heard them talking about installing the participant software, or something like that," she said. "I didn't know what it meant at the time, but they could have been talking about the antidote."

"That has to be it!" Arthur said. "Software is a set of instructions for a computer to perform specific operations."

Beacon felt something flutter inside his chest then, a tiny batting of wings. Hope.

"If you're right, this means I can hack the system," Galen said. "Disable the programs. We can stop the attack."

"Then what are we waiting for?" Everleigh said. "Let's do it."

"I'll need access to a real computer," Galen said. "I can't do it from the ship."

"Okay, so where's the closest one?" Arthur said.

"We can go to the inn," Beacon offered.

"That computer is older than me," Galen said. "I'll need better tech than that if I'm going to have any chance at this."

"We can't go to the base," Everleigh said. "That place will be full of Sov."

"Unless it's not," Daisy said.

Everyone turned to her.

"I'll create a distraction. I'll fly the ship nearby and take the Sov on a chase while you gain access to the building. They won't expect you to go back after you freed your dad, so they won't see it coming."

"That sounds awfully dangerous," Arthur's grandma said.

"And you don't know how to fly a ship," Galen added.

"No. But *she* does." Daisy jerked her chin at Everleigh, who did a double take before she threw her shoulders back.

"Yes, she does," Everleigh said.

"You can't be serious, Dais." Galen had dropped his voice to a harsh whisper, even though the ship was small and they could all hear everything he said. "You can't put yourself at risk like that. You know the consequences."

"I don't need to be lectured by you, Galen." She unbuckled her harness and stood up, letting the blanket fall off her lap. In that moment, she looked more like the queen of the Sov than ever. "I make the rules around here. It's about time everyone remembered that."

Beacon thought Galen would be angry, but a small smile played at the corners of his mouth.

"About time," he said. "So what's the plan, boss?"

Daisy looked uncertain for a half a second before resolve stiffened her jaw.

"We'll drop you off in the forest close to the base," she said. "You can travel the rest of the way on foot. They'll think you're out here in the mountains, so they won't expect you, and especially not on foot. Then we'll get their attention and make a spectacle while we lead them away from you. Galen, you do your magic, and we beat the bad guys."

Everleigh and Arthur let out a cheer, but Beacon couldn't join in.

"I don't know about this plan," Arthur's grandma said, echoing his thoughts. "A lot could go wrong."

"Yeah, like what if they shoot at you?" Beacon said. "You're just banking on the fact that the Sov wouldn't shoot at a ship with the queen on board."

"They *won't* shoot at me," Daisy said. "They'd never hurt a hair on my head."

"What about *her* head?" Beacon said, nodding toward his sister.

"She'll be safe with me," Daisy said. "Your dad can stay with us, too. He'd be a liability inside the base. Your grandma is welcome as well," she added to Arthur.

"I'm going with the boys," Arthur's grandma said. "I couldn't in good conscience let you kids enter that base without adult supervision."

The kids exchanged a glance. They'd done a lot of dangerous

stuff without any adult supervision, but she didn't need to know about that.

"You don't have to do this," Beacon told Everleigh quietly.

"I *want* to do this. Beaks, none of this matters if the Sov win. If they take over, we're all screwed. We need to do everything we can to stop them, even if it means taking the biggest risks."

Beacon chewed on his lip for a moment, before he finally nodded. "Okay."

"Great. Because I wasn't asking for your permission." She sat next to Galen. They immediately began talking shop, going over the control panel as if no one else was on the ship.

Before long, they were airborne again.

Snowcapped mountains and trees flashed underneath them. Beacon couldn't see the on-land base under the swirl of snow and cloud, but it must be close. Too soon, they were touching down in a small clearing surrounded by pines. The hatch opened, and a gust of snow crystals rushed in on a bitter wind. Beacon zipped up his jacket all the way.

"Go east," Daisy called over the noise. "There's an entrance near the service doors that's rarely manned."

Beacon nodded.

"Take this," Daisy said. She rooted around in a drawer, then tossed something into the air. Beacon caught it. It looked like a two-way radio.

"We'll keep in contact with you this way," Daisy said.

Beacon flicked on the power switch. Loud static filled the air, and he turned the volume down.

"Take this, too." Daisy handed Arthur's grandma a small keycard. She flipped it over. On one side was some type of bar code, and on the other was a picture of Daisy. "That'll get you in any door."

Arthur's grandma pocketed the card.

Daisy looked at Galen then.

"I guess this makes me officially not a coward, huh?" Galen said.

Beacon had no idea what that was supposed to mean, but it must have been an in-joke, because Daisy gave Galen a small, sad smile that he returned. "You never were a coward."

They looked at each other for another long moment, so long that Beacon got the distinct impression they were communicating telepathically. Galen frowned, then nodded. Daisy swallowed hard, then tore her eyes away from him and took a deep breath. "All set?"

"Yeah, just one thing," Beacon said.

Daisy raised her eyebrows expectantly.

"Which way is east?"

Daisy closed her eyes, Everleigh let out an exasperated breath, and Arthur's grandma mumbled something about this not "boding well" for their mission. Daisy pointed.

"Right. Perfect, thanks," Beacon said brightly.

Then he looked at his sister. He opened his mouth to say goodbye, but she said, "Don't," in a tone that left no room for argument. "I'll see you later."

"Later," Beacon said. Then he peered back at his dad, who was staring blankly into the middle distance. "See you later, Dad. I love you."

His dad said nothing. Beacon almost ordered him to say "I love you" back, but that seemed too sad and pathetic, so he clamped his mouth shut.

And then they were off.

21

They ran through the trees, their heads down against the punishing wind. Snow swirled down the back of Beacon's jacket, chilling him to the bone. Before long, his fingers felt numb with cold. He didn't know how Galen was going to operate a computer if they managed to get inside the building, but that was a problem for *after* they got inside.

Beacon was just beginning to think that they'd gone the wrong east when the base appeared. He squinted through the swirling snow and spotted the entrance Daisy must have been talking about. It was a small, nondescript door next to an industrial garbage bin. Only it wasn't unmanned. A knot of guards was clumped outside the door, standing stiffly in their starched uniforms, their belts shining with weapons.

"What now?" Galen said.

Beacon pulled the radio out of his jacket pocket and brought it close to his lips.

"We've got a problem," he whisper-hissed. "There are a million guards at this door. Is there a different one we can use?"

Static crackled from the radio for a moment before Daisy's voice came through. "No. Any other entrance will be much worse."

"Then what do we do?" Arthur's grandma whispered back urgently.

"I vote Galen goes Squidward on them," Arthur said.

"Then what?" Galen said. "I hack the computer with my tentacles? Great idea if you want this to take twice as long."

"You can transform back to human after," Arthur said.

"With what energy? I used all my EpiPens to stay awake. I'm already running low on time."

"I don't know what EpiPens have to do with anything," Arthur's grandma said. "But in any case, that's not exactly discreet. The idea is to slip past the guards."

"Just hang tight," Everleigh said. "I have an idea."

A moment later, the ship swooped in low over the building, sending Beacon's hood flying off his head and the air whooshing out of his lungs. A guard yelled something into his radio and they all ran inside, the door sliding shut behind them.

Beacon smiled. *Thanks, Everleigh.*

"Now!" Galen said.

They ran for the doors.

As Beacon bolted through the yard, it suddenly occurred to him that the place very well could have snipers manning the property like he'd seen in prison movies. The thought sent a jolt of adrenaline racing through him, and he ran faster. They finally reached the door. Beacon, Arthur, and Galen flattened themselves against the brick like secret agents as Arthur's grandma swiped Daisy's badge over the red light. The door slid open.

Arthur's grandma poked her head inside, then waved for them to follow. They ducked into an empty hallway glinting with harsh green lights.

"We're in," Beacon whispered into the radio.

He waited for a reply, clutching the radio. When a second passed, then another, and no reply came, Beacon's throat clenched with fear. What if their ship had been shot down? What if the building really *did* have snipers and—

"A little busy right now," Everleigh said between crackles of static.

Beacon let out a small breath.

"What's going on? Are the Sov after you?" he asked.

No reply.

"Come on, we don't want to distract them," Galen said. "Plus, we can't stand here forever. Someone's going to find us."

Beacon pocketed the radio. Arthur produced his map of the building, which was now tattered and ripped.

"Which way?" his grandma asked.

"Computers would be in the office areas, right?" he said. "That should be here." He pointed at a spot on the map. "One floor up and down a few halls." He folded up the map and shoved it back into his pocket.

They slunk forward through the quiet, neon halls. The ice crystals inside Beacon's jacket and rimming his socks melted, making him colder and wetter than ever. His skin burned and prickled as feeling returned to his body.

They followed Arthur up a set of wide stairs to the first floor, then through a labyrinth of empty halls lined with labs, file rooms, and doors with blacked-out windows that held who knows what. They hadn't seen a single person the entire time, which is maybe why they got a little too comfortable and didn't peer around the next corner before they turned it. Arthur slammed right into a squid. He skittered back on the tile, nearly slipping in the goo. The creature stood on its rear tentacles, its flesh rolling in a constant wave even as it stood still. Gelatinous snot oozed from the monster's uncooked chicken meat skin. A chilling rattling noise issued from its mouth.

"Run!" Galen yelled.

Beacon was already on it. He forgot all about how frozen and tired he was and ran down the hall so fast, he knew that if he thought too much about it, he'd go tumbling down.

Arthur's grandma loped along beside him.

Beacon had never had the occasion to wonder how Arthur's

grandma would fare during a chase, but he never would have guessed that she would be so fast. She more than kept up with the kids as they raced down hall after hall.

"I'm going to need an awful lot of ibuprofen if we survive this," she grunted, as if she could hear Beacon's thoughts.

They careened around a corner.

Another squid was waiting for them. They doubled back in a riot of elbows and shouts, thumps and slurps. They weren't running anywhere in particular now, just away. Their boots squeaked loudly, but they were past being stealthy.

Beacon skidded around another corner and froze. The doors to the queen's room were thrown open. Inside, a massive squid had Perry and Sumiko backed into the wall. It hadn't even occurred to Beacon to be fearful for their safety. Sure, they were humans, but they were on the Sov's side. But the Sov seemed to have forgotten all about that now. The squid slithered in front of them, darting a tentacle out at the Gold Stars every now and then, making them shriek.

It was playing with its food.

"P-please. We're Junior Guards!" Sumiko stuttered.

"Let's go!" Galen whisper-shouted.

But Beacon couldn't leave them—even if that was what the Gold Stars would have done to him. What they *deserved*. He knew if he left them to die, he wasn't any better than the Sov.

"Behind you!" Beacon screamed. "There's a door behind the tapestry!"

Sumiko fumbled behind her and yanked the tapestry out of the way. She found the knob and they fell through the door, slamming it shut just as a tentacle clobbered it.

The squid reared back, revealing its razor-sharp teeth.

"Note to self. Don't make the Sov mad," Arthur said.

They ran. The next hall was empty, and Beacon had a moment of hope that they'd get away. But when they reached the next corridor, his heart sank. There was a squid on the floor. Two suctioned to the walls. One running along the ceiling. Beacon froze, feeling the blood drain from his face. This was bad. Really, really, bad.

Some corner of his mind that wasn't freaking out registered that they hadn't passed a single human since they'd reentered the base. He wondered if the Sov were giving up on blending in now that they'd started their takeover.

Arthur's grandma was shouting something that Beacon couldn't hear. He felt himself being ripped away. His feet moved without his body's command, and the next thing he knew, they were crashing into a room. A door whizzed shut behind them, muting the sounds from the hall. Beacon slowly got his bearings, and sound funneled back. He took in his surroundings. High-tech computers lined a large, circular desk that took up the entire room. From the look of triumph on Galen's face, this was exactly what they'd been looking for.

Galen jumped into a chair at the desk and pulled the keyboard close. Beacon's limbs were still buzzing with adrenaline, and he could barely think. He shook his head, trying to clear the fog. They needed to keep Galen safe while he worked.

"Come on, help me move this." Beacon raced over to a filing cabinet. If those things figured out they were in here before Galen finished up, they were in deep trouble. Arthur's grandma was bent double, trying to catch her breath. She held up a finger in the universal "one minute" gesture.

"I got it, Grams!" Arthur ran over and grabbed the other side of the cabinet. They slid it across the floor. Galen looked over his shoulder. The look he gave them said he could slap that cabinet aside with one swat of his tentacle, but it made Beacon feel better to be doing something. Once the cabinet was in front of the door, Beacon pulled out the radio.

"How's it going? You guys okay?" he asked.

A crackle of static, then, "We're good!"

Relief flooded through him at the sound of Everleigh's voice.

"What happened?" Beacon asked as Arthur crowded close to the radio to listen.

"The Sov sent a few ships after us," Daisy said. "I think they were trying to pen us in. Got a little tight for a minute, but Everleigh got an idea to—" Static cut out her next words, before her voice came back through. "Your girl's got moves!"

"And we'll never hear the end of it," Beacon joked.

"How are things over there?" Daisy asked.

"Almost got slaughtered by some Sov," Arthur said, "but we found the computers, and Galen's working on getting in now."

"Almost got slaughtered?" Daisy and Everleigh shouted together.

"We encountered a few Sov in squid mode," Beacon confirmed, giving Arthur a look to shut up when he opened his mouth to protest that it was more than just a few. He didn't want his sister worrying about him while she was trying to fly a freaking alien ship.

"We've got it all under control," Arthur's grandma said, pressing her hand against a stitch in her side.

"Just . . . be careful," Everleigh said warily.

"Same goes for you," Beacon said.

There was nothing else to say after that, so Beacon, Arthur, and his grandma went over to see what Galen was doing.

Fragments of code filled the screen. It might as well have been written in alien for all the sense it made to Beacon.

"Any progress?" Arthur whispered.

"Shhh," Galen said, typing.

Arthur drummed his fingers on the desk until Galen shot him a dark look.

"Sorry, sorry!" Arthur said, raising his hands.

Beacon looked back at the door, his fingers clenching around the back of Galen's chair.

Sweat glittered in beads on Galen's forehead. For several long, anguishing minutes, the only sounds were the clacking of the keyboard, the occasional scream of a Sov through the thick metal door, and the even more distant sound of missiles outside. The tension solidified.

Then Galen let out a hysterical laugh of triumph.

"What happened? Did you do it?" Beacon asked.

"Not yet. But you were right about the antidote being a computer program."

"I was?!" Beacon said, at the same time as Arthur said, "He was?!"

"The software is all right here. And they haven't even encrypted it!" Galen cracked his knuckles and went back to work.

Arthur blew out a relieved breath, and his grandma grabbed his hand, giving it a squeeze.

Everything was going according to plan.

Just as he thought it, a deafening boom sounded, and then everything went black. For a horrible moment, Beacon thought he'd been killed. That a missile had struck the building, and now he was in some kind of afterlife. But then something slurp-slithered on the other side of the door three feet away. Arthur yelped and jumped back, his heel digging into Beacon's foot. Beacon smothered a hiss of pain and shoved him off, while Galen shushed them both.

Dim emergency lights flickered on in sconces in the wall. Galen punched the computer's power button about a hundred times, but it didn't boot up.

"No, no, no, no!" Galen cried.

"What happened?" Arthur's grandma said.

"They shut the power off." Galen gave up trying to restart the computer and sank forward onto the desk, rubbing his temples. "It's all over."

Beacon shook his head. "It isn't over. It can't be over."

There had to be a way to get these computers up and running again. They couldn't give up now. He pushed past the fear that they would all die here and thought hard. "A building this big must have a source of backup power, right?"

"There's probably a generator on the mechanical floor," Arthur said.

"How are we going to get there?" Arthur's grandma asked.

There was a long beat of silence, punctuated by the sound of something slithering outside the room. Then Arthur said, "I-I'll go."

Beacon spun to face his friend.

It wasn't like when Daisy had announced her plan to lure away the Sov, when she'd looked and sounded so confident, she practically dared anyone to disagree with her. Arthur's lips trembled, and even in the dark, Beacon could see that his skin had gone sickly pale.

"Don't be silly," Arthur's grandma said. "You're not going out there."

"Those things will eat you for dinner," Beacon agreed.

"We need Galen to hack the system," Arthur said more confidently. "And you wouldn't know the first thing about how to find a generator," he told Beacon, "much less how to fix it. It has to be me."

"No." Arthur's grandma shook her head.

"Look, it's like Everleigh said before," Arthur continued. "If we don't stop the Sov, we're all majorly screwed. What do we have to lose here? If we do nothing, we die. If I do this? We have a small chance. It's like that saying goes: You miss one hundred percent of the shots you don't take."

"Is . . . that from the poster in the guidance counselor's office?" Beacon asked.

"Yes," Arthur said guiltily. "But that doesn't make it not true."

He was right, but that didn't mean Beacon had to like it.

"I'm coming with you," Beacon said.

"Okay."

"You're not even going to try to convince me to stay back?" Beacon said.

"No, man, I'm not that stupid." Arthur grinned.

"I'm coming, too," Arthur's grandma said.

They didn't bother to argue with her. It was clear she wouldn't back down.

"I hate to interrupt," Galen said. "But how are you even going to get the door open with the power out?"

He had a good point. It was an automatic sliding door. There was no handle.

"The ventilation shafts!" Arthur said after a beat of silence.

Beacon looked up at the ceiling warily. There weren't drop tiles on the ceiling, like in the old church.

Arthur produced the building plans again.

"Yes, they're definitely up there." He flattened the map on the desk and stabbed his finger at an area where a maze of ventilation shafts ran through the building.

"Should I point out how that plan worked out for us before?" Beacon said.

The last time they'd crawled through a ventilation shaft, they'd literally fallen into the middle of a Gold Stars meeting.

"If you have a better idea, I'm all ears." Arthur hunched over the map, and they all crowded around him. "All of the automatic doors and elevators will have been affected by the power outage, but there's an emergency stairwell here." He pointed to a corner of the page. "If we can just crawl close, we can drop out near the stairs and shoot down without running into any Sov. Hopefully," he added.

"Galen, as soon as the power is back up, you need to work as fast as you can."

"On it," Galen said.

Arthur folded up the map and shoved it back into his pocket. "Now we just need to cut away the drywall on the ceiling somehow. There has to be something here we can use." He began whipping open drawers. He shoved aside boxes of paper clips and highlighters, until he proudly produced a box cutter.

But before Arthur could get to work, a tentacle whipped out of Galen's chest, punching into the ceiling. Drywall blasted around them like fireworks. Beacon coughed, but when the dust cleared, there was a human-size hole in the ceiling and the side of the exposed ventilation shaft.

"That's one way to do it," Arthur said.

"Won't you have to sleep now?" Beacon said in a panic.

"Nah," Galen said. "Partial shifts don't have the same effect. I'll just be a bit tired. Now go. Stop wasting time."

Arthur's grandma peered up at the gap in the ceiling. "That passage is awfully small . . ."

"You can stay behind, Grams. Help Galen," Arthur said.

She scoffed. "What does an old lady like me know about computers? No, I'm coming with you."

Then there was nothing left to do but get into the shaft. Beacon climbed onto the desk and pulled himself up. He was just reaching down to help Arthur when someone banged on the door. Beacon froze.

"I know you're in there," Victor said calmly.

The door rattled, but it didn't open. The power outage was the only thing standing between them and death.

"Go!" Galen shouted.

"But what if he gets in?" Arthur said.

"I can defend myself. We need that power up."

Beacon had seen Galen battle Victor. It was true, he *had* held his own. But Galen still hadn't recovered from his previous transformation. Would he have the energy for a battle with Victor?

"Go!" Galen said, clearly reading Beacon's thoughts.

"Be safe," Beacon said.

He gripped Arthur's hand and hauled him up. His grandma must have climbed up next, because a moment later she was whisper-shouting at him to "go, go, go!"

Beacon tried not to imagine Victor shooting the ventilation shafts action-movie style while they were trapped like sitting ducks and crawled forward.

Static crackled, and then Everleigh's voice came over the radio.

"They're starting to drop the acid rain!" she said. "I can see it falling from the UFOs!"

Panic and terror blazed through Beacon's body.

"Go faster!" Arthur hissed.

"I'm trying," Beacon cried.

He shuffled forward as quickly as the tight space allowed.

They had no flashlight this time, so they moved in the dark. It didn't take long for Beacon's already sore knees and palms to hurt like bruises being prodded. He thought of the acid rain, of the effects he'd witnessed in that lab, and pushed past the pain.

They'd only been traveling for a few minutes when Beacon heard a noise behind them. He froze, and Arthur bumped into his feet. His grandma muttered, "What in tarnation?" farther behind him.

"Shhh!" Beacon turned his head to the side, listening. There was thumping and slithering below them, muted from the thick drywall. But that was it. Paranoia was getting the better of him again. He was just about to keep moving when he heard the creak of metal.

Someone else was inside the shaft.

22

Arthur gasped.

Beacon was trying to figure out how Victor had managed to fit inside the shaft when Arthur's grandma could barely fit at half his size, when he heard a girl call out, "Don't bother running!" in a calm, singsong voice.

Every nerve in Beacon's body tingled.

Jane.

Of course. Victor was too big to fit, but Jane wasn't.

"Go, go, go!" Arthur's grandma yelled.

"There should be an intersection up ahead," Arthur said. "Move!"

Beacon crawled forward as quickly as he could in the cramped space. Behind them, the shaft rumbled with noise. It felt like the shaft went on forever, and he started to worry that they'd gone the wrong way or that Arthur's map was outdated. Finally, Beacon reached an intersection of shafts that branched off in three different directions.

Arthur frantically tapped his back, gestured to the path to the left, then put his finger over his lips. Beacon instantly understood. If Jane went the wrong way, it would at least buy them some time.

Beacon banked left, sliding quietly through the shaft. Sweat dripped off his forehead, splattering onto the metal beneath him. Beacon hoped and prayed that Everleigh or Daisy wouldn't try to communicate with them just then. They'd be so totally screwed if the radio in his pocket went off again.

"Hmm, now where could you have gone?" Jane sang from farther behind them in a faux-curious voice. "I wonder if it's the shaft with all the hand and knee prints in the dust?"

They were *so* totally screwed.

"Forget about being quiet," his grandma called. "Just move your butts!"

They scrambled forward, but Beacon didn't know why they bothered. It was only a matter of time before Jane reached them.

Then he saw light up ahead.

"That's not on the plans," Arthur said.

"Who cares?" Beacon said. It was an exit.

Beacon crawled toward the light like he was stranded in a desert and he'd just spotted an oasis. Only his oasis turned out to be some type of maintenance access covered with an iron grille. A set of ladder stairs fed from the shaft onto a platform that circled nearly the entire ceiling of the mechanical floor. Which was absolutely crawling with Sov. But they had no choice but to go down there. And fast, judging by the clambering sounds coming from behind them.

Beacon gripped the grille and pulled with all his might. The cover came away easily and he slid it aside. He swallowed hard, then crawled through the access and stepped down, into the open. So far none of the Sov had spotted him, but he felt as exposed as if he'd just walked into his classroom naked.

Arthur was right behind him, then his grandma. As soon as they'd descended, they scurried into the shadow of a huge pipe. And bumped into someone.

"Nixon?" Beacon said.

Arthur's grandma yanked Beacon behind her, glaring at Nixon's Junior Guard uniform.

"It's okay, Grams," Arthur explained. "Nixon's on our side. He's immune to the antidote, too."

Nixon made frantic throat-cutting gestures at them, then peered anxiously past the pipe.

"What are you doing here?" Beacon whispered.

"Trying to hide," Nixon said.

"What happened to trying to free the prisoners?" Beacon said.

"I *was* trying to free the prisoners, and then everyone went wild! It's like no matter what I did, they wouldn't stop following the Sov guards. What are *you* doing here?"

"Trying to get to the generator," Beacon said.

There was a loud thump. When Beacon peered around the pipe, he saw Jane dusting off her hands at the bottom of the ladder. The Gold Star hummed a cheery tune under her breath as she strolled along the platform with a giant tentacle bulging out from between her torn-open buttons. Arthur's grandma yanked Beacon behind the pipe. Nixon brought a finger to his lips, as if anyone needed a reminder.

Out of the corner of his eye, Beacon saw the tentacle slithering left to right. Without warning, it slid around the pipe. Arthur's grandma clapped a hand over Arthur's mouth to keep him from crying out. They kept as still as possible as the appendage writhed around the pipe, inches from their faces, so close that Beacon could see the blood pulsing under its wet, translucent skin. Then as fast as it had come, the appendage retreated.

When they were sure she was gone, Beacon let out a huge breath.

"You don't get used to it," Arthur's grandma said, swallowing hard.

Nixon peeked around the pipe. "Why do you need to get to the generator?" he asked, even more quietly than before.

"We're trying to hack the system that's controlling the prisoners. But we can't do that without power. The generator must be somewhere in this room."

"Well, good luck with that," Nixon said.

They gazed out at the mechanical floor. It looked like a scene out of an apocalypse movie. One where the humans were about three seconds away from being cornered by a mob of flesh-eating zombies and eaten for lunch.

They could really use one of Everleigh's distraction techniques right about now. Beacon was wondering if he should risk radioing for help, when Arthur pointed at a big yellow contraption that looked like a train car.

"Over there!" he said.

The generator was in the middle of the room, and there were at least seven Sov between them and the machine. Beacon chewed his bottom lip. There was no way they'd get there without being clobbered by squids first.

"I'll cause a distraction," Nixon said. "Then you need to run for it."

"No," Beacon said firmly. "We saw a squid try to kill Perry and Sumiko. They don't care that you're a Gold Star or a Junior Guard anymore. If you get caught, you're dead."

"Then I better not get caught," Nixon said.

He launched himself out from behind the pipe, curls bouncing as he ran across the platform.

"Hey, over here, you slimy scumbags!" Nixon yelled and waved his arms in the air. All of the squids whipped around to face him. There was barely a millisecond of hesitation before they were moving toward the stairs to the platform like gulls spying a french fry at Deadman's Wharf.

"Idiot," Beacon muttered.

"What are we waiting for?" Arthur's grandma said. "Let's go!"

They scampered across the platform in the opposite direction, then descended the stairs to the main floor, moving quickly and quietly. When they reached the generator, Beacon and Arthur's grandma took cover while Arthur immediately bent over the engine.

"How do we get it running?" Beacon said.

"It should have booted up automatically when the power went out. Something went wrong."

"No, duh," Beacon said.

Arthur didn't dignify that with a response.

Beacon anxiously looked over at Nixon. The narrow platform stairs had slowed down the Sov, forcing them to ascend single file, but they were catching up to him now. Nixon raced to the end of the platform, then stopped abruptly, pinwheeling his arms.

The platform had ended. Nixon would have to circle back to get to the stairs, and about a dozen squids blocked that route. One had even figured out that it could forgo the stairs altogether and had launched itself up with its powerful tentacles. Now it clung wetly to the underside of the platform. Nixon tried to back away from a squid that thumped toward him, almost stumbling over the rail. He looked down, and Beacon knew what he was thinking: that if he jumped, he would break something. Probably a lot of somethings. He might even die.

He was trapped.

The squid reared up on its hind tentacles, towering over the Gold Star. Its tentacles rippled and curled at its sides. Beacon didn't know how he knew, but he just did: It was Jane.

"Unbelievable," Arthur muttered. Beacon assumed he was talking about the horror scene taking place in front of them, but he was looking at the engine. "It wasn't even set to auto. Who do they have running this place?"

"Just get it working," his grandma hissed.

Arthur said something back, but Beacon was barely listening. He couldn't wrench his eyes away from Nixon's impending death.

He couldn't let this happen.

Beacon made a split-second decision and jumped out from behind the generator, running for Nixon. But someone walked out and blocked his path.

A wolfish grin split Victor's face. "You're so predictable," he said. "Always playing hero. What is with you? Don't you have any interest in self-preservation?"

"It's called being a good friend," Arthur called from behind Beacon. "You should try it sometime."

Victor laughed riotously, as if Arthur had said the funniest thing in the world.

The main lights blinked on suddenly. Machinery hummed as it came to life. Arthur must have gotten the generator up and running.

Victor's smile faltered. His eyes narrowed dangerously.

"Speaking of friends," he said, stepping forward, regaining his composure, "I just had a conversation with one of yours. I have to admit, though, I never really liked the guy."

It took Beacon a moment to realize who Victor was talking about, and when he did, his stomach sank with dread.

"If you hurt Galen, I'll kill you," Beacon said.

Victor stared at him dead-on. "I'd love to see you try."

He fell onto all fours like a dog. By the time his hands hit the ground, they were already tentacles. There was the sickening sound of goo squelching under wet tentacles, and then Beacon's feet went out from under him. A strangled cry left his mouth as a tentacle wrapped around his body, locking his arms against his sides.

"Let him go!" Arthur screamed, pounding on the tentacle.

"He's just a child!" Arthur's grandma clawed at Victor.

Without breaking his grip on Beacon, Victor plucked Arthur into the air with another tentacle and threw him against a wall like he was nothing but a pesky bug he was swatting away. Arthur's grandma let out a horrified cry right before the tentacle swung back around and clomped her across the chest, sending her flying in the opposite direction. She landed with a horrible, dull thud that couldn't mean anything good for an old woman.

The tentacle gripping Beacon's chest strangled his scream. He tried to suck in a breath, but he couldn't get air. Stars burst in his vision.

Victor rose on his hind tentacles. The mouth on the underside of his body yawned open, revealing row upon row of razor-sharp teeth dripping in slime. There was movement deep in the shadows of its mouth the moment before a gooey pink organ slid out. Beacon had seen this before, back in the underwater UFO. A Sov posing as a human had eaten a hamburger this way. He'd watched the organ close around the burger and dissolve it in a hiss of steam. *They're like sea stars*, Everleigh had said. *They evert their stomachs outside their bodies to eat. The digestive enzymes absorb the food, and the liquefied food is then absorbed through the body and transferred to other organs. Pretty neat.*

Yeah. Neat. He was going to be eaten alive.

Beacon swallowed hard—as hard as he could with the tentacle wrapped tightly around his chest, restricting his breathing. Victor lifted him up as the pink organ pushed out farther, widening like gum being stretched between fingers.

Beacon squeezed his eyes shut.

He'd heard you were supposed to think of happy memories in stressful situations, so he thought of Jasper. Maybe it was because of the recurring nightmare, but the first thing he thought about was their games of hide-and-seek back in LA. One time, Jasper had found the best hiding spot. It had taken Beacon over an hour to find him, but when Beacon had pulled aside the rolls of wrapping paper in the hall closet and Jasper was there, the pleased grin on his face had told Beacon that the long wait had been worth it.

Beacon almost smiled then, because he could see Jasper's twinkling brown eyes and the dimple that popped out on his cheek so clearly.

Almost, because he was about to become squid food.

Or was he? Beacon had a half a second to wonder if he was imagining things, or if the viselike grip around his chest was loosening, right before he was unceremoniously dropped on the ground. He landed with an *oof*, sprawling across the floor. He scrabbled back from Victor as fast as he could, but the squid wasn't even paying attention to him. Victor was looking at the tentacle that had held Beacon up moments ago, slowly coiling and uncoiling the appendage. His movements were as slow as molasses, as if he'd suddenly been shot with a tranquilizer dart. What was going on?

Just as Beacon had this thought, Victor started to go down. Beacon rolled out of the way, narrowly avoiding a flying tentacle as Victor hit the ground. A thunderous boom resonated through the mechanical floor. Beacon scrambled up as Victor let out a screech so loud, Beacon winced and covered his ears. He didn't have to understand alien to know exactly what Victor was trying to say: that he was furious, that he'd get his revenge, and that he'd destroy anyone who stood in his way. And then make a meat pie out of their remains.

Another thunderous boom sounded. Then another, and another.

Boom, boom, boom, boom.

Everywhere Beacon looked, squids were hitting the ground and screaming in rage.

Arthur and his grandma stumbled over. Beacon was so horrified and confused by what was happening all around him that the relief of seeing them safe barely pierced through his fear.

"We need to get out of here," Arthur said, shaking his arm and jolting him back to the present. "Where's Nixon?"

Beacon scanned the platform. Nixon was picking his way over Jane, trying to avoid her flailing tentacles.

"Nixon, you okay?" Beacon called.

"Never been better," he shouted back, slipping and sliding in goo.

"What's happening?" Arthur shouted.

"I—I think they're dying," Nixon answered.

"But . . . why?" Arthur's grandma said.

"It doesn't make sense," Arthur chimed in. "What would make every single Sov keel over at the same time like this?"

Every single Sov.

The realization hit Beacon like a lightning bolt.

"Galen!" he gasped.

He was one of the Sov, too.

Victor reached up a tentacle and grabbed Beacon's leg, but his grasp was so weak that Beacon easily broke free. Beacon ran, skidding through the halls, around flailing squids and over one that wasn't moving at all, before he finally reached the room where they'd left Galen. He shoved aside the file cabinet with shocking ease, then realized that he needed a keycard to enter the room now that the power was up and running again. Just as he had this thought, Arthur, Arthur's grandma, and Nixon ran up.

"What's going on?" Arthur said, gasping.

"The keycard!" Beacon said, shaking his hand desperately at Arthur's grandma. "Hurry!"

Arthur's grandma frantically dug inside her pocket, then produced the card. Beacon snatched the card and swiped it over the access panel. The door slid open. Beacon had hoped that whatever had happened to the other Sov wouldn't have affected his friend, but Galen was slumped in front of the computer. His skin was so pale, Beacon could see the veins pulsing weakly underneath his eyelids.

Beacon rushed over and dropped to his knees in front of his friend. "Galen, are you okay?"

It was a stupid question—he obviously wasn't okay. But he didn't know what else to say. He patted Galen from head to toe, trying to find the source of the damage, but he couldn't find anything wrong.

"Galen, wake up!" Beacon shouted, shaking his shoulders. A wild, untamed feeling roared through his body.

Galen's eyes fluttered open.

"Oh, thank God," Beacon said. "I thought you were dead. Don't do that ever again."

"We did it," Galen whispered.

Beacon frowned. "Did what?"

"You hacked the computer?" Arthur asked.

The others crowded around Galen. Arthur's grandma checked Galen's temperature with the back of her hand. She pursed her lips and didn't say anything. Nixon hovered awkwardly behind him, looking like he didn't know what to do with his hands.

"What's going on?" Beacon asked again.

"What happened to you?" Nixon added. "All the Sov are down."

"Is there something we can do to help you?" Arthur's grandma asked.

"What about an EpiPen?" Arthur said hopefully.

But Galen only shook his head.

"There has to be something we can do," Beacon said. "Someone get him a glass of water or something."

"There's got to be a first aid kit around here somewhere," Arthur's grandma said.

"Don't." Galen swallowed hard, as if speaking had taken a lot out of him. "That isn't going to help."

Beacon was about to argue with Galen, when he heard footsteps in the corridor. Nixon went ramrod straight, and Beacon shot up and whirled around. Someone was here. They formed a circle around Galen, frantically looking around for something to defend themselves with. But it was too late. The person entered the room.

For a moment, Beacon thought he was seeing things.

"Everleigh?" He squinted at her.

How could his sister be here? But it was her, grease smeared on her cheek and the radio hanging limply from her hand. His dad was there, too, standing obediently in the hall behind her, waiting for a command.

Despite everything, relief washed over Beacon. He ran over and embraced his sister, then his dad, who just stood there with his arms straight at his sides.

"How are you here?" Beacon asked.

"Did you land the ship?"

"Where's Daisy?"

The group volleyed questions at her. Everleigh swallowed hard before she spoke.

"Galen sent a message that you guys needed help," she said in a shaky voice. "He said things were going badly and you needed backup. Daisy told me to land the ship on the roof, and I did, but when we got out of the ship, she didn't follow. She locked us out." Everleigh's lip wobbled. "I yelled at the doors, but they wouldn't open. Then she just took off. I tried to radio her, but she wouldn't answer."

"Why would she do that?" Arthur said.

Beacon turned to Galen, but he didn't look shocked. Whatever Daisy had done, he'd known about it.

"What did you do?" Beacon asked.

"What we had to," Galen said sadly. "Hacking the program was never going to be enough. It had to be the necklace."

"What does the necklace have to do with anything?" Beacon started. But even as he said it, the puzzle pieces started to click together. Suddenly it all made sense. Why Galen had said he was officially no longer a coward. Why the Sov had all dropped like flies at the same time. Even the sad look Galen and Daisy had shared when he'd been sure they'd been communicating telepathically took on new meaning. They'd planned this all along.

"The necklace," Beacon said. The necklace Daisy couldn't remove. "You destroyed it."

"What do you mean?" Nixon said.

Galen didn't deny it.

"Daisy—she sacrificed herself to kill all the Sov," Beacon said, his throat tight. "To save our planet."

"Is this true?" Arthur's grandma asked Galen.

"No, it can't be." Everleigh whipped her head from side to side. "Galen, tell Beacon he's wrong."

"I'm sorry," Galen said.

Tears streamed down Everleigh's cheeks. She furiously paced the room.

"This isn't okay, Galen!" she shouted. "We didn't agree to this!"

"It wasn't up to you," he said.

"Okay, we need to calm down," Beacon said. "It isn't too late. If you're still alive, that means Daisy is, too, right? There has to be another way."

"There isn't," Galen said.

"We'll think of something," Everleigh said. "Nixon's a Junior Guard, he knows this place, these people. Maybe he can—"

A voice came through on the radio. Everleigh yelped and almost dropped it before she realized what was happening and clutched it desperately to her lips.

"Hello? Daisy, are you there?" she asked.

Static crackled, before Daisy's voice broke through. "I'm here."

Everleigh released a huge breath. "Oh, thank God. Listen, whatever you and your idiot friend were planning, you can forget about it. We're coming up with Plan B."

"It's too late." Daisy's voice was so soft it was almost inaudible against the hum of machinery in the room, but it had an air of finality that shut Everleigh up. "Is Galen there?" she asked.

Everleigh swallowed. She nodded, then seemed to realize Daisy wouldn't be able to see her and sniffled hard. "Yes. He's here."

"Can I talk to him, please?"

Everleigh brought the radio to Galen.

Galen licked his lips and took a deep breath. "Hey, Dais."

"Hey, Gales," Daisy said. "Our plan worked."

"You did good. I'm proud of you."

"Are you in pain?" Daisy asked after a moment.

"I'm okay," he said.

"You're a bad liar," Daisy replied. After a beat, she added, "I'm sorry it had to be this way."

"Don't be sorry for being a hero," Galen said.

Quiet descended, as if neither of them knew what to say.

Beacon wondered then: If he'd had a chance to say goodbye to Jasper, what would he have said? How do you say goodbye to someone forever?

Static crackled. Beacon waited for one of them to talk again, but it didn't happen. That's when he realized that Galen was staring unblinkingly ahead.

Galen and Daisy were gone.

A surge of emotion welled up inside him. He would be sad later. But right now? Right now he was *furious*.

He screamed and kicked a chair, sending it smashing across the room. He thought someone would stop him, tell him to calm down and that it would all be okay, or some other patronizing junk he didn't want to hear. But after a few moments, Everleigh joined in, too. She screamed with her whole body. The sound tore through the room like shards of glass. They screamed together until Beacon felt an artery bulging in his neck and he had no air left in his lungs. It felt so good to get it all out. Everything he felt about this unfair world. About losing people he cared about over and over. Therapy and long talks and self-reflection had their place, but there was something to be said about a good scream.

When he was done, he slumped onto the floor. Everleigh let out one final roar before she slid down the wall next to him and laid her head on his shoulder. Silence fell over the room. He felt more drained than he ever had in his life. Like he was just a husk of a human.

After a while, a hand landed on his shoulder. Beacon sighed heavily and peered up. He was expecting Arthur or even Nixon, but he froze when he saw his dad. His dad smiled wearily at him.

For a solid twenty seconds, Beacon just stared. His dad looked tired and weak and pale, but there was an alertness in his eyes and a softness in his expression that told Beacon everything he needed to know: He was Off-Program.

"Dad!" Beacon shouted.

Beacon and Everleigh jumped up as fast as they could and crushed their dad in a bear hug that made him hiss in pain, then laugh as the kids rushed to disentangle themselves from him.

"Are you okay?" Everleigh asked.

"I'm fine!" he said. "Get back over here."

"Are you sure? Are you hurt?" Everleigh said.

"Just hug your old man," he said, smiling.

They tried again, gentler this time. Their dad wrapped his arms around them, and Beacon was pretty sure he'd never been so happy. He felt horrible for feeling anything other than pain after Galen and Daisy's sacrifice, but it was so good to have his dad back that he let himself have this moment. He closed his eyes and squeezed his dad and let the happiness soak into his bones. Several times Beacon tried to speak, but all that came out were unintelligible croaks.

"How?" Beacon finally said. He wasn't sure when he'd started crying, but his dad's shirt was soaked at the shoulder. "How are you normal again?"

"Was it the necklace?" Everleigh asked. "Did the program lose its power when Daisy . . . when Daisy made her sacrifice?" she finished.

Arthur quickly walked over to the computer. He typed something into the keyboard, his eyes scanning the screen. He shook his head in wonderment.

"The program," Arthur said. "Galen did it. He hacked the antidote software."

"Antidote software?" the twins' dad asked, frowning. "I think I remember something about that."

"It will all start coming back," Everleigh said. Beacon almost asked her how she could be so sure, but then he remembered she'd once been brainwashed by the Sov.

"Let's get out of here," Arthur's grandma said after a while.

The group picked their way through the wreckage of the base. There was slime everywhere, tentacles sprawled all over the floors. The last of the Sov clinging to life had finally stilled. Without the roaring and flailing, the building was eerily quiet. Through a blown-out gap in the side of the building, Beacon could even hear a bird chirping. He felt something heavy and cold move through him, all the way down to his knees. The Sov were dead. All of them. Victor, Jane. He had to remind himself that it was a good thing. That they'd done all of this to save human lives.

A sudden thought occurred to him.

He turned around and ran back the other way.

"Where are you going?" Beacon's dad called.

Nixon sighed, and they all ran after Beacon. They caught up with him in Daisy's room. Beacon stepped over a downed Sov and peeled back the tapestry on the wall.

"I'm pretty sure we can just use the front door," Everleigh said.

But she shut up when he opened the door and Perry and Sumiko stared out at them.

"What's happening?" Sumiko said in a quavering voice.

Beacon, Everleigh, Arthur, and Nixon exchanged a glance.

"Come on. It's safe now." Beacon extended a hand.

Perry and Sumiko peered hesitantly out of the secret exit at the dead Sov on the ground. Then Perry took Beacon's hand and stumbled out. Sumiko bypassed Everleigh's hand and pushed through the door.

They trailed back through the base and, finally, outside. The storm was over. The wind had died down, and the clouds had broken apart. The sun shone so brightly that the snow was already beginning to melt, and Beacon had to shield his eyes as they stepped through the front doors. There were no Sov. No guards. No fighting or ships.

"Is it really over?" Everleigh asked.

Footsteps crunched over the snow, and Beacon froze. So did the guard who stumbled around the corner. Donna. Everleigh stepped forward, ready to defend them. But it turned out it wasn't necessary. Donna just looked at the group for a moment, then at the base, before she shook her head and walked down the road toward town.

"It's really over," Arthur said.

"Well, what happens now?" Beacon asked after a moment.

His dad looked out at the road. "Now we go home."

SIX MONTHS LATER

"Good morning, children. I trust you've read up to page sixty-eight in your history textbooks?"

Arthur's grandma smiled at the class before bending over the laptop on her desk and tapping at the keys. She frowned, and a white tendril drifted loose from her bun and fell in front of her lined face.

"Let me help you with that, Grandma N," Nixon said.

"That's Mrs. Newell to you," she said, though there was a twinkle in her eye as Nixon popped up to help her get her lesson going on the projector.

At first, it had been kind of weird seeing Arthur's grandma at school like this, but it turned out she'd had a background in teaching before she retired, and she'd said she wanted to keep a close eye on the kids to make sure there was no more "funny business," as she'd called it. Beacon thought that was partially true. But he also thought that she was just bored now that there was no rebel operation to front.

Beacon didn't mind a little boredom.

After they'd left the base that day, they'd learned that, partly thanks to Driftwood Harbor being so rural, the other Sov ships hadn't managed to get too far before Galen and Daisy's world-saving sacrifice. The formerly brainwashed humans had somehow landed the ships back at the base and then gone home, dazed but alive. Only twelve people had died as a result of the acid rain.

Only twelve.

That was hard for Beacon to understand, but his dad had said it could have been so much worse.

Beacon had thought there would be no way for the government to cover up what had happened that day—UFOs, toxic rain, giant squids—but they had. They'd claimed the ships were part of an Air Force drill, and blamed the deaths on a particularly lethal outbreak of the flu. Any squid sightings were put down to conspiracy theories. And when Beacon and the others had returned to the base to collect Galen's body for a funeral, not only was he not there, but the entire building and all of the ships were gone. Every last sign that the Sov had ever been there had disappeared.

The world was only too happy to believe, and just like that, everything was back to normal, and school was back in session.

The bell rang for lunch. Beacon and Nixon gathered their books and joined the flood of kids heading for the caf. Arthur pushed his way through the crowd and fell into step beside them.

"You won't believe this," he said, panting. "I got Sumiko to join YAT! She's coming to our next meeting."

"Really?" Beacon said. "How'd you manage that?"

Perry and Sumiko remembered everything from their time as brainwashed Sov minions. While Perry had instantly joined YAT and become one of their most active members, Sumiko had preferred to join Driftwood Harbor, and the rest of the world, in pretending nothing had ever happened.

"Tell 'em," Nixon said.

"Well, I kind of agreed to join the Gold Stars," Arthur said sheepishly.

"WHAT?!" Beacon cried, so loudly a few people looked over.

"It's not a big deal," Arthur said defensively. "It's just a normal volunteer group now. With Nixon, Perry, Donna, and your dad, our YAT membership is up to eight people!"

"Next step: world domination," Nixon joked.

....

"Hey, wait for me!" Beacon dragged the boat the last few feet up the shore, then jogged after Everleigh and Arthur, Boots trotting happily alongside him.

They'd gone back to New York to get Boots from the kennel after all the dust had settled. It hadn't seemed right to leave him there, waiting for an owner who would never come back, so he and Everleigh had convinced their dad that they needed to be the ones to find him a good home. Well, Boots had practically knocked Beacon over with slobbery kisses when he saw him, and that was it: He was officially their dog. Pretty much the only place Boots didn't go with Beacon was to school, and that was only because of Nurse Allen harping on about health code violations.

The sun was out, birds were singing, and the flowers bloomed. It seemed wrong. Like everything should be as dark and foggy as Beacon felt inside. But it was as if the world wanted to remind him that life would go on.

Before long, they arrived at the mouth of the cave. Galen had once said that he came here a lot to think, and Beacon thought Daisy might have liked this place, too, when she sneaked out of the ship with him, so it seemed like a fitting place for their funeral.

"Did you bring the stuff?" Arthur asked.

"Honestly, what do you take me for?" Everleigh shucked her backpack and took out two plants, handling them as if they were bombs that might detonate. They went to work digging two holes, then they tucked the plants into them and filled the holes with dirt. Some light in all the darkness.

"Well, that's done." Everleigh dusted off her hands. They admired their work for a moment.

"Should we say something?" Arthur said.

Everleigh cleared her throat. "We didn't know you that well, but I like to think that we would have been great friends. Your sacrifice won't be in vain."

A bird trilled, and a brook babbled somewhere nearby.

Beacon wanted to say something, but he couldn't find the right words. One second passed, then two. He could have let it go. But then he remembered Jasper's funeral. He hadn't spoken then, either—he'd been too overwhelmed, too unsure of what to say, and the thought of speaking in front of hundreds of people had paralyzed him. But the regret of not speaking had eaten at him, and when he was falling asleep at night, he'd sometimes replay in his mind what he would have said about Jasper, perfecting the epic tribute to his brother that he should have delivered. Now he knew that for him, the only wrong thing to say would be nothing at all. So he took a deep breath and let out everything he'd been thinking lately.

"When Victor told me I was going to save the world, I thought he was wrong. I figured the elders had screwed up, maybe got the wrong kid or something. After you did what you did, I was even more confused. I didn't do *anything*. It was all you two. But now I think Victor was right. I did save the world—we did," he said, looking at Everleigh and Arthur. "But we were only able to do it because we met you two. We did it together. And I guess what I'm trying to say is you're always going to be a part of our team, even if you're not actually here anymore."

Everleigh linked fingers with him, and Arthur clasped his shoulder.

And that was it.

It didn't seem like enough. They'd saved the world, and history would never even know their names.

They had a picnic in the warm grass, talking and laughing about Galen and Daisy, until the sun began sinking on the horizon. It was the weirdest funeral Beacon had ever been to. Kind of the best, too. He thought this was how it should always be: focusing on the happy times, instead of the grief. He'd had enough of grief lately.

"Well, we better get back," Arthur said, looking at his watch. "Our YAT meeting starts in half an hour."

"Everyone collect your trash," Beacon said. "I've got a separate bag for recyclables, too."

"Yeah, yeah, we know the drill, Captain Planet," Everleigh said, picking up her soda can.

They booked it back to the boat.

Soon, they were cruising down the main road toward Arthur's house, Everleigh and Arthur on bikes, and Beacon on his board, Boots trotting happily on his leash beside him. It wasn't his favorite board—that one had been lost in the apartment squid fight debacle—but he was just happy to be riding again. He couldn't believe how much he'd missed the feeling of the road bumping along under his feet.

Beacon was in his own world, enjoying the wind in his face, when Boots jolted forward so suddenly, he went flying off his board. He stumbled, nearly losing his grip on the leash. Boots started barking.

"What the heck, dude?" Beacon said, just as a pair of headlights blinked into existence up ahead.

"Someone's coming," Arthur said.

"Nothing gets past you," Beacon and Everleigh said at the same time, then laughed. But Beacon's laughter died out when Boots's barking got louder and crazier. He'd never seen him act this way before. Well, he had one time, he remembered, thinking of that day outside the pawnshop. Beacon tried to shush the dog, but his barking just got worse the closer the car came, until Beacon had to dig his heels into the road and haul on the leash with all his might so Boots wouldn't go racing off as the car roared past.

Boots didn't stop until the car was long gone.

"Who was that?" Everleigh said, looking after the vehicle as its taillights disappeared into the dark. "I didn't recognize that car."

"More importantly," Arthur said, "what's wrong with Boots?"

A chill shuddered down Beacon's spine.

It couldn't be a Sov. They were all dead. The queen was killed, and—

Beacon gasped.

No. No, no, no. It wasn't possible.

"What?" Everleigh said.

"The Sov left their home planet with the queen, right?" Beacon said.

"Yeah . . . ," Arthur replied warily.

"So what happened to all the Sov they left behind? How did they survive without their queen?"

"The jewel's power must have reached really far," Arthur said, though he was frowning now, as if he couldn't quite believe he hadn't thought about this before.

"What if that's not true?" Beacon said. "What if the jewel is only strong enough to cover one planet?"

"That doesn't make sense," Everleigh said. "Then everyone

back on their home planet would have died when they came here with Daisy."

"*Unless* Victor crowned another queen who could power the home-planet Sov before they left," Beacon said.

"Then why wouldn't he have told Daisy about that?" Everleigh asked.

"To keep her under their thumb," Beacon said. "Think about it—if you've been told you're responsible for the lives of everyone on your planet, would you be likely to act out of line? Disobey commands? Take any big risks?"

No one said anything.

"Victor kept her in the dark to protect himself," he said. "The Sov aren't all dead. And there's at least one of them here in Driftwood Harbor."

Boots's barks filled the silence as they exchanged a terrified glance.

THE END